IRMA'S GUN

IRMA'S GUN

MONET THOMPSON

Copyright © 2021 by Monet Thompson.

Copyright Registration Number: TXu2-224-428
Library of Congress Control Number: 2020924439
ISBN: Hardcover   978-1-6641-4660-0
         Softcover   978-1-6641-4659-4
         eBook   978-1-6641-4658-7

All rights reserved. No part of this book may be reproduced or transmitted in any form or by any means, electronic or mechanical, including photocopying, recording, or by any information storage and retrieval system, without permission in writing from the copyright owner.

This is a work of fiction. Names, characters, places and incidents either are the product of the author's imagination or are used fictitiously, and any resemblance to any actual persons, living or dead, events, or locales is entirely coincidental.

Any people depicted in stock imagery provided by Getty Images are models, and such images are being used for illustrative purposes only.
Certain stock imagery © Getty Images.

Inspired by a true story

Print information available on the last page.

Rev. date: 12/11/2020

To order additional copies of this book, contact:
Xlibris
844-714-8691
www.Xlibris.com
Orders@Xlibris.com
822189

CONTENTS

Chapter 1 1
Chapter 2 5
Chapter 3 18
Chapter 4 32
Chapter 5 39
Chapter 6 47
Chapter 7 52
Chapter 8 68
Chapter 9 77
Chapter 10 92
Chapter 11 97
Chapter 12 101
Chapter 13 108
Chapter 14 118
Chapter 15 123
Chapter 16 128
Chapter 17 139
Chapter 18 147
Chapter 19 156
Chapter 20 169
Chapter 21 180
Chapter 22 193
Chapter 23 207
Chapter 24 219
Chapter 25 231
Chapter 26 244

Ms. Cynthia Toney,

Thank you so much for your support. I promise to make you a loyal fan! This is my 1st book and I hope you really enjoy it! Please tell me what you think. I respect your feedback. Luv...

Sincerely,
Monet "She M.D." Thompson
2021

443-537-5815

Dedication

Irma's Gun is dedicated to my daughter Adriana Thompson. I wish I knew you better. I know one day you'll have questions. Hopefully this book will answer some of them.

Epigraph

Life is but an illusion, a game to be played with great vigor.

-anonymous

Irma was full-blooded Cherokee Indian. Both her mother and father were killed when their home and land was overtaken by the United States government. Irma was raised on a reservation by her grandmother who died when she turned twenty-one. Irma always said that her grandmother, who was ill for a long while, held on to see her to adulthood. She wore a locket with her grandmother's picture in it.

In the early 1800s, the president of the United States visited her reservation to look around and introduce a new act that supposedly would help the Indians there and on other reservations. The men on the reservation were still angry about their ancestors being run off their land by white settlers. One stood up and shot an arrow into the president's chest. Irma went into action. She saved the president's life. She single handedly treated him with herbs and wrapped the flesh wound, but more importantly she protected him from further attack. The men respected Irma; and although they were angry, she held them back. The president never forgot.

Time went on, and Irma desperately wanted a better life for herself. She fell in love with and married a white man. She moved from the reservation and onto a few acres of land owned by her husband. On the land was a trailer and a patch where they grew fresh vegetables and fruits. In the back was a homemade pig pen where they raised hogs to slaughter and sell and have pork for themselves. They weren't rich but were hardly poor. This is Irma's story.

CHAPTER 1

The day was breezy and chilly. The gold and brown leaves were blowing all over the few acres of land they shared. However, that couldn't stop Irma from harvesting the corn and okra she had planted just a year ago. She would boil the corn and make okra soup for dinner. Life had been fruitful for Irma and her husband, Joe. They had plenty of food from their small farm for themselves and extra to sell at market. They had accumulated savings and lived for themselves. Life was good unless Joe would drink and beat Irma. He would have no reason most times. Joe had demons haunting him and would simply take it out on Irma.

She stayed because Irma had seen hard days before Joe. She had memories of losing both parents to white men taking their land. Even after she was placed on a reservation with her grand mother, life was still difficult. It was ironic that she would marry a man the same color as the ones who killed her parents. She only wanted more. She wanted security that could not be found with the other poor Indians in her community. She knew some blacks, but they were mostly slaves, and she did not want to invite the trouble.

So she settled for Joe, a man with some land and a small home. He had no children, and they would bear none together. She thought this was a new beginning. In a way, it was if it were not for the abuse.

One day she was in the house folding clothes she had just pulled in from the lines outside. Joe staggered in, asking questions, "Where were you last night? Who were you with?"

Irma told Joe not to be silly. She was in the bed last night with him. He was too drunk to remember. Then the assault began. Irma was tired. She was tired of being pummeled for nothing. She asked herself, was it all worth it? What would she do if Joe were suddenly gone? Could she assume her duties on their small farm by her self? It seemed she did anyway because Joe was always gone. Then the blood started. This time, her whole face was wet. She didn't know if it was blood or tears. She broke loose from Joe for a second and ran into their bedroom. She reached under the mattress for his gun. She told Joe if he took another step towards her, she would kill him. He said she didn't have the guts to do it.

Then she thought. She had entered the threshold of death. If she didn't kill Joe, he would kill her for pulling a gun on him. So she shot twice, and his rigid body dropped to the floor like it had fallen from the sky. Now what? Joe was a frail man, and Irma had the strength of an ox from working the fields every day. She let him bleed to death on the floor until he was no more. She thought of dragging him outside into a shallow grave she could dig, but the shock of what had just occurred left her in a stupor. Joe lay on the floor all night while Irma slept in their bed.

During the night, Irma slept so soundly she did not hear the clip-clop of horse's hooves entering her yard. It was only the brisk knock at the door that woke her up. Still sore and bloodied, she staggered to the door, walking around Joe's dead body. A feeble voice cried from her body, "Who is it?" A man answered, "It's the law, ma'am. Somebody heard gunshots. Are you okay?" Irma cracked the door and peeked onto the porch. "Do I look like I'm okay?" The man gently pushed the door open and peered down into Irma's face. "Looks like you need medical attention, ma'am. You should come with me."

As the man walked in, he was stunned to see Joe lying on the floor in a pool of blood. You could still smell the alcohol reeking from his pores. "Looks like we have a casualty, gentlemen." Another man put

Irma on his horse and took her to a hospital while the others investigated and cleaned the mess.

At the hospital, it was confirmed that Irma had no broken bones. She was just a little swollen and would take some time to heal. Irma knew the drill. This was not the first time she had been beaten. However, it was the first time that the law had gotten involved. It took a tragedy. They said they would let her stay the night until an officer could come to take her back home the next day.

She slept until the law came and knocked on the door of the infirmary. She thought she was going back home until they explained that she was being arrested for the murder of her husband. Then came the newspaper reporters. They were taking pictures and asking questions as the officers loaded Irma into a police car. They took her to jail. She stayed there about a week until she had a visit from the president.

He was dressed in dungarees and a cotton white shirt. Usually accompanied by the secret service, he came alone today. He greeted Irma with a firm hand shake and a wry smile. He began, "Irma Smith . . . I understand that you've been charged with the murder of your husband, Joe. I read about it in the newspaper. Do you remember me?"

Irma paused. She wondered what the president was doing here in jail. Her consciousness was somewhat muddied by the prospect of spending the rest of her life in jail. So she asked him, "Why has the president come to visit me?" He smiled again and answered, "Do you remember saving my life? Were it not for your quick thinking and careful bravery, I would not be here right now. I feel like I owe you something. Thanks was not enough. Now I know that was seven years ago. I have thought of you often, and when I saw that article in the newspaper, I thought, *Here's my opportunity to do something meaningful.* So here I am."

Irma responded, "I have enough money in the bank to live off of. I continue to make money from selling produce from the farm. I may have to hire some help, but I can afford to do so. I don't need your money."

The president was proud to offer another remedy to this conundrum, "No, Irma, I'm not here to offer you money. I'm here to first erase your charges and send you back home to your farm. Then I want to offer you further protection for you and the women who come after you in your family. From this day forward, you have an unspoken license to kill anyone who threatens you harm. When you die, this license will be passed on to your daughter, then her daughter, and so on. You've more than earned it as far as I'm concerned. I've already written this into law to be passed down. This is why you are now exonerated of these murder charges. Do you understand?"

With tears in her eyes, she asked the president how she could ever repay him. He told her she already did. It was said and done. With that, he turned and left her there. Several minutes later, a warden unlocked her cell holding all her belongings. She told her to get dressed. Someone would be there shortly to take her home.

CHAPTER 2

Irma climbed the three steps to her porch as if she was about to die. She wanted to go in and lie down, but instead she sat in a rocking chair outside and cried profusely. She just couldn't believe that with no trial and after all she had been through that she was a free woman. Her life now had a new beginning, and she knew it. She wiped her face and tried to think of what she would do next. The first thing that crossed her mind was not telling anyone of what the president had divulged to her. She did not want to become a target of the envious and wind up dead herself. The second thing she thought of was what she would tell everyone about Joe.

She had always kept the abuse from him a secret. It was their cross to bear. It was their business. Their nearest neighbor was a half mile away. So no one would hear the thumps and bumps in the night. No one would see the black eyes and bloody noses. No one would notice the bruises that Irma would cover with long sleeved shirts in the summer when she would travel somewhere. Once she thought further, that license was a blessing in disguise. She could never prove the abuse in court because she never recorded it with the law. She told no one. A jury might have thought that she was simply making up a story. Irma would have gone to prison for sure. She would have lost everything in the process including her life. She couldn't believe how blessed she was.

She went inside and changed her clothes. She got a bucket and filled it halfway with water from a pump out front. She went back inside and began the arduous task of cleaning up Joe's blood off the bedroom floor. When she finished, dusk was looming. She had a renewed strength and energy, so she went outside and picked her butter beans. Now, since she was the only one who lived on this small farm, she would have to go into town to hire some help. That was the only way she could continue to sell her produce and have a steady flow of income. She surveyed a small patch of land behind her rows of vegetables. She would bury Joe there. That would eliminate her having to pay for and find a burial plot. She could find a small tombstone to mark the grave. She would post the proper announcements in the paper in the morning. A small funeral could be had at the chapel in town.

The next morning, she slept longer than usual. Normally, she was up before dawn; but today the only thing that woke her up was the crowing of a rooster off in the distance and the sunlight of half of an orange sun peeking into her window. She sat up nearly at her bed and stretched. Irma pulled a small pink basin from underneath her bed and went out in the front yard to the pump to fill it with water. Careful not to spill it, she sauntered back up the steps, across the porch, into the house, and back into her bedroom. She placed the basin on the floor in front of her bed. She found something nice to wear just beyond her church clothes and laid the dress out on the bottom half of the bed. Retrieving under garments from her dresser drawers, she too laid them across the bottom half of the bed.

Then she undressed and put yesterday's clothes in a basket on the other side of the room. Getting a piece of soap and a wash cloth from the bathroom, Irma sat nearly at her bed and washed up thoroughly. She got dressed and was ready for the day.

Smokey, a gray-and-white horse tied to the back of the house, was her transportation. Irma threw a basket filled with vegetables over the horse's saddle. She rode him into town, going over in her mind what she would say on the announcement of her husband's passing. The day was beautiful. The sky was blue, and clay ribbons provided an appropriate back round for her trek into town. The silver, brown, and beige mountains moved from the front to the side and then finally behind her view. The earth crunched below Smokey's hooves as he progressed at a slow pace. When she got there, she tied him to a post outside of the market and removed the basket filled with vegetables from Smokey's saddle.

Irma entered the market with confidence. Two colored boys stood outside, asking everyman who walked by if they could shine their shoes. Most said no. One man threw a nickel to the foot of the boys as they quickly fetched it from rolling under the chairs. Irma didn't notice a thing. Her skin was almost the same as every white patron who occupied the store unless the sun hit it. It turned a reddish brown instead of pink. No one noticed her walking in. Three white ladies were competing for the store owner's attention. Irma waited patiently until no one was at the counter. The store owner called her by name to approach the cash register and asked to see what was in her basket. Never looking the man in the eye, Irma stood there as he studied and picked through the vegetables. He put money on the counter. She said thank you and left the store.

Then she went next door where they printed the town newspaper. She approached the printer and told him she wanted to make an announcement of her husband's death in the obituaries. He asked her if she could read. She said yes, and he handed her a pen along with a paper to fill out. The man pointed to a small desk over in the corner where she could write. Irma said thank you and pondered over what she would say in the announcement:

> Joe Smith was shot by a burglar on Sunday May 4th, 1830, around 6:30 p.m. His going-home service will be held at the town chapel this coming Sunday. He will be buried on his farm outside of Washington, D.C. All are welcome.

Irma handed the paper to the printer and asked how much it would cost. She gave the printer money and waited for her change. The printer threw the change on the counter. Irma picked it up as she looked at it. She said thank you and walked out. Next, she walked up to the two boys still soliciting to shine shoes outside the market. She asked them their names and ages. One was fifteen; the other was twelve. She asked them if they would like to work for her instead of asking white men to shine their shoes.

The boys wanted to know what they would be doing. Irma said the work would only be once a week from dawn until closing the stores in town. They would come to her house and assist in harvesting vegetables and doing some light cleaning around her yard. She would pay them, but she could only hire one because Smokey could only carry two people at a time.

The fifteen-year-old spoke up swiftly. His name was Edmond. He said that his little brother wouldn't be able to leave the house by himself anyways, so he would be happy to work for Irma. They arranged and agreed to meet at the market on Mondays starting a week after Joe's funeral. Edmond said his family would be pleased.

So Irma returned to her home feeling like she had accomplished things in town. She mentally prepared herself for Joe's funeral, for speaking to all the people who would ask questions about her husband. She went over in her mind how she would answer the questions not to arouse suspicion about the fact that she had killed him and gotten away with it. Irma still couldn't believe what the president had given her. She couldn't believe that the gift would be handed down to future generations of women. She didn't believe it. All she knew was that she would not become some roving outlaw running around killing people just because she knew she could get away with it. She would take her blessings and run. Today was a new day.

Sunday came, and Irma prepared her black dress suit to wear along with a black bonnet she had tucked away for safe keeping. She wasn't sure if she was ready for the day's charade, but whatever she was ready for would just have to do. There was no turning back now. She had some breakfast and tidied up her house if she brought someone back with her. Then she ascended Smokey and rode to the town chapel.

Joe was prepared and waiting for her at the front of the church. She stood there a moment to get one last glimpse. She had to admit to herself that in his final appearance he did look handsome. It reminded her of when they first met and how he courted her. Irma couldn't remember exactly where things went wrong. She concluded that he was only a wolf in sheep's clothing waiting to pounce on his prey. He was wrong all along. She just never noticed.

The pastor walked in and took both her hands in his. He bowed his head and said a brief prayer and then apologized for her loss. Irma thanked the pastor and then assured him that Joe had left her well-off and that she would be just fine going on. The pastor asked if there was anything she wanted him to mention at the eulogy. Irma said no; and little by little, people filed in. The church never filled up, and the participants sat in small clusters besides one another. A bunch of strangers came to see who this Joe was that the newspaper had mentioned.

Just then, Edmond walked in and like everyone else apologized for Joe's passing before taking a seat. He introduced his father, Edmond Sr., as a widower who could understand her pain. Edmond Sr. thanked Irma for hiring his son. He explained that since his wife died, they were a little short on cash. They made do with two incomes; but now since there was only one, his two sons would have to step up and fill in the gaps. Irma couldn't help but notice what a strapping young-looking fellow Edmond Sr. was. His son took after him, but he was the real deal. Edmond Sr. offered Irma twelve white roses and said he hoped he'd be seeing more of her around. Irma said likewise and excused herself.

Now that all introductions were final, Irma gasped at how easily everything flowed. No one asked how Joe died. They were just concerned for her present state of mind. She sat on the front pew with tissue in hand, constantly wiping her dry eyes. She had to keep up appearances. When the sermon was over, just as everyone entered, they said their final apologies one by one then filed out of the church. Irma was alone again. She was the only one to see Joe back to the house where his tombstone awaited the grave diggers. The moon greeted the sun from the other side of the sky as one rose and the other fell. The men took their time filling the hole with dirt just as they took their time digging. Joe was at the bottom now. He had seen his last day. Irma went inside to have dinner.

On a full belly, she cleaned enough dishes and pots for one. She retired into her bedroom and took off her black boots. Her black dress suit followed. She stretched out in her black slip and lay across the bed spread. She tried to remember the good times she had with Joe, but they were few. So instead, she went over those sparse ones again and again. Soon she was dreaming about him. She missed him still despite all the hardships, and where would she go from here?

When she awoke, she sat up in the still of the night. There was no sound. Only the moonlight entranced her bathroom, which she followed. She looked into the mirror and noticed lines of dried tears on her face. She splashed some water from a basin on her face to remove the unwanted evidence she had been crying. Then she patted her face with a towel and went back to sleep, this time under the covers and without her black slip.

These nights turned into days, and then the days turned back to nights several times before she was to meet Edmond Jr. in town to bring him back to her home to work for a meager wage. Edmond was delightful. He was a fast learner and quick on his feet. Whatever Irma suggested he do, he did. He assisted in doubling her profits at the market, and she would tip him on top of his daily wage. Edmond said he gave most of the money he made to his father and saved some for himself. He had dreams of learning how to read and maybe going to a trade school some day.

Irma was so impressed that she said he didn't have to pay someone to teach him to read; she would do it. Edmond would work on Mondays, learn to read on Fridays, study the whole weekend, and then return on Monday to practice while he worked. While he was in the garden, he would go over his alphabet and spell new words to prepare himself for the books on Friday.

One Monday Irma went into town to pick up Edmond Jr. To her surprise, Edmond Sr. was with him. The father of the pair sat atop a sandy-brown horse while his son waited on foot. Eye to eye, the senior greeted Irma and then thanked her for allowing her son to work for her. He let her know that with the money his son gave him he saved up for a horse and now it would not be necessary for Irma to ride into town twice a week to pick up Edmond Jr. He could ride to her house and back home himself now. Besides, he was sixteen now and responsible enough to handle the task.

Junior walked a ways off to give them some privacy. Irma and Edmond Sr. chatted like old friends. They talked about the president and the state of the economy, race relations, and slavery. Then Edmond Sr. dropped a bombshell. He was no longer a slave. He had bought his freedom about twenty years ago, met his wife, started a family, and then she died. He had been alone ever since. Irma was sorry to hear about the details surrounding her death. She wanted Edmond Sr. to know he had a friend, so she invited him to her home. She left him an open invitation. She told him about her farm and the pigs out back. Irma explained how she cooked often; but since she lived alone, most of the food she cooked would go to slop the hogs. If ever he showed up, he would have a meal waiting for him.

Edmond Sr. was happy to hear that, so happy he took her up on her invitation right that second. He said he and his son could follow her home so he could see this magical but quaint place she spoke of. Irma was ecstatic to oblige. So off they went. The two Edmonds followed Irma.

When they arrived at her place, Edmond Jr. got to work without instruction. He gathered the trash and threw it into a hole behind the house where he burned it. Then he gathered the leftover food in a bucket in the house and went out back to slop the hogs. His father stayed behind to finish talking to Irma. This time, they talked about Joe.

Irma started with the good times but told Edmond how he would abuse her. She wanted to tell him she had killed him too, but she stopped herself. "Good thing those burglars came along when they did. It was a blessing in disguise." Edmond agreed and they left it at that. Irma made him a plate after she warmed up some leftovers. She accompanied him on the porch as he ate.

Before they both knew it, Edmond Jr. came around the corner, saying he had finished his work. He gave his boss a summary of everything that he did and where he would resume next Monday. He told her was looking forward to Friday because he was learning a lot. His appetite for reading was ferocious. He was always ready for more. So the duo said their goodbyes and were on their way. Everyone was all smiles. It was an amicable union. Irma was just happy to have some company for once.

These meetings went on for quite a while. The father and son would show up together on Mondays. Junior would do his work while Irma and his father would sit on the porch and talk. Irma loved entertaining him. She would always cook something special on Mondays, expecting company besides her employee.

Then one day, out of the blue, Edmond Sr. showed up alone on a Saturday. Irma was surprised but pleased. She offered him a plate, but he refused. He said he was thinking about Irma and just wanted to see her. There was a gathering place near his home, and he asked if Irma wants to come, first to meet his friends then to see his place. He felt obligated to extend his hand since she was always so gracious towards him. Irma smiled a wide smile and grinned for a while before answering. Then she asked Edmond if he would help her pick out something to wear. He did; and while Irma got ready, Edmond sat on the porch like the gentleman he was and waited patiently.

She sauntered out looking gorgeous. Edmond helped her onto his horse. Then they rode off to the watering hole on his side of town. They talked the whole way there mostly about the community of freed slaves who worked and played together. Their families were raised among one another, and they were tight knit. He also talked about his family. It was a family inside of a family, and Edmond was proud of it.

They arrived, and Irma requested, "Is this it?"

Edmond said, "Woman, don't you hear the music?" He helped her off his horse.

They stood there and admired the falling- down planks of wood with bent nails hanging from them. They crept across a boarded- up stoop and into the bar area. Edmond ordered two whiskeys and pulled up a rickety stool while he stood to continue their conversation. Almost everyone there stopped by to greet Edmond and see who this Indian woman was that he brought to their neck of the woods (literally). Edmond was so pleased to introduce his new friend to his friends.

Then like clockwork, everyone left them alone. They talked until a slow song was being played. They took their tin cups with them to the dance floor. Edmond wrapped his arms around Irma's neck while he held his cup. She wrapped her arms around his waist in the same fashion. The top of Irma's head reached his chin. They fit perfectly into each other's space. They danced until the music turned boogie-ish again. They held hands and exited from the dive. Edmond wanted to get her over to his place before it got too late.

When they got there, both of Edmond's sons were sitting on the porch waiting for him to get home. They weren't expecting a guest. The boys giggled and then ran into the house never to be seen again. Edmond apologized for their childishness and invited her in. He was a good cook himself and wanted to show off his skills in exchange for all the meals she had offered him. Irma ate gingerly although she had worked up quite an appetite. By the time she finished, the moon was upon them and Edmond was yawning. Irma told him she'd hate to impose by having him ride all the way back to her house then all the way back home, so he might take her home and then spend the night at her house. Edmond said he'd rather have her spend the night there because the roads were no place for a black man after dark.

She agreed and said she would stay the night. Edmond offered her his bed. He would sleep with his youngest son.

When morning came, Irma woke up to the smell of bacon and eggs. Edmond left a towel and wash cloth with a small piece of soap on the dresser in his room. Irma took advantage and presented herself at the table in the kitchen. The boys were all smiles, still giggling. Edmond made her a plate and poured her some coffee and orange juice. He asked if she wanted sugar and cream. She said yes but offered to do something for herself. This time, she wanted to express how hungry she was and how good the food was; so she wasn't as careful in eating this time, and this was on purpose.

Edmond asked if she was going to church. He said he could have her back in time to make the early service. Irma said she would like that. Again they were off on Edmond's horse headed toward church.

When they got to the church, they sat together in the back so as not to stir up confusion, but it didn't matter. Sundays were usually a day for Edmond and his two sons. He had only one horse, so his sons stayed home this Sunday. Irma usually came by herself, so everyone was whispering, but no one said anything to either of them directly. They enjoyed the service but didn't stay for refreshments. They left promptly to take Irma home. It had been a long weekend.

From then on, Sundays were an event. Irma would meet Edmond and his boys there, and they'd sit together and talk before and after church. Sometimes they'd have Sunday dinner at Irma's. They didn't know it but they were becoming a family.

There was never any intimacy. Talking was their intimacy. Edmond Sr. always showed Irma the utmost respect. Then one Sunday he pulled her away from the crowd and his sons and asked her to marry him. He got down on one knee and professed his love. Edmond said that they were already a family and that he looked forward to blending by having more children with her. His past as a slave and her past as an Indian who lost her parents and land made them the perfect match. They understood each other.

Edmond had overcome by saving his money to purchase his freedom. Irma had persevered by killing Joe and leaving her past behind her. They had things to offer each other, and they worked well together. The boys, now eighteen and fifteen, contributed to the family environment and enjoyed it. They too respected Irma and all she offered, so they got married.

Irma's trailer was bigger, so Edmond sold his house, and his sons moved into Irma's spare room. Irma settled more into the kitchen while the men made use of the farm and expanded their pork business. They made more money together than apart, and their love blossomed.

People at church would gossip. It had been ten long years since Joe died but Irma and Edmond made it work. The town's people would gossip about how Joe died and how Irma was turning his meager farm into a small enterprise with Edmond's help. Some people felt like she had set Joe up, and it didn't sit well with them that Joe was buried in the same place that Edmond was now calling home.

No one still knew about the abuse that Joe subjected her to, so it just didn't make sense to them. No one ever came to justice for Joe's murder. They never found the intruders who supposedly shot him, so some felt unsafe, as if they could be next.

When Irma heard about the rumors, she asked Edmond if maybe she should have sold her place and moved into Edmond's house. Edmond said no. It worked better the way they did it. He said that they did nothing wrong. People were just jealous because they were making out like fat rats and they got along so well. Irma's secret was wearing at her, and she had to tell her new husband. She just felt like someone knew. She hadn't spoken a word to anyone; and unless the former president told someone, no one should have known.

One night, when the boys had finished their dinner and left Irma and Edmond Sr. to clean up, she told him.

Irma went on and on about how the president at the time came to her cell in jail. She explained in great detail about their conversation and how he promised to protect all the women who came after her by allowing them to kill anyone who threatened their lives. She still couldn't believe it, but he said that. For the first time, Edmond hit the roof. He couldn't believe that Irma was naive enough to believe that a white man would grant her, an Indian, such privileges. Irma retorted, "They let me walk free. I never even went to trial. They just swept it all under the rug like it never happened. That has to mean something!"

Edmond's silence was deafening. He knew she was right. However, his past and position as a colored man in a world that did not belong to him would not allow him to just settle on words. He had questions, "How do you know they won't hold you responsible later? What will happen to his promises after his term is up? Did he offer you any papers or proof of what he said, and how will you prove what he said to your future generations?"

Edmond was convinced that this was all just a ploy to have something over Irma. Anyone who knew what happened could come back later to blackmail her. Edmond was suddenly uneasy. He paced the floor and dropped a dish. He was so nervous. "Why didn't you tell me this before we got married?" Irma was hurt. "Now you don't want to be married to me?"

Edmond said he just needed to know what he was getting himself into. There was a long pause as if they were rethinking their vows. Then Edmond apologized. He took Irma into his arms. "I still love you. I just need to know what we're up against. It's not easy for a colored man to walk a straight and narrow path. There's always someone looking to cut you down and say you don't deserve what you've worked so hard for. I think it's nice that he wanted to reward you for saving his life, but what about the future? He's not always going to be around. How can we be sure that men in these racist times will honor his words? We can't be sure. Did you tell anyone else?"

Irma said, "No. You're the first one."

Edmond made her promise she would tell no one. They would just have to let the cards fall wherever they may.

That was how it was for the duration. They never spoke of it again. Their secret renewed their love for each other and made them watch each other's backs in a way they had never done before. They grew even more found and protective of each other and their boys, and then Irma announced that she was pregnant.

The doctor had just left their room after examining her. He smiled at Edmond and showed himself out. Edmond and Irma danced around the room like they were newlyweds. They had been married about five years now, and there were rumors that slavery was going to one day end. That didn't stop plantation owners from having slaves, so Edmond had to keep his freedom papers on him wherever he went. They were living a dream.

As Irma got bigger, her responsibilities around the house lessened. Edmond didn't even want her riding a horse anymore, so she was confined to the house. The men took over all chores around the house and in town. This was Irma's first child, so no one had any indication of how her pregnancy would develop. They all treated her like a porcelain china doll. She followed what her husband and her sons and her doctor told her to do. Edmond hired a midwife from his old community; and in the last two months of Irma's pregnancy, he moved her in to be with Irma.

One day, the three men returned from town to find Irma in labor. The midwife summoned Edmond to get more clean water from outside. Edmond came back spilling water everywhere. He dropped the silver basin down next to the midwife and ran out of the room to be with his sons. They waited outside on the porch until they heard a baby wailing. The three, all wide-eyed, stiffened toward one another and stood up together, not knowing what to do. They hugged until Irma and the midwife called them into the bedroom.

The three men stood in the doorway, grinning. Irma told them they could come in now. "It's a girl!" Edmond joined his wife, and they kissed like never before as she held their baby girl. Irma said, "She'll make a fine addition to this family, and with a father and two big brothers to look after her, she'll be well protected. Welcome to the world, little girl. What should we call her?"

Edmond looked back at his sons. The younger yelled out a name. They all had suggestions, but they settled on Irmeina after Irma. They thought it's only befitting since Edmond had his namesake. Now Irma had hers. They were all complete now. Edmond and Irma had something to call their own now.

CHAPTER 3

Irmeina was two years old when Irma put her on a horse to ride her into town to church. By then, they had four horses, each for an adult in the house. Already, they were outgrowing the small trailer with its two bedrooms, so, Edmond Jr. built a second house behind the first one. It was for himself and his brother. Irmeina would have her room in the boys' old room. They thought only right that a little girl have her room. Then Irma fell ill.

She was throwing up every morning and didn't have an appetite. That was unusual for Irma, so Edmond was worried. He invited the doctor over to check her out. This time, Edmond stuck around in a concerned stupor. He didn't know what to do. Then the doctor said he had some news to deliver. Irma was pregnant again. Edmond was so relieved. It wasn't like Irma to not have an appetite; but now that he knew why, he could cater to his wife. He was happy to do it. Edmond took care of Irmeina and cooked more than usual. Irmeina would listen to her mother's belly whenever she could. She knew something, not someone, was in there. Irmeina was so excited never-the-less.

Irmeina looked like a miniature Irma. She favored her mother something terrible. She had long flowing black hair and tan skin. Her eyes looked like small pieces of coal that darted out from her long and thick eyebrows. Irma was so proud. Just as Edmond Jr. had taken after his father, Irmeina took after her mother. Edmond Sr. was a looker himself. He was at least six feet tall and as handsome as could be. He had dark curly hair, and his skin was only two shades darker than that of his wife's. His mother was very dark, and his father was rumored to have been his master on the plantation although he never lived in the big house. This fueled his rigor to save his money and eventually buy his freedom.

When their second daughter was born, Edwina combined both of her parents. She had her mother's temper and would fuss and throw things when she was hungry. When adults would talk to her, she would get quiet and peer into their eyes as if to understand every word. Then when you asked her to do something, she would take control and execute beautifully. Edwina had long curly dark-brown hair and long eye lashes. She looked like a fusion of both Irma and Edmond.

Then finally came Louise. When she came along, she caused a temporary rift in the family. Edmond assumed that Irma was cheating on him. His sons initially felt alienated. The whole family's skin tone was the same. There was an unspoken pride in sharing the same hue. They understood and saw issues from the same perspective because they had similar experiences, and then came Louise.

Louise was brown skinned. When the sun kissed her, she wouldn't get darker like her sibling; but a reddish tone would emerge from her brown, like clay. Irma loved her all the same; she loved her from the beginning.

Her mother would vouch for her all the time, looking for a way to explain away what seemed like a difference. Irma would expound on her strengths. She would hold Louise up to the light to make up for all the awkwardness she might feel in sticking out in a family of light-skinned people. Irma never cared, but everyone would notice: "Are you babysitting?" "Did you step out on Edmond?" "Is that a slave child you adopted?" Irma's feelings would be hurt, but she would never let on. She would just defend her child by scolding nosy people, "You know how funny genes can be. Her grandmother on her father's side was very dark. I guess she showed up in Louise, but she's ours never-the-less! She is a part of this family, and I gave birth to her. I was there fully awake when she came out. She's mine!, and I love her just the same as my other children." The looks she would leave on people's faces spoke volumes. Irma would only excuse herself and walk away.

When they went places, she made sure that Louise always rode with her. She was the best at speaking up for her child. Louise couldn't help it; but in a world that saw skin as both a badge of honor and a badge of debasement, she caused more trouble than good. Her brothers loved her and doted on her at home but were not as well versed at explaining things to people who knew their family. Her sisters played with Louise and would exhibit a quiet anger when folks would ask questions. They didn't understand the difference. They all came from the same parents. They lived on the same land. They ate the same food and worked the same field. They played with the same toys; and although they knew there was a definite difference between them all and white people, they couldn't always deal with the subtler disparities among the members of their family.

Louise was intelligent, though. She knew how to downplay when with whites to stay safe. She was smart enough to realize the danger in sticking out but brave enough to fight on her level. Like the times Irma would take her into town with her, Louise was five now but would hold her mother's hand when going into different shops. She knew she was supposed to stay outside and wait, but Louise would not be separated from her mother. Irma approached the clerk at the counter with her usual basket of fruits and vegetables. With one hand in Louise's and the other laying her array out on the counter, she made small talk with the clerk, "That corn is rather large this season."

The store owner was silent. "Is that your little girl?"

Irma answered, "Yes . . . she's my baby."

He went on, "Better keep her away from your husband. No telling what another man's child could bring in your household."

Irma returned the silence, accepted his money, and walked away. Louise stared at the man behind the counter as he turned red. On the way out, she asked, "Momma, what did he mean by that?" Irma told her not to worry. People were just ignorant, and Louise seemed to understand what she meant by that.

Louise took in everything around her. These interactions never scared her. They only made her thirst for knowledge. She seemed to read more voraciously and ask more questions when these things happened. She wanted to know what was going on. She more than knew her place as a child. When out in public, she was always quiet. If she wanted to speak, she would always pull an adult to the side to make sure it was okay, although one day she could not hold her tongue.

The whole family was traveling across the forest to Edmond's old community. Besides the bar, there was a church there and many homes of other former slaves who had bought their freedom or were born into it. Edmond was proud of his family. He was also proud of where he came from. He loved the people who raised him and who made him the man he was. Occasionally, he would go back to visit. Today he took his whole family. They anticipated spending the whole day there, so they left early so they would not have to rush. Between their home and the old community was the plantation where Edmond Sr. was born. Edmond knew many folks there but never dared to go back. Although he bought his freedom long ago, he always feared they might try to take it back; so he cut his losses once he left.

He thought of saving enough money to buy his mother's freedom but didn't want to ruffle any feathers. He didn't want to be the trouble maker, returning to buy everyone's freedom. He just stayed away. Edmond didn't even share any stories of his past with his children. Sometimes they would ask, but he would just get quiet and then change the subject. Today, Irma inquired about his mother. She knew they had more than enough money to buy her freedom, so Edmond said once they got back to the old community he would learn some information about her and look into it.

Just as they passed the old plantation, the family noticed clouds of dust kicking up in the distance. It was a troupe of horses being occupied by white men. The tribe got quiet and rode along at a cautious pace, waiting for the men to pass. They did not. "You all coming from the old plantation over there?"

Edmond spoke up, "Naw, sir. We headed to Stone Haven."

The white men wanted to know. "That's that place where the free niggas go, ain't it? You'll free, or you'll running from the plantation?"

Edmond Jr. butted in, "We is free!"

Edmond Sr. excused his son, "I got my papers right here, sir." He reached into his shirt pocket and unfolded his freedom papers, holding them high enough for the white men to see. The white men froze and looked around at one another. None reached for the papers to look. Then they responded, "We know what's going on here. You'll done snatched that baby up from her master to get her to freedom."

One man looked at Edmond Sr. "That your love child or something? Wanna bring her in with the rest of the family, huh?"

Then Irma raised her voice, "That's my baby. I gave birth to her!"

The white men looked around at each other again. "Well, we'll just see about that." With guns drawn, the white men said they would take the family back to the plantation to see what was going on. They asked if there was a ransom on Louise's head. Edmond Sr. frantically tried to explain. It was to no avail. Then Edmond Sr. said that the law was on his side. He had his papers and had no intentions of going back to that plantation especially under these circumstances, so he challenged the leader of the white men to a fight. He threatened to get the law involved. The white men assured Edmond that the law was not on his side. The leader also let him know that he was not interested in fighting, so they argued. The rest of the family tried to get past the men; they pulled the reigns of their horses, and they raised their front legs and neighed. Clouds of dust rose around the commotion, and then there were gunshots.

The white men galloped off in the direction they came from. When the dust cleared, Edmond Jr. was laying on the ground, clutching his chest. Irma dismounted to examine her stepson. "Junior, let me see." She removed his hand to find a small pool of blood on his shirt. Looking up at her husband, she said, "Edmond, he's been shot! We've got to get him to a doctor!" Edmond Sr. responded, "Well, he can't ride himself there!" The patriarch appointed Irmeina, now nine, to ride Edmond Jr.'s horse. Edmond Sr. put his son on the horse with him, and they all

IRMA'S GUN

rode to Stone Haven as fast as they could. There was a medic there who worked in a doctor's office in town.

By the time they arrived, Junior was out of breath and riving in pain. The community rallied around the family as Edmond quickly told them what happened. Someone got the medic, and he did what he could. They took Junior into someone's house and laid him on a bed where he was treated. About two hours later, the medic came out and pronounced Junior dead. Edmond was silent. He glared at Louise. Then he looked at his wife. "We need to talk."

Irma cried as the family gathered to hold one another. They all cried. Then, one woman from Stone Haven suggested they come in to see Junior one last time before he was prepared for a funeral. All of Stone Haven sympathized with Edmond Sr. and his family. The people of Stone Haven put the family up in an abandoned house for a few days while they prepared the funeral at a church in Stone Haven. A grave was dug in the local cemetery for Junior. The family felt safe there.

After the funeral, Junior was buried. At the burial, Louise asked her mother if Junior died because of her. Irma assured her she had nothing to do with Junior's death. She went on, "Some people will not like you because of the color of your skin. They may try to cause problems for you because they don't understand you or where you come from. That is what happened a few days ago when Junior was killed. It wasn't you, baby." Louise said okay and shed a tear. She was there to witness everything that happened. She knew her brown skin made the white men think she was a slave and that her family was doing something wrong. She felt so guilty but as a child could not express it. All Louise could do was hang on to the words her mother had said.

The ride back to their home was silent. The sun hung in the sky as the wind was still not stirring a thing. The only thing you could hear was the clip-clop of the horse's hooves moving at a slow pace. The ride back without Junior was a glum one. When they arrived home, everyone retreated to their rooms to change clothes and get ready for dinner. As soon as the girls and their older brother disappeared, Edmond broke down and cried. Irma tried to console him, but he did not want her sympathy. He just sat in a chair outside of the kitchen and sobbed as Irma prepared dinner.

Irma made everyone a plate and sat them on the table at their usual place settings. She called for dinner, and they all dragged in. In silence they sat at their places. Edmond was the last one to sit down. By then his eyes were red and his face pale as he wiped his face with his hand. No one said a word. Everyone just picked over their food as they all tried to ignore the empty place where Junior would usually sit. After dinner, there was a lot of scraping of plates into the slop bucket outside the kitchen. The lone son asked if Irma needed help cleaning up the kitchen. She said no, she would be okay. He went to the new house out back to be alone.

Once the kitchen was clean, Irma settled into her pajamas and lay across the edge of their bed. Edmond came in, visibly shaken. "Irma, we need to talk."

Irma was disturbed. "You keep saying that. What do you mean? What is there to talk about? Junior's gone now."

Edmond had plenty of questions. "And do you know why? Do you even understand why my son is dead? When Louise ain't around, this family gets along just fine. When she is around, it's always a million questions! Is she yours? Is she a slave? Why she look so different?"

Irma butted in, "Edmond, she looks like your mama."

Edmond was hot. "My mama is a slave on a plantation, and Louise may as well be right there with her!" Irma couldn't believe her ears. Was the man she loved trying to oust the little girl she loved? Would she have to choose? It wasn't Louise's fault that her skin differed from the rest of her family's. Irma cried, "Edmond what are you saying?" He turned around. "I think you know what I'm saying. I worked too hard to get off that plantation to have somebody drag me backwards. Now I know a good white family, the Augers. They're an older couple, and they'll have a lot of love in their hearts for a girl like Louise. They'd be happy to raise her. With them, there wouldn't be so much suspicion surrounding her existence. When she goes somewhere, she won't be attacked and questioned all the time. She'll be better off and happier with them, and our family can continue to prosper. Irma, you really need to think about it."

Irma rolled over and sat up on the bed. She was agitated. "You want me to just give away my baby? What is the purpose of a family? A family is supposed to love and protect each of its members. Without a family, what do you have? How do you know she'll be better off with a white family? They can't protect her like we could!" Edmond came back, "I'm telling you, Irma, look at what happened to Junior. We couldn't protect him, could we? Who's gonna die next? My other son? One of our daughters? Me? You? Who, Irma, who? Besides, with the Augers, people won't harass her the way they do with us. I'm telling you, she'll be better off!"

Just then Louise stormed in, crying, "I knew it was my fault! Momma, you said it wasn't! I don't want to go and live with a white family! I want to stay here with you! I promise I won't cause any more trouble, I promise!" Louise jumped into Irma's arms and held her as tight as she could. Louise apologized to her father. Edmond kneeled down, stroking her hair; and with tears in his eyes, he told her, "Baby, you'll be better off. They can take better care of you than we can. You'll be safer with them. They can protect you."

Louise inquired, "What about my brother and sisters? Will I be able to visit them sometimes?"

Edmond said, "Sure, baby. Now go back to your room so Mommy and I can finish talking."

Louise sulked and walked back to her room. Irmiena and Edwina wanted to know what all the commotion was about. "Louise, are they really going to send you away?" Louise answered, "Yes. They want me to go live with a white family. I don't like white people. I like you'll! I want to stay here."

Irmeina instantly understood the logic of sending her sister away. She loved her and wanted her to stay, but Irmeina realized the seriousness of what had just happened. She was scared too. She trusted her parents' judgment; and if this was best, Irmeina was all for it. "Louise, I'll bet those people have money. Think of all the beautiful toys you'll have and all the nice dresses you'll get to wear. You'll go to the best schools and have better opportunities than us. Then, once you get settled, you can come back to visit. Look at it that way."

Louise cried again, "You want me to go?"

Her sisters rallied around her with hugs. "We don't want you to go. We want what's best for you. You know we love you. You have a chance to go on and be better than us. Represent us in all that you do, and we'll keep you in our hearts."

Louise got quiet. She didn't know what to say. Her confusion gave in to what everyone was trying to convince her of. She acquiesced. She went to her dresser to gather her things. Irma walked in. "Louise, what are you doing?" She answered that she was putting her things together to go live with the white family. She explained to her mother she would miss everyone but if it were for the best she wanted to go.

Irma couldn't believe what she was hearing. Her baby wanted to leave? Maybe it was for the best. She wouldn't be giving her away for good. They could always visit and keep tabs on one another's whereabouts and good deeds. It wouldn't be permanent, just a move to keep everybody safe like Edmond was telling her. The more she went over it in her mind, the more she changed her mind. Everyone was slowly letting Louise go, hoping for a better outcome. It was done.

The next day Irma and Edmond went into town to the Augers' home. They were uninvited; so when they knocked and a butler came to the door, he almost slammed the door in their faces. Irma intervened, "Are the Augers home? We're here on some very important business."

The butler's visage went from angry and irritated to concerned and displaced. He said, "One moment." Then he closed the door.

Irma and Edmond stood there for about ten minutes until the butler reappeared. He opened the door, surveying the couple from head to toe, and then cracked the door just enough for them to walk through. The butler was silent. He just waited, so Irma and Edmond walked in. "Right this way."

He led them into a living space where the Augers were sitting with curious faces. They summoned them to come in and have a seat. Their first comment was, "Do we owe you something? We don't recall having done business with you before."

"No, ma'am. We're here on some different business. We would like for you to take our daughter for raising. She's become a bit too much for us to handle, and being as though you don't have any children, we thought you might like to raise her for us. We know you could do a better job than we ever could, and she would probably be safer here anyways. See, our eldest son was recently murdered by some thugs on our way back to my old community."

"Well, what did you do to bring that on?"

"We didn't do anything. It was all a big misunderstanding. We tried to explain, but they didn't believe us, so they shot my son. We don't want a similar fate for our youngest child, so we would be much obliged if you would take her on for us."

"Why? What's wrong with her that you don't want her?"

Edmond and Irma looked at each other. "Why, nothing's wrong with her. She's as bright as a whip. She can read well for her age and wants to go to school. Well, you're smart people. No need for exaggeration. Her skin is brown, and she is darker than the rest of us. The color of her skin has stood out like a sore thumb and in the past has caused problems for our family. We love her dearly, but since my son was killed just about a week ago, well, we just don't want any more trouble."

Mrs. Auger said, "I see . . . and how much do you want for this child?"

"We don't want anything for her. We have a small farm and a piece of land. We sell our produce at market and fetch a fair penny for it. We getting along just fine, thank you. We just want you to guarantee that you will take good care of our Louise and raise her up right. We want you to do what we can't. Besides, she'll be safer with you than with us."

"Is that her name, Louise?"

"Yes, ma'am."

"Do you have a picture of her?"

"Yes, ma'am. . . right here."

"Why, she's a pretty little thing. What a shame she's causing you trouble. Is she lazy?"

"No, ma'am, not at all. She's strong for her age and gets along just fine."

"Well, of course we'll have to discuss it amongst ourselves first. You can wait out on the porch while we talk about it."

"Yes, ma'am."

Edmond and Irma crept onto the porch led by the butler. He left them alone and said he'd be back when they were done. The middle-aged couple was nervous. With no other recourse, they were not prepared to turn back with a no. They had done all the convincing they could do. Now it was up to the Augers.

About twenty minutes had passed; and they both were pacing the creaky porch, making more noise than they realized. Just then the door opened, and the butler motioned for them to come in. The trio made their way back into the living room where the Augers were all smiles.

"We've made a decision."

Edmond jumped at Mrs. Auger. "Yes, ma'am?"

"Now, wait a minute. We also have stipulations. We are willing to take on your child, but before we commit, we'd like to meet her."

"Yes, ma'am."

"And she'll have to go to school, no more working in fields and on farms. If we are to raise her, she'll be raised right with a good education and a strict upbringing."

"Will she be able to visit us sometimes?"

"No, ma'am! If we find her suitable, we'd like to adopt. She'll be ours for the keeping. No going back and forth. She'll have a new life with new friends and a whole new world to live in, no going back and forth. She'll soon forget her life with you anyway."

With tears in her eyes Irma said, "Yes, ma'am."

"So when can we meet her? Can you bring her by tomorrow?"

"Yes, ma'am. Tomorrow will be just fine." Irma cleared her throat.

"Well then, it's settled. We'll meet Louise tomorrow at three. You can let yourselves out. We'll see you tomorrow."

"Yes, ma'am. Thank you."

The butler closed the door behind them. They hugged like they had not in a long while. There were mixed emotions. They had overcome. They knew the Augers would fall in love with Louise, and they were elated that she would be living a better life, but they missed her already. They mounted their horses and talked about it on the way home.

"Edmond, I'm okay with everything except the fact that we won't see her anymore. Are you sure we're doing the right thing?"

"Baby, we don't have a choice. People already think that you stepped out on me. They think Louise is a love child I'm taking care of. Now you know somewhere down the line that's bound to cause more trouble just like Junior getting shot."

"Deep down inside, I know you're right. I already feel a hole growing in my heart."

Irma cried the rest of the way home while Edmond was silent. When they reached the trailer, they tied the horses up and sat on the porch for a while before even letting the kids know they were home. They wanted to give them one last night to play together before Louise left. They knew once Louise met the Augers, she would not be coming back. How would they tell the other children they would never see their sister again? They wouldn't tell them that's how. Edmond and Irma decided that it would be their secret that Louise was never coming back. If they told the kids the truth, it would be too hard to sever ties. They just hoped that they eventually forgot about one another, although they knew that was the furthest thing from the truth. They vowed to keep the secret never-the-less.

Irma finally went inside to start dinner. Then her husband stopped her, "Let me cook tonight. I'll make something special."

"We can cook together."

"No, I've got it. Go and spend some time with the children."

Irma was impressed. She smiled a shy- school- girl smile and walked away to look for the children. She checked the girls' room, but it was empty. There was no sign of them. Then she went across the way to the boys' house out back. Before she got there, she could hear the chuckling of little girls and one distinct male voice above all the others giving orders. They were not taking him seriously because they would quiet down just long enough to listen and then upend his conversation in laughter.

Irma peeked into the humble house. "What are you guys doing?"

"Momma, Walter was showing us a game of house. See, my doll is the mother. Irmeina's doll is the father, and Edwina's doll is the baby. We are sending her away to school, but don't worry, she'll be back in the summer."

Irma choked, "Why is she going away to school? Don't they have a school that she can walk to or ride a horse to?"

"She's been bad, Momma. She must learn, so she's going off to school to become a better girl. Good girls make excellent women, and excellent women go on to get married and have children and live wonderful lives. Don't worry, she'll be back."

Irma gazed at her daughter as her eyes glazed over. She said nothing then she walked away. As the voices became more and more distant, a large tear made its way down to Irma's chin and held on until she wiped it with her sleeve. By this time tomorrow, her youngest child would be nothing to her but a memory gone forever. She made her way to Louise's room to pack her things.

By the time the girls had worked up an appetite for dinner, Irma was all done.

"Mommy, you packed up all my stuff? Am I leaving tonight?"

"No. You'll be leaving tomorrow around two. The Augers want to meet you. If they like you, you will probably stay."

Now Louise was excited. "Do they have any children?"

"No. You'll be the only one, so you won't have to compete with a brother and two sisters. All the love will be yours."

"Will I be going to school to continue learning how to read?"

"Yes. You'll learn other subjects too like math and history."

"Will I learn *my* history, like how the Indians ended up on reservations and how colored people became slaves?"

Irma sat erect. "Now, Louise, you listen to me good. The Augers are white people. They ain't no different than the whites in town or the whites at the market. They got good hearts, is all, and they're older so they'll be depending on you to help them with things like the chores or carrying bags from the store. They want to give you a chance, but you have to remember they're not like me or your dad. They will love you just in a different way. I want you to get along. Listen to them and mind them. Don't ruffle no feathers or give them a hard way to go. You'll make trouble for yourself that way, and that's what you don't want. Do you hear me?"

"Yes, ma'am . . . I hear you." And just like that, her excitement vanished. She now knew this was serious business, but something in her still looked forward to it.

"Girls, let's get ready for dinner. Daddy's making something special."

"Oooohh weee . . . what is it?"

"I don't know. It's a surprise to me too. C'mon, let's go see."

Edmond had set the table with the good dishes. He poured freshly squeezed orange juice into everyone's cups. Then he put the baked chicken on the table. The green beans and rosemary rice followed. Everyone sat down, trying to ignore Junior's empty chair. Now there would be two.

CHAPTER 4

The two parents didn't understand it. The girls and Walter talked a mile a minute, asking one another questions and reminiscing about all the things they did together. Then they talked about a reunion, how they would preserve Louise's bed and her space. They said it would always be hers for whenever she came back.

Edmond and Irma tried to interrupt and change the subject, but the children would not hear of it. They went on. Usually, Irma would clean up any mess she made while cooking, but tonight, everyone pitched in. Walter washed to dishes while Irmeina and Edwina dried them and put them away. Louise was too small to help, so she just danced around and talked purposely in the way wanting her siblings to shoo her away and tell her to move. Edmond swept. Then it was over and time to go to bed.

The next day everyone slept in. The rooster crowed, and Louise just turned over. No one bothered getting out of their pajamas until around noon. By the time lunch was made, consumed, and cleaned up, it was time for Louise to leave. They would take two horses to the Augers : one to carry Louise's belongings and the other to carry her. Louise asked questions the whole way there. Her curiosity about this adventure could not be quelled. Then when she got there, she suddenly remembered the long talk her mother had with her about how to conduct herself, so she hid her excitement and put on her noble face.

The Augers were waiting on the porch, "Well, well, lookey here, and what do we have here?" Mrs. Auger bent down to get a good eye full of Louise. "You *are* pretty."

"Yes, you are. I hear you're just as smart too."

"Thank you."

"How old are you?"

Louise held up her whole hand with her fingers spread wide to see. "I'm this many."

The Augers laughed in delight. "Well, I see. You're five years old. Do you have a middle name?"

"No, ma'am."

"I see."

Irma butted in, "Maybe you can keep her last name Taylor as a middle name and give her your last name. That way, she can always know from whence she came."

"I won't hear of it," Mrs. Auger snapped. "Her new name will be simply Louise Auger. She's ours now. Leave her things on the porch. The butler will be out to help her put them away. We'll be in touch if there are any problems. So if you don't hear from us, just know that all is well and that she is taken care of. Okay, okay, fine, then it's settled. Thank you, and you can be on your way now." After they gave her a few last hugs and kisses, the departure was an easy one. Everyone anticipated the reunion, but there would be none. Louise Auger would be headed in to town the next day to get adopted.

"So, Louise, come sit next to me. Would you like a snack?"

"Yes, ma'am. What is it?"

"Don't ask questions, love. If someone offers you something, you take it. Charity is not about pride. Remember that, okay?"

"Yes, ma'am."

"Now come with me into the kitchen."

Louise followed Mrs. Auger as she was told. So far, things were going okay. These white people didn't seem so bad. They were nice to her, and they seemed generous. Louise already wished that there were at least other children around, but that was all right. She would see her siblings soon enough. As she enjoyed her red seedless grapes, she entertained Mrs. Auger's conversation. The new matriarch informed her of what her new life would entail, where she would go to school, how she would behave both at home and with others, and when and where she would learn with a tutor.

The Augers assumed Louise would be behind the other children her age since she had never been to school. They didn't know that Irma was vigilant in teaching her children all they could handle, everything from their ancestry as Indians and colored children to reading and counting numbers and money. She also taught them how to handle themselves around white people. Louise would discover soon enough that the Augers lessons in etiquette differed greatly from Irma's. Irma showed her children how to have pride in the ways they interacted with others no matter how they had to adjust themselves to get along. The Augers taught Louise how to maintain her "place" not just as a child but as a person of color. They taught her how to be less, but it was too late. The damage had been done. Irma and her biological family had instilled a self-esteem that could not be removed with simple displacement. Louise only shrank in the face of adversity only to regain her confidence when around people who looked like her.

"Come and take your bath, Louise. I'll lay out your pajamas and your clothes for tomorrow. I've put a towel, a washcloth, and a piece of soap in the bathroom for you. Do you need help washing?"

"No, ma'am. I can wash myself. My mother taught me how."

"Now Louise let me make you understand something. There will be no more talk of your mother or your siblings. You're with us now. We are your parents. If you need anything, you come to us. Everything you learned with Irma and Edmond, you can just as well abandon. We will re teach you everything and I do mean everything. Do you understand?"

Louise cried, "You want me to just forget about my family?"

"They're not your family anymore. We are." With that, Mrs. Auger walked away and left her to bathe herself. Louise sobbed quietly as she removed her clothes and threw them to the floor. She had never felt naked this way before, not even in front of her siblings, and she was all alone. She eased into the warm water and squeezed water on her face to mask her tears. Not that anyone was looking, but she was learning to be strong for herself. She put her hands together and prayed a little prayer for her family and finally for herself that she could live and survive in this new world. When she was done washing, she dried herself and put on her night clothes. Louise climbed into bed and pulled the covers up to her chin. Mrs. Auger came in and reminded her to say her prayers.

"Louise, we go to church every Sunday around here, and we believe in God. You will too. I don't know if you've ever been to church, but we will teach you. I'm going to get you a Bible, and you will go to the children's Bible study on Thursday nights. You need to learn about the stories of the Bible. Now get from underneath those covers and get on your knees with me. We're going to say our prayers."

Louise reluctantly removed the covers. She wanted to blurt out that she had said a prayer for her family but instinctively withdrew her notions and went through the motions of praying with Mrs. Auger. She got on her knees and repeated what she was told to say. Mrs. Auger also kneeled close to Louise. The warmth and softness of her body comforted Louise and made her sleepy.

After prayers, she pulled herself back into the bed and Mrs. Auger tucked her in. Mrs. Auger drew the curtains and turned out the lamp. Louise felt like a queen. She had never had a whole room to herself before. She was exhausted from the day's events and fell fast asleep.

The next morning Mrs. Auger swished into Louise's room wearing a magenta dress pulled taut at the waist and flowed out from the hips down. She pulled the curtains back to let the sun in. Louise turned over in her bed with sleep in her eyes as Mrs. Auger stopped to pose and tilt her head to admire her new baby the perfect age for molding. Louise was old enough to understand but still impressionable, and now she belonged to the Augers.

"Wash your face, Louise. Put your clothes on and come into the kitchen for breakfast. We have to hurry now. We're going into town this morning."

"Yes, ma'am."

Louise walked into the kitchen and sat down at the head of the table like she normally would at her original home. Mr. Auger was swift to inform her that that was his chair. He pulled out a chair and told her she could sit there. Then he pushed her underneath the table. Her legs dangled from the tall chair as she reached over the table to pull her plate close. She waited. The Augers were now seated and ate. Mrs. Auger summoned her to "eat up" they had to make it into town by a certain time. Louise put her hands together and closed her eyes.

"You silly girl, no need to pray now. Just eat your food. Go ahead."

Louise felt awkward. She ate anyways. When she was done, she looked around for the slop bucket. There was none. She wouldn't dare put her good scraps of bacon and that piece of biscuit in the trash. Then Mrs. Auger snatched up her plate and scraped what was left over a paper bag near the back door. Louise looked at her like she was crazy.

"What's the matter, child? You didn't want that bacon."

"No, ma'am. I'm full."

"That's what I thought. Now wash your hands and go sit on the porch."

Louise did as she was told. She looked around for the horses. There were none, only a black and dark-green automobile. She had seen them only in town when traveling with Irma but never rode in one. Today was her day. Was she rich suddenly? She didn't dare ask.

They drove past the market where her mother would sell her produce. This was another part of town she didn't know about. They parked the car, and the trio walked into an office together but separate. Louise thought the man behind the desk knew Mrs. Auger because he seemed so happy to see her. "Good morning, ma'am. What can I help you with?"

"I'm here to initiate an adoption."

"Are you the biological mother?"

Mrs. Auger was offended. "Do I look like the biological mother?"

"Oh is this the subject of this adoption?" The man bent towards Louise. "Hello, little girl. How are you today?"

No white person had ever cared to ask how she was doing. She didn't answer. She only stared at the man while swiping at Mrs. Auger's hand. Mrs. Auger held the child's hand.

"Say hello, Louise."

"Hi."

"Ma'am, I'm afraid I will need the biological mother's signature to properly process the adoption."

"Well, the biological mother already said I could have her. Just ask Louise. She'll tell you."

"Ma'am, that won't be necessary. On the paperwork, it needs to be proven that the child is being given up by the natural parents, not taken by someone else."

Mrs. Auger butted in, "Are you suggesting that I'm a thief!?"

"Well, no, ma'am, not at all. I'm just telling you what the procedure is. I cannot process this adoption without at least the maternal parent's signature . . . at least an X if she can't write."

"Well, I can mark an X if that's all you need!"

The man paused and excused himself. He said he'd be right back. He went into an office where another man peered out through a window and said something in a curt fashion to the man. He returned and apologized with the proper paperwork. The Augers filled it out, and Mrs. Auger placed a large sloppy X where she was told to. Just like that, it was done. Louise had been adopted. Louise and Mrs. Auger walked out hand in hand. It was a beautiful day.

While they were in town, they shopped for a few knick-knacks: an old basket with a handle to carry the things in and some fabric in an assortment of patterns and colors to make dresses for Louise. Mrs. Auger wasn't satisfied with the dowdy dresses that Irma sent with her. They all had wild colors, some with strange patterns and turquoise and orange beads sewn into them. Mrs. Auger hated those beads. She said they would all fall off in the wash.

They stopped at a few other places and ended up at the market. Louise got excited, and the Augers didn't know why. She was looking for her family. They were not there, but the nostalgia of the place made her happy. She held on tight to the hand of her adult until she got to the counter.

"Say good day to the clerk, Louise."

Louise flinched. The clerk flinched, "I see your back where you belong."

"This ain't my mama!" Louise snapped.

"Louise! Well, if you don't watch your tone with grown folk! Please excuse her. She's only been with us for a day and some change. She's not all the way acclimated to the ways of a child, a colored one at that."

Mrs. Auger held on to her hand while snatching her arm as if to say "bad girl." Louise just glared at the clerk like she always did; and this time, she wasn't scared. Mrs. Auger finished her business. When they got outside, she gave Louise a good brisk talking to.

"Now I see why your people gave you away! You are a pistol! You can't talk to grown folk that away. That won't get you anything but trouble. Now today you're in luck. We are good, decent people and get respect around here. That'll get extended to you once people know you're with us, but you got to know your place! Getting all uppity 'bout things won't get you anything but trouble, you hear? And you'll be in it by yourself. No harm won't come our way only yours you hear?"

Louise shifted her glare from the clerk to her care giver, "Yes, ma'am."

"Don't get that-a-way with me! I'm the one taking care of ya! Now come on!"

Mrs. Auger snatched her up, and into their car they went. It was quiet the whole way home as Louise missed her peoples already. Irma would have never chastised her in front of all those people; and when the clerk made his remarks at her, Irma would have taken up for her child. What kind of people were these Augers? And what kind of life did she have to look forward to? Louise just wondered as she took in the scenery passing by the window of the car.

CHAPTER 5

As the years passed by, Louise learned to get along in this new world. She was the only colored girl in her school. Her white friends were far and few between, but she did have colored friends. They would treat her a little different than they would one another. Sometimes they would have to explain things to her that were not apparent in her white world. She loved the contrasts and soaked up her culture. Although she would have to hide it once she got home, she was getting the best of both worlds: the etiquette and cultivation of her white world and the couth and refinement of her colored world. She was becoming what they called a mixed breed (like her sisters) although her skin did not reflect it.

She mastered her lessons quickly and rose to the top of her class; but when it came time to render scholarships for college, she was passed up. No one thought she wanted to go because she was colored. This was unchartered territory she was treading upon, so no one knew what to do. Her path was for the taking, and that's what she would have to do: take it. It was all up to her. Everyone stood idly by as she thrived. No need to worry, though. The Augers had plenty of money; and as long as Louise kept up appearances and always did what was in their favor, she could have whatever she wanted including college.

Her colored friends were not going to college. Some only completed their educations up to the sixth grade and then went to work on a farm or in someone's house as a maid or butler. Some of her other friends studied up to the twelfth grade only to work in a store in town or become a teacher. Teaching was the noblest of professions especially for a colored woman, but Louise did not want to do that either.

More than anything, she wanted her family the people she started life with. She hadn't seen them since they dropped her off that fateful day at the Augers. She never even ran into them in town at the market. Mrs. Auger made sure of that. She never took Louise into town on Mondays when Irma was there selling her produce; and she refused to get her a car, saying there were white kids without cars and it would only be trouble. Louise figured she just didn't want her to find her way back to Irma, but Louise would find a way even if it was only in her heart.

Once her eighteenth birthday came around, the Augers said they wanted to have a talk with Louise. Mr. Auger had a friend who worked in the White House close to the president. He was even in some meetings to listen in and give his opinion on certain matters. His name was George. One day he came across some information he thought Mr. Auger might like to know about.

"George, what brings you here today? Haven't seen you in a while. Can I offer you a beer, some ice water, or some orange juice?"

"Sure, Augie. I'll take a beer. You might want to have one too."

"Why you say that, George?"

"Well, when I say what I have to say, well, you might wanna take a seat."

Mr. Auger sat down. "What is it?"

"It's that girl of yours, Louise."

"She in some trouble?"

"No, not yet, and she might be better off if you don't tell her what I'm about to say EVER."

"Well, say it, George!"

"That girl is in possession of a license to kill anyone who threatens her including you."

"WHAT! Well, that's just ridiculous! Who the hell would give a colored girl something like that?"

"She got it from her momma. Years ago, her momma killed a man. The president at the time pardoned the whole thing because she saved his life one time. Said that license was to be passed down to all the women folk throughout the years. And sure 'nuff, one of her girls killed a man. Heard him talking in a bar 'bout killing her brother, so she slipped his pistol out of its holster and shot 'em with it!"

"Now, George, that can't be"

"I'm telling you it is. But see, this girl was an Indian passing for white. So when the whole thing never went to trial, no one got suspicious. But I'm telling you Louise got it too. I know she's got a temper on her and smart as a whip. But if you ever cross her, you'll be a dead man, and she'll get away with it."

"Noooo . . . they wouldn't let her."

"Yes, they would. I've seen the ordinance with my own eyes."

"So what should I do, George?"

"Don't tell her, that's what. She doesn't need to know."

"Thanks for the heads-up. She just turned eighteen. I promised her an endowment so she can start herself a life of her own. That'll get her out of our hair. There's really not a lot of places in the world for a girl like that to go. She doesn't wanna be a teacher, she can't go to college. She ain't courting anybody. I reckon it's just time to turn her loose."

"That sounds like a plan to me, Augie."

"Yeah, that's what I'll do." Mr. Auger called Louise into the room.

George was still seated. He looked Louise up and down. "Hello there, Louise. Haven't seen you in a while."

"Hi, Mr. George. What brings you here?"

George glanced at Mr. Auger with fear. "Oh, just dropping by 'cause I happened to be in the neighborhood." His voice was tense.

Mr. Auger jumped right in. "Have a seat, darlin'."

Louise followed his instructions, "Yes, sir?"

"Well, you know your eighteenth birthday is coming up, right?"

"Yes, sir."

"I want you to start thinking about your future. I'm going to give you a good amount of money that I've been saving up for you since the day you came here. You can buy yourself a house and start a life of your own, no use in hanging around here. You're a grown woman now. Time you started acting like it." Louise stood up and gave Mr. Auger a big hug. "Thank you, Mr. Auger. You know, when my mother brought me here, I didn't know what to expect, but you all have done right by me. I'm gonna buy me a few acres of land and build a house on it just like my mother had. I remember how to work the land. I'll turn a profit off it and everything . . . just like my momma, just like my momma."

"And so it will be, Louise. You can come back and visit anytime you wish."

"Speaking of visiting, would you know how I could find my mother and old family?"

"Now, Louise, you've asked us this a million times, and we always tell you the same thing. The day you came to be with us, you said goodbye to your old family. We're your new family, and that's that, okay, honey?"

Louise felt like crying but had no more tears left. She'd been through this enough times before to know as for finding her roots she was on her own. She made a note to herself to put this high on her priority list. She was eager to start her new life. In her mind, she went over repeatedly what Walter and her sisters looked like now. She wanted to hear all the stories of what happened while she wasn't around, good and bad.

She didn't know it, but all she wanted was love. She knew that with the backing of the Augers she could have pushed to go to college. She could have learned a trade. Louise knew the many opportunities afforded her, although because of her skin color the Augers didn't believe in her the way they should have. They let her fall by the wayside because they didn't know what to do with her. Louise was just elated to have the chance to be out on her own now. The world was hers for the taking.

She took her endowment and purchased two acres of land. She built a house and bought two horses. She hired some help and planted many fruits and vegetables: watermelon, corn, string beans, collard greens,

IRMA'S GUN

onions, carrots, lima beans, and on and on. At first, it was so exciting to be away from the Augers and out on her own. Then loneliness set in. She thought about her biological family again and went back to that office in town where Mrs. Auger adopted her when she was five. She had always kept her eye on it whenever they would go into town. Since the Augers were not cooperative in helping her find her mother, parents and siblings, Louise never had the courage to explore completely; but she was on her own now. It was time.

She wore a dress Mrs. Auger had made for her to go to church in. It was green with yellow beads sewn around the neckline. She wore her black boots with the small heels and put her hair up in a bun. She wanted to be taken seriously. She wanted to look like she had come from money. She felt like she had to compensate for being colored. She thought about facing rejection because of that fact and didn't want her search for her family to suffer just because she was a color that someone wouldn't understand or might fear. She wanted to succeed.

Louise took a deep breath and stepped into the office. A lady was behind the counter and asked if she could help Louise just as she walked through the threshold. Louise hadn't been in this place since she was five.

"Yes, ma'am. I'm here to see if you can help me find the parents that I was born to. I was adopted by a family with the last name Auger thirteen years ago. Any information as to the whereabouts of my born family would be so helpful."

"Well, you do know you're in the county court house?"

"No, ma'am. I was not aware."

"Yes. You'll want to go around the corner and make a left. Adoptions are handled there now."

"Yes, ma'am. Thank you."

"Sure." The lady nodded and walked away as Louise traveled around the corner looking for a door that said *adoptions*. She tapped lightly and waited for a response.

"Yes. Come in." When Louise entered, a different woman stood up and asked to help her.

43

"Yes, ma'am. My name is Louise Auger, and I'm here looking for my born family. I was adopted thirteen years ago by the Augers, and any information as to the whereabouts of my biological parents and siblings would be so helpful."

"Well, where's your adoptive mother? You couldn't just ask her about your biological parents?"

"Well, ma'am, I tried, but I was told she didn't have any information about them."

"That's sounds a bit fishy to me." The woman looked Louise over and hesitated, "Here's a piece of paper. Write down your full name, your biological mother's full name, and your adoptive mother's full name."

"Yes, ma'am." Louise tried her best not to get excited. She purposely took her time sliding the piece of paper over to her side of the counter. She handled the pen ever so delicately, writing down the information the woman asked for. When she was done, she waited patiently for the woman to return.

"Are you finished?"

"Yes, ma'am. Thank you."

The clerk looked over the information and checked the spellings with Louise before utilizing what was on the paper. She disappeared for about twenty minutes while Louise sat on a bench near the door. Louise wasn't sure if she should be sitting there; but since she was the only person in the office, she didn't worry over it too much. If someone walked in, she would just have to stand until the clerk came back.

She returned with a stern look on her face. "Honey, I found your adoption records, but there wasn't much to go on. I don't know who filled out your paperwork, but there were no birth records, there was no mention of your mother's name, and there was no record of where you were born. Could your mother read and write?"

"Yes, ma'am. She taught me."

"Well, I'm afraid not, honey. She marked her signature with an X. That's a sure sign of a person who could not read or write. Are you telling me a fib?"

"No, ma'am. Are you sure you have the right records?"

"Are you challenging me? I'm helping you now, and I don't have to. Don't be unappremciative!"

"No, ma'am. Of course not. May I take a look at the records myself?"

The clerk slid the papers across the counter and waited. Sure enough, the papers included the whole names of Mr. and Mrs. Auger and her mother's name, but that was it. The biological mother's address and the child's information from the birth certificate were all left blank. There was no mention of her siblings or her father. It was a dead end.

The only other thing she could think to do was to return to the market on Mondays hoping her mother still came in to sell her produce. That's it. That is what she would do. But what if that didn't work? The trail would end there. She almost didn't want to go afraid of the failure of not running into her mother or siblings. However she had to, she had no other choice.

Monday came, and Monday went. She sat in the same spot where when Junior and Walter were children they would wait for men to stop so they could shine their shoes for money. The August heat wilted her something terrible, but she didn't care. Running into her real family would prove the perfect excuse anyways. She waited. Every girl who walked by was eyeballed white or not. She knew her sisters were Indian and colored and under the August sun probably a little darker than usual, but she looked at every girl. She didn't know the circumstances they were living under. Maybe they walked with parasols to prevent from getting tanned. She remembered that in the winter their skin got so pale. She hadn't seen them in thirteen years. Every female had to be inspected. Louise had to contain herself, though. Only God knows the trouble that could come from staring at a white woman.

The market closed its doors with a slam. Louise was exhausted, disappointed, hurt, and abandoned. She thought about it. They never came back to visit in thirteen years. She didn't know the Augers told them not to. She revisited the situation that led to her to being adopted. Then she hated her parents for giving her up. They couldn't just love her unconditionally. Then she recounted her venom. Junior died that day, and it was because of her. How would she have felt if the same thing happened again and someone else died because of her? Maybe her being adopted was for the best and she just couldn't see the reality of it. She sure did miss her family, especially Irma. She hadn't felt that love in a long time.

Louise missed Irma's hugs and kisses and mostly the way she would take up for her. Her father didn't even do that and not the Augers. If ever someone accused Louise of wrongdoing, it was always Louise's fault no argument, no investigation. The Augers took good care of her, but their concern was downright different. She missed Irma and vowed that if ever she had children, she would love them the way Irma loved her when she was little. That's it. That's all she could do, so she went on with her life.

CHAPTER 6

Louise found herself at the market every Monday morning selling her produce just like her mother would do. She hoped she'd run into Irma there. Growing up in the care of the Augers, Louise developed a rapport with certain white folk in town; and the clerk at the market was one of them.

"Step right up, Louise. Whatcha got in that basket for me?"

"A few goodies, Mr. Willis corn, green beans, some collards. I'm not stepping on anyone's toes by selling my produce here, am I, you know, preventing anyone else from selling?"

"No. Don't be silly. I run out of things from time to time here. Business is good. Any selling is welcome long as the produce is quality. Got a reputation to keep up, you know."

"I understand. I guess what I'm really getting at is my mother. Have you seen her?"

"Oh, Mrs. Auger? No, not lately." He rifled through the vegetables.

Louise laughed. "No, my real mother."

"And who's that?"

"You know, Irma, an Indian lady about yea tall who sells her produce here every Monday."

47

Mr. Willis's whole face dropped. He discontinued his eye contact. "No, I don't know who you're talking about."

Louise lost her composure. "Yes, you do! You know who I'm talking about. She used to bring me in here when I was a little girl! Then once you saw me with Mrs. Auger, you always acted like she didn't exist anymore! What happened to her? I demand to know!"

"Don't you take that tone with me, young lady!" Mr. Willis hushed her away. "Now I told you I don't know what you're talking about, and that's final. Why don't you ask Mrs. Auger, *your real mother*?"

Louise snatched her vegetables and stormed out of the market, running into a gentleman who seemed to catch her and save her from her own devices.

"Are you okay? Is everything all right?"

Louise brushed her dress off and looked back at Mr. Willis. "Yes. I'm fine, thank you. Why do you ask? Who are you?"

"My name is Samuel Emmerling." He took off his hat. "And your name is?"

"Louise . . . Louise Auger."

"Mr. Willis is a stern man. What happened back there?"

"Well, I was looking for my mother, and he wouldn't help me. He knows something. He just won't say. I hope nothing bad has happened to my mother."

"Well, why would you expect *him* to help you?"

Louise looked into Samuel's eyes and then, frustrated, looked away. "It's complicated." She took her basket of vegetables and threw them over her horse's saddle, never looking at Samuel until he forced her to.

"Tell me about it. I have time."

"Well, I don't. Excuse me."

"Please don't leave. I'd love to talk to you again if you don't have time now. Maybe I could meet you here again and we could sit here on the bench and talk."

Was he trying to court her? He didn't even know Louise. Never the less, she was impressed in her all her fury. "Meet me here tomorrow at twelve thirty sharp!" She galloped off, not waiting for a response.

"Will do, ma'am. Will do." He waved his hat at the dust kicked up by her horse, smiling like a fool.

The next day at twelve thirty, he was waiting on the bench smelling like Sunday morning. Louise didn't arrive until twelve forty-five. She took her time, stepping up to the stoop.

"Hello, Mr. Samuel. I see you're on time."

"Likewise, miss lady. It's good to see you again. I didn't think you would show."

"I'm a woman of my word, Mr. Samuel." She sat down next to him. "Now what did you want to talk to me so bad about?"

Samuel asked her to recount what happened in the market the day they met. Louise obliged; and naturally, she talked about her mother, which led her to her biological family, which led her to the Augers, which led her to Junior and how she wound up getting adopted. Samuel listened intently. She admired his brown skin but never said so. Deep inside, she was still angry with her father for suggesting she be adopted. She was still angry with his bright hued skin. She was still upset he didn't understand that she needed his love more than he needed to live, and she still couldn't understand that he had to choose. If Samuel was talking right, she would choose him just because he was dark. She began her investigation.

"Are you married?"

"No."

"Do you have children?"

"No."

"How old are you?"

"Twenty-two."

"Are you educated? Can you read and write?"

"Yes, both. I graduated from the twelfth grade before going to work on Mr. Weatherfield's farm. I'm his chief share cropper."

Louise was impressed. "Do you have a girlfriend?"

"No."

"Why not? A handsome strapping young available man such as yourself with no missus? What's wrong with you?"

Samuel laughed. "Ain't nothing the matter with me, just focused is all. I'm saving my money to be prepared for the day I meet my missus I'll be able to take care of her."

Louise wanted to tell Samuel how Mr. Auger gave her an endowment to start her new life with. She didn't explain how *they* were rich and, therefore, *she* was rich. She kept to herself the fact that she could take care of him if she wanted to. She wanted him to bait her in. She could always give him the other details later.

"Well, how much do you have saved?"

"About $100."

"Really? That much, huh? Were you born a slave since slavery was just abolished?"

"Yes, but I'm free now . . . a free man in a world that's for the taking."

"Wow. You're ambitious, but you know this ain't our world. We free, but we ain't free. We still have to overcome."

"That's true, but I got a lot of energy, and I'm willing to try. Are you?"

"Sure, but sometimes I need a little bit of help."

"What kind of help? The help of a man?"

"Yes. Could that be you?"

"Perhaps. Let's see."

They walked around the town arm in arm, just talking and getting to know each other. The sun hung low in the baby-blue sky, threatening to set. They agreed that they should have parted ways until their next meeting, which was the next day at the same place and time. This time, Louise invited Samuel to her new home. She showed him the way as he followed on his horse. They became inseparable. From Sundays at church to long walks in town and rendezvous at each other's homes, they couldn't stay away from each other. Soon Louise was pregnant. She became angry at the fact because it was improper to have a child out of wedlock, so Samuel married her. He still didn't know that she was rich. She told him that the land and house were gifts from the Augers, and now she just lived off the land. He moved in to help.

Their first child was a girl named Mary. After her, they had nine more all boys. Mary's life was very interesting. The oldest of ten, the only girl, the second mother, once she reached eighteen she was *ready* to leave. Samuel and Louise were good to her, though, but enough was enough. At home, she had led the life of a well-seasoned adult. She was ready for the world; and with nothing to tote, she made a way for herself.

Mary Emmerling graduated from the twelfth grade and then went to a specialty school where she learned how to type and do secretarial work. She got a job at the local courthouse where fifty-five years prior her mother had been adopted. Mary made tremendous strides for a woman of color. She was the first to be hired at the courthouse and kept her job for forty years.

She got married and had children of her own, two girls named Melanie and Margaret. Melanie was autistic and confined to a mental hospital at twelve. She remained there until her death at sixty-eight. Margaret never married but had a daughter named Lois. Lois had a daughter named Paige. Then in 1975, Paige had a girl named Bryce; and Irma's gun was still a go. Only Bryce didn't know.

CHAPTER 7

Paige knew little about her family's history. All she knew for sure was that the women in her past had a habit of raising children alone. The further back she went, the more children the women had, and usually, they were married; but more recently (like the last fifty years), they were single with only one or two kids each. Paige was determined not to repeat those statistics. At forty, pickings were getting slim, so she settled for Rocco. They met at a bar in the city. Paige and Rocco were from Baltimore.

Rocco kept a job and some money in his pocket, but he was an alcoholic. He was also abusive, more physically than verbally. His way was to hit his wife, leaving a bruise or scar, and then come back with a barrage of kind words like "I love you," "I didn't mean it," "It'll never happen again," "Was I drunk?" "I'll try to cut back."

He was dependable in some ways, though. For instance, he always paid the rent and gas. Paige was responsible for the water bill, the light bill, and the groceries. When they met, they didn't have a vehicle. After they got married, they saved up enough to buy a used car from the auction out in Laurel. Rocco's best friend Leon drove them out there to see what they had. They had $500 in cash, and all the bills were paid that month. Financially, they were on the up and up, so things were looking great, Paige thought. Never mind the bruises or controlling behavior. A little piece of heaven was better than none even if hell came with it. Paige didn't want to know what being alone was like without a man especially now that a baby was on the way.

Rocco seemed excited, and his appetite for sex was unparalleled. Paige assumed he got her pregnant on purpose. She wasn't sure, though. At night, he would lie on top of her big belly, seeming to want to suffocate the baby. He would put all his weight on the baby like he wanted to squash the baby right out of her. Paige would yell at him to stop; and after a while, he would, nonchalantly rolling over to go to sleep. Paige thought that was strange but had nothing to compare it to. This was her first child. They say being pregnant is one of the happiest times in a woman's life, but Paige wasn't certain. What was happiness? Did it include all the times Rocco would hit her?

Amazingly, Paige was not afraid of Rocco. After a while, she actually got used to being hit. It didn't hurt anymore. What bothered her was the way he would act afterward like he was the king of the castle. First he would go into the kitchen and put some ice in a Ziploc bag. Then he would wrap it in a wash cloth and gently hand it to Paige to place on her swollen area. Then he would watch her no phone calls, no leaving the apartment. And if it were late at night, he would not sleep until she went first. Wherever she went in the apartment, he would follow. If Paige sat up in bed, he would lie down next to her. If she moved to the living room, he would go to the kitchen.

That was his favorite place after hitting Paige. His beers were in the refrigerator, his whiskey was in the cabinet, and the knives were on the counter. There was a whole set of them. He'd never cut her before, and he never threatened to at least not with words, but he'd loom. He would sip his beer and pour his whiskey and stare at them and then look at Paige. With a child in her stomach, that scared her. She'd read the paper one time, and it said that pregnant women who died were usually killed by the father of the child. She remembered thinking that was the strangest thing, to think enough of someone to create a life with them and then want to extinguish it. It was as if they'd changed their mind right in the middle. Who would do that?

Anyways, when Rocco would go through these motions, Paige would close her eyes and see him cutting the baby right out of her. Then she'd shed a tear. He had accomplished the fear that locked the doors and kept the phone off the hook. It was done. Again. Eventually, Paige would lie down and fall asleep, hoping for a better day, forgetting the night's events but remembering the pain of the betrayal of their union. Sleeping next to him, fixing him breakfast the next day, and letting him get on top was forgiveness enough. He never needed the words.

Paige was entertaining. She cooked dinner every night. She would warm up left overs for Leon whenever he came over. Paige would rescue the two from the bar by picking them up to drive them home when they were too wasted to drive themselves. She hosted get-togethers. On the outside, they were the perfect couple. If only the world could see how it was rotting from the inside.

Paige was seven months and two weeks when Rocco's abusive behavior became increasingly worse. The slaps were fueled with more vigor, and the punches left bruises that lasted a little longer. For all the times she wasn't afraid, she was getting afraid. All Paige did was go to work and come home. What could be sustaining his anger and making it worse in what was supposed to be such a happy time? Maybe he didn't want this child, but they were married. A child was the most natural thing to have after marriage. Paige could understand his anger if they were only dating, but they had committed to each other. Did he not want children? They never discussed it.

Then one day they were talking about baby names, and Paige just came out and asked him, "Do you even want this baby?"

"Of course I want the baby. I wouldn't have made it if I didn't want it, right?"

"I don't know. You tell me."

"Yes, yes, yeesss. I want a boy so I can raise him up to be like me."

Paige was quiet. She was thinking what a farce that would be another alcoholic in the world to be beat his wife or girlfriend when he grew up? Then it dawned on her. What was she doing? Too late now, she would have to make the best of it and just try to balance out the karma that her husband was putting forth. She would set the good example and show her children the way to go while Rocco would show them what not to do. But who was she fooling? It would be an uphill battle, and she knew it, but it would be even harder to be alone.

"What will we name the baby if it's a girl? I want a girl."

"It's gonna be a boy. You carrying low."

"Let's pick a name that will suit a girl or a boy . . . so we'll be prepared either way!"

"I like Junior. Name him after me."

"I like Sam . . . Samuel for a boy or Samantha for a girl."

"Junior."

"How about Bryce?"

"That's a good boy's name. I like Bryce too. That's what we'll name him. I see you're good for something."

They both laughed. Rocco did have a good sense of humor. Only Paige would wonder how often he was serious when comically putting her down. She didn't let it worry her. The new baby would make everything better. He or she would give them something to concentrate on besides themselves.

Tonight Rocco didn't want to lie on her or the baby. He didn't want sex, and he didn't want to pleasure himself. He didn't want to talk, and he didn't want to start an argument, and he didn't want to hurt his wife. Tonight he just wanted to sleep, so he got under the covers and turned over. Paige didn't know how to read this. She didn't want to anger Rocco, but she was worried. Was he messing with another woman? More than anything, she feared losing her husband. She too meandered underneath the covers and faced her husband's back. She gently laid her hand on his shoulder to let him know she was there. He brushed her hand away as if he didn't even care, so Paige turned over. Now her back was facing his back, and she watched the wall until she fell asleep.

Her slumber was deeper than usual because she was released from all matrimonial obligation for a night. Inside her dreams, she tried to enjoy it, but she just couldn't. Her dream turned into a nightmare. Rocco had hit her; but this time, she got mad. Normally, she would eat her anger and just let it subside, but today she wanted to fight. The attack happened in the bedroom, so she refused to sleep with him. She went to sit on the couch and listen to some music. Before she knew it, Natalie Cole was playing "This Will Be." Rocco was in the kitchen acting out his usual routine. She could hear him putting ice in a plastic bag. He went to the hallway closet to find a wash clothe. He returned to his wife, and she was livid. "What difference does it make? Let it stay swollen!"

She snatched the bag and threw it back in the kitchen. Ice cubes were everywhere. She thought Rocco ran to clean up the mess. He came back with a knife. Paige quickly piped down, but it was too late. Rocco stabbed not on her face or her chest but on her stomach. Just then she woke up in a panic, clutching her belly. Rocco was snoring.

Paige turned over to look at the wall again. This time, her anxiety got the best of her. What if her dream came true? What was she doing? Was having a baby with this abusive man the best she could do? Too late to ask now, her first child was on the way. Did Rocco even care? He said he did whenever asked, but did he care? He seemed gone more since Paige's stomach grew.

Before her pregnancy, Rocco ran the streets with the best of them. He wasn't into drugs, but liquor was his thing. He sold cocaine on the side and worked a part-time job as a mechanic. He was excellent at paying the rent and maintaining his bar tab. Financially, he was responsible; and he must have been faithful because between the streets and his jobs, he couldn't have time to cheat. When he wasn't at work or in the streets, he was at home; but emotionally, he was disconnected. Rocco never rubbed Paige's stomach. He never massaged her shoulders or rubbed her aching feet after a long day at work. He never asked if the baby kicked lately or put his ear to her belly to see if he could hear the baby's heartbeat. Was he even invested? Or was that just his way?

Leon wanted to know. "Man, you rubbed your lady's belly lately?"

"For what? That baby ain't ready to come. When they get here, I'll do plenty of rubbing then."

"You ready? You been saving your money or drinking it up?"

"What you think? I been saving, and yeah, I'm ready. That baby ain't ready. That's who ain't ready."

"You ever seen a baby kick its feet clear outta that momma's belly button? One time I seen my baby pokin' at me through my lady's stomach. It was so funny, but it scared the hell outta me! I didn't want her to have that baby then'cause I thought she was having an alien!"

"When that baby came out and you saw them big ole ears, I bet you thought he was an alien, didn't you?"

Leon roared, "You know I did! I said, 'Get back, alien. You ain't welcome here. Betta go back to where you came from!' Just then, my lady stopped me and said, 'Uh-uh, ain't no going back. He here to stay.' So we had to keep him. Been wit him ever since."

Rocco laughed back. "That's your little man, though."

"Yeah, he is. Love him to death, and you'll feel the same way 'bout yours as they grow. I know you're scared right now, though you won't admit it. You'll learn to love that baby be they boy or girl."

"All I know is Paige betta be actin' right. I ain't takin' no mess from woman or child."

With that, Rocco paid for that round of drinks and settled his week's tab. Leon chopped up some blow right on the bar. As he snorted a line through a rolled-up dollar bill, the bartender complained that he was going to leave razor-blade marks in the wood on the bar. Leon acted like he couldn't hear. When he was finished, he wiped the bar clean with his hand and licked his palm. Leon's bottom lip slid to the side. Rocco asked him if he was having a stroke. Leon got mad and walked home.

Rocco returned to the bar to have one more. The phone rang, and the bartender said it was for him and handed Rocco the phone. It was Paige. She was going into labor and waiting by herself for an ambulance. She was upset he was not there. He said he was on his way. Rocco hung up the phone and ordered one more. He finished both drinks before he left.

He arrived at the street where they lived and waited at the corner until the paramedics arrived. He watched as they nonchalantly got out of the ambulance and wheeled a stretcher up to their apartment. About fifteen minutes went by, and out came Paige and her enormous belly on the stretcher. She was calm and wiping her eyes while looking at the sky. Rocco followed the ambulance to the hospital. He parked his car and waited more. Then he went in and found her just in time to help her experience more labor pains. He saw the scrubs on the chair and asked if they were for him. He put them on and asked Paige if she was okay. She said she'd be okay once that baby was out of her.

Just then, the doctor came in and felt her stomach. He said he thought she was ready and made a phone call. A whole team of nurses came in and rearranged things in the room. Slowly, they gathered the bed and all its attachments and moved to a room down the hall. As they set up, Paige had a contraction. Rocco panicked. A nurse stepped in and showed Rocco his place and told him not to leave it. She could tell that he was not comfortable with that, but his angst went ignored. There was too much going on.

About three hours went by, but it felt like just thirty minutes. Paige was pushing, but nothing seemed to happen. The doctor was getting frustrated.

"Push!"

"I am!"

"Push harder!... One more time!"

Paige gave it everything she had, and a joyous noise came out of her womb. It was a crying baby.

"Is it a girl?!"

"Yes, ma'am, it is!"

Rocco was dumbfounded. He couldn't speak. He just stood there trying not to fall. The team of nurses huddled around the new life until a bloodied and defiled lump of life was now a yellow, curly haired, and wrapped-in-white-cotton-cloth baby girl. The nurse placed her on Paige's chest. Paige told her husband to come closer. She could smell the liquor on his breath, but she didn't pay attention. She wanted nothing to ruin this moment.

"Here . . .hold your daughter."

"No. Not right now. I'll hold her a little later."

Paige ignored his refusal and cuddled her child. "Are we still naming her Bryce?"

"Whatever you want, but don't you think Bryce is a little too mannish for a girl?"

"Well, baby, this is a rough-and-tumble world we live in. Maybe if they think a man is coming, they won't be so hard on a girl. I like Bryce. Let's call her that."

Rocco was quiet for the rest of the night even as he sat up and held his first child. Paige enjoyed admiring him, although he was as stiff as a board, but she didn't care. She just liked watching her husband hold their daughter. In her mind, they were a real family now whole and complete.

When they got home, Paige put Bryce down to sleep and Rocco slept soundly too. Paige tried to lie down because she figured she should try to sleep while everyone else was, but she was wide awake. She just lay there looking at the ceiling. She thought about what her new life with the baby would be like now. Would Rocco stop hitting her and focus on the baby? Would he spend more time at home and stop drinking so much? She wondered what kind of father he would be. She went over how she would braid her child's hair and what she would look like in her first-grade pictures: light skinned with shoulder-length hair and a gap-toothed smile like her father. Then Rocco suddenly woke up.

"What you smiling about? You don't hear that baby crying in the other room? Get your lazy self up and feed her! I certainly can't do it!"

"Sorry, honey. I was asleep. I'm going now."

"Well, go ahead then! And hurry up!"

Paige went to tend to Bryce in the other room. Rocco followed her and swiped at the back of her head. "Get in that room!" Reality had her eyes wide open now. He would not stop even with a precious new life in the house. She knew she couldn't go on like this. She had to do something. She just didn't know what. Rocco put his pants on and stormed out of the apartment. He didn't even put a shirt on. He just wore his white tank top in the June heat, so Paige thought he wouldn't be gone long since he wasn't properly dressed to be out and about in the streets, but Rocco was gone for three days.

When he finally returned, Paige was upset but didn't want to rile him. "Where have you been? Bryce was crying for her daddy."

"That baby ain't but a few months old. She don't even know who I am."

"Sure, she does. She knows you. She knows when you hold her, and she knows when you're not around. I notice when you're not here. I sure missed you. Where were you?"

Rocco ignored her question. "You just take care of the baby." Then he walked off. He went into the kitchen and poured himself a whiskey. After swallowing it whole, he went into the bedroom, took off his pants, and lay on top of the covers. With his back turned towards Paige's side of the bed, Rocco fell fast asleep, snoring, drooling and all. Paige was hurt. She was convinced now that he was having an affair, but she wasn't sure if she should confront him. A tear streamed down the side of her face. She looked out of the window and held on tight to Bryce.

Rocco's disappearances continued. They would usually be for days at a time. Once, he was gone for a whole five days. He went on paying the rent, but sometimes it would be late, and Paige would have to bug him for it. There was a gentle knock at the door. Paige rarely got visitors, so she cautiously looked through the peephole. It was Leon.

"Hey, stranger! Haven't seen you in a while. C'mon in!"

Leon crossed the threshold. "How you been? Sorry, I haven't been by since the baby was born. I been working a lot."

Paige pried, "You and Rocco been spending a lot of time together, huh?"

"Naw, not really. I assumed he was busy with you and the baby. What, he ain't been home lately?"

"No, he hasn't been."

"Well, where's he been?"

"I don't know. I was hoping you would have some answers."

"Naw, babe, I don't know where he been at. Did you ask him?"

"You know how he is. I don't want to get him upset, so I just let it go."

"Whatchu mean you don't want to get him upset?"

"You know he got a temper."

"Yeah, but that's all it is, right? He ain't taking it no further, is he? You seem scared. Are you afraid of him, Paige?"

Paige paused. "Yeah, I am afraid of him. He puts his hands on me, Leon."

"WHAT! He does what?"

"He puts his hands on me. You don't think he'll hurt the baby, do you? I get so scared about that. I can take care of myself, but if he put hands on the baby, I don't know what I'd do, Leon"

"Leon what? Paige, you gotta get outta here. I ain't know my man was hurting you. I mean, I knew he was a hot head, but I ain't know he was taking it that far. I do know that he's stubborn. If it's been going on this long, he most likely won't stop. How you feel about that? Do you have a plan, or you just putting up with it?"

Paige put her head down. "I'm just taking it, Leon."

Leon moved in to give her a hug. It was much appreciated. Paige cried, and Leon held her closer. He hugged her until Bryce whined in her crib. "Let me see what's wrong."

"Go ahead. Take your time." Leon followed Paige into Bryce's room. "Let me see that baby."

"Go ahead and hold her. Look, she's reaching out for you, Leon."

"Give her here." Leon caressed Bryce, and she cooed. Bryce mumbled, "Da-da." Leon blushed and with a guilty disposition and gave her back to Paige. "She miss her daddy, huh?"

"I guess. I wish you were her father instead of Rocco. You'd make an excellent daddy. Why you ain't got no kids, Leon?"

"Can't find the right woman. You gotta have a good foundation and a good relationship fore you can start bringing kids into the world."

"Wish I woulda thought about that before I let Rocco get me pregnant."

"You having regrets? That's your husband till death do you part. I was there."

"It might be till death do we part, but I don't know if it's gonna be on his part or my part. I'm worried, Leon. He been gone since yesterday."

"When's he coming back?"

"I don't know."

Paige put the baby down and invited Leon to come into the living room to finish their conversation. They sat on opposite ends of the sofa and talked for two hours. The dialogue was mostly serious and about

Rocco, but they laughed sometimes too. Finally, Leon excused himself and said he had to go. Paige was sad to see him leave. This was the most love she had gotten in a long while. She invited him back whenever he wanted to come back. She said he was always welcomed there, and he said he would take full advantage of the opportunity to speak with her again because he enjoyed himself that day. He'd be back.

With that, Paige let him through the door but not without giving him another hug and this time a kiss on the cheek. Paige leaned in to kiss him one last time on the cheek; and this time, Leon turned his head to catch the kiss on the side of his lips. They said goodbye and let each other go.

Paige closed the door and with her back to it just stood there for a while daydreaming. About what she didn't know. All she knew was that she hadn't felt that good and warm inside in a long, long time. She hoped he'd come back. Then she heard keys turning in the door. She quickly moved away from it and ran into Bryce's room. It was Rocco. He was drunk as a skunk. He belligerently called out, "Paige . . . where you at?" and stumbled into the baby's room. He reached out for his wife and flailed his arms around her. The smell of alcohol made Paige turn her head and put her arms between her and Rocco in defense. He threw wet kisses all over her face and neck and told her how much he loved her.

Bryce cried. Relieved at her baby's rescue tactics, she pushed Rocco away and almost dove into Bryce's crib to pick her up. She walked away shaking her in her arms asking her what was wrong and if everything was okay.

Rocco went into the bedroom. Paige stayed in the living room with Bryce until she calmed down. She fed Bryce and burped her. Later she returned her to her crib. Just as she was putting Bryce down, Rocco stumbled in. She heard him before she saw him. He was in his birthday suit with lust in his eyes. Paige said no, but she couldn't stop him. He was too strong. She ran from him, and he slammed Bryce's door shut.

He chased her around the apartment for a short while; and when she ran into the bedroom, she was all his. He threw her on the bed and lifted her sun dress. He didn't even bother to try removing her underwear. He just took what he wanted. Paige tried to fight him off but eventually gave in by just laying there. It was cold and sloppy. After it was over, Rocco collapsed on top of her, drooling. Paige felt used and abandoned simultaneously.

Years went by. Variations of this went on whenever he came home. Paige tried to get used to it but could not. She lived for the times when Leon would visit. He would always pop up when Rocco was gone, which was all the time. The visits became more and more frequent as time went on. Leon was her rock. He was her shoulder to cry on, her confidant, her friend. She would tell him about Rocco, and he would suggest how to deal with him. Leon knew Rocco from a different angle, so his comments were always helpful. Paige would have crumbled without him.

Then one day there was a gentle knock at the door. It was Leon again. He had come over earlier that day but came back in the evening. He told Paige to sit down. She did and stared at him with a blank face.

"Paige, I have something to tell you."

"What is it, Leon?"

"Paige . . . Rocco is seeing another woman."

Paige was silent for a moment. "I knew that. I just couldn't prove it. He's never home. The little bit of romance and peace that we used to have is gone. I knew he was taking it somewhere else. Whenever we have sex now, all love is not there any more. He just takes it. I'm just something he uses whenever he wants to fulfill an urge."

"Aaawww, honey . . . I'm sorry to have to be the one to tell you that. What are you going to do?"

"I don't know."

Leon saw the tears coming and stood up to hold Paige. They embraced for a long while, and Leon gently rubbed her back. He held her tighter and tighter. She caressed his back. They kissed. A few pecks turned into a long passionate tongue kiss. Leon pulled her into his body. She felt the strength of his manhood against her pubis. They were making out. They didn't stop as their feet moved towards the bedroom. Once they got there, they took each other's clothes off. Leon told her to hold up as he went over to close the bedroom door. They made love in Rocco and Paige's bed.

This was only the beginning. Every time Rocco went away, within hours, Leon was there. They would talk. They would eat. They would make love. Paige fell hard. She made plans to leave Rocco. She worked hard and saved much money. Whenever Leon came over, they tried hard to hide their relationship from Bryce. They didn't want her to indicate to Rocco what was going on. This went on for over a year. Bryce was four years old and talking.

Then Paige got frightened. The few times that Rocco was at home, Bryce would always ask for "Uncle Leon." Rocco knew he was coming by, but he had no idea just how often. He thought his secrets about his affair were safe with Leon, but Leon was telling Paige everything. Rocco thought he was getting away with murder, but little did he know his world was about to turn upside down.

One day Paige sat him down. She had been saving her money and was prepared to leave him. She had put a deposit down on another apartment for her and Bryce. She had worked so much overtime. Rocco was hardly there, so he didn't even notice. Then she could entertain Leon at her leisure. Paige had moved on, but how would her husband take the news? Leon said he wanted to be there to protect her from Rocco, but Paige said it was best if she broke the news to Rocco on her own. Leon would not let her do it without having someone there, so they made a compromise. Leon picked out a bouncer from a club he would frequent. He told him just to sit in Rocco and Paige's apartment while Paige delivered the news. His job was to keep Rocco from hurting Paige further. Leon knew it would work because he knew his best friend. Rocco would never hit Paige with someone else around because he knew he was wrong. He started by asking about this guy.

"What, Paige? You leaving me for this clown?"

"He's not a clown. He's an old friend of mine. He's just here to make sure you don't fly off the handle."

"I don't need no other man in my house watching me!"

"He's not here for you. He's here for me. Just ignore him and listen to what I have to tell you."

Rocco stormed off. "You ain't going no where, Paige! You belong to me! You mines! You and Bryce!"

"Rocco, come back, sit down, and listen to me!"

Her acquaintance was calm as if nothing was going on. He just sat in the kitchen, oblivious to what was going on. Rocco stomped back into the living room. "Whatchu want? Whatchu got to say that's so important? I already know where this is going. You need help packing?"

"No. I don't need anything from you except a divorce. I'm moving out tonight, and I'm taking Bryce with me. I'm tired of you hitting me and never coming home. I want better for our daughter. I don't want her to grow up and get a man who will hit on her like you do me. I'm leaving."

"Well, go on then. I won't stop you. In fact, you better be gone by the time I come back."

With that, Rocco left again. Paige thanked her acquaintance for fulfilling his duties and asked him to stay a while longer while she packed a few more items for her and the toddler. She loaded up her car with as much as she could. She almost forgot to leave space for Bryce. Then off she went to her new home. Her acquaintance suggested that she not come back without him. He said he didn't mind being there for her as a favor to Leon. He said he and Leon were tight, so he didn't mind. Paige thanked him again. He also said it would be a good idea if she didn't give Rocco her new address. All he would do was wreak havoc in her new life, dragging his old ways into her new dwelling. Paige agreed and promised not to give Rocco any information.

In her new apartment, the only rooms decorated were her bedroom and Bryce's room. They were furnished and had pretty pictures on the walls. Paige unloaded their clothes and other belongings with Leon's help. She even gave him a key. This was her way of letting him know how serious she was about him. Was this turning into love? It had the makings. There was trust, Leon protected her and provided for her and Bryce, and he was passionate and gentle. This was the happiest Paige had been in a while. She was glad she had decided to move. She could relax now, and her and Leon's relationship could flourish.

A few months went by, and Paige filed for a divorce. Leon pressed her about telling Rocco about them. He said Rocco wanted to spend time with him sometimes, and he felt awkward. Knowing how he was now, he didn't want to be his friend anymore but he couldn't just walk away. He didn't want Rocco to realize that Leon had scooped his woman. He wanted to tell him to officially end their friendship. Paige was opposed. She didn't want Rocco to retaliate. Leon said she had nothing to worry about because he didn't know where she stayed and as long as she had someone with her whenever she went back to Rocco's apartment she should be fine. He consoled her and eased her mind. Paige eventually gave in and gave Leon permission to tell Rocco about their affair, but she said she wanted to be there. As Leon wanted closure on his friendship, Paige wanted closure on her marriage. They were in this together now, Bonnie and Clyde.

So one day Rocco and Leon were hanging out at the bar. He called Paige and told her to meet him at Rocco's apartment. The three just stared at one another for a while. Then Leon broke the silence.

"Bro . . . me and Paige got something going on, and since it's now a conflict of interest, we can't be friends anymore. You're a sick man, and you need help. I'll be there for you to get some help if you need me, but other than that, I'm gone."

"Leon, you just gonna take my wife and leave me, man?"

"You did this to yourself, man. You had the perfect life and didn't know what to do with it. Now it's gone. Maybe if you're lucky enough to find another woman like Paige again, you'll know how to treat her next time."

Rocco cried. Paige couldn't believe it. He was always so hard, so militant. He never showed emotion before. What a moment. Paige and Leon left hand in hand as Rocco stretched out on the couch with his hands over his face, bawling like a baby. It was finally over, Paige thought.

Rocco stalked Leon. He would call him several times a day and wait for him at the bar. He ran his tab up but wasn't taking care of it like he used to. Then Rocco babbled about how Bryce wasn't his. He complained about her skin tone. Rocco said she had darkened up and looked more like Leon than him. He accused Paige and Leon of sleeping together the whole time they were married. He wanted nothing more to do with Bryce or Paige. He was so hurt and felt so betrayed. He went into a deep depression, and Leon was the only person who could help him out of it, so he tried.

He convinced his former friend to go to counseling and Alcoholics Anonymous. He sponsored him and went to meetings. Leon didn't want to, but he knew that without his help Rocco would go under. He didn't know how that would affect Paige, so he had to do something. Rocco slowly came out of his funk and concentrated on politics. He had always loved chopping it up with Leon about the city's policies and what was going on in the ghettos as opposed to what was going on in the suburbs. He had always joked about running for mayor, but it was just that until Paige left him. He wanted her back, and he knew he had to prove that he could be a better man. He had to show her something. He had to give her a reason to want him back too. Leon was just a factory worker. Rocco had to top that, right? He decided to try. What did he have to lose?

Rocco investigated. He went down to city hall to talk to a few councilmen to inquire about what it would take for him to run for mayor. Enthralling conversations about politics made people take notice. Rocco knew what he was talking about. He created cronies throughout the city; and before you know it, he was a councilman for the third district. He served two terms and did his district well. He created recreation centers and after-school programs for the kids. He looked out for the elderly and helped church programs for senior citizens. The people loved him. He was a sure candidate for mayor. As soon as he became mayor, he would ask Paige to go out on a date with him. He had his mind made up.

He took two years of recovery, six years of being a councilman, and finally two years of being mayor before he had the courage to ask his ex-wife out on a date. It was too late. Paige had moved on with Leon. She was happy for Rocco, though. It was nice to see him get himself together and to know that he was in a better place, but she could not be with him. The damage was done.

CHAPTER 8

Bryce was fourteen now and without a father. Leon was the closest thing to it, but Bryce knew the truth. She wanted her real father, but he didn't want her. She was becoming a young woman now; and with no man in her life, she looked elsewhere for father figures in males who took a liking and cared. Maybe that's why Bryce developed into a tomboy. She was into basketball and hip-hop, and most of her friends were boys.

She wasn't promiscuous, but you couldn't tell her mother that. Paige was convinced that Bryce was screwing every boy who called the house. She thought Bryce was in a gang. Hip-hop wasn't around when Paige was growing up, so she didn't understand the dynamics. She didn't understand the crews of guys with just one or two girls. She didn't understand how Bryce rapped, and she didn't understand the respect boys had for a girl who could rap.

However, what Paige did understand was her daughter's need for a father. Although she didn't want Rocco anymore, she did want Bryce to have a relationship with her father; so she let Bryce meet Rocco at his apartment. Things didn't go well. Paige talked to Rocco first, and he expressed so much doubt that Bryce was his that Paige thought that their meeting was a bad idea. She didn't want to dampen her child's self-esteem. She had never realized it before but Rocco was waging an all-out war on his daughter.

As mayor, he had access to information that others did not know about including the knowledge of Irma's gun. Paige knew too. She just never talked about it.

"So, Rocco, what exactly are you planning to do?"

"I'm planning to be mayor for a very long time as long as the people allow me to be."

"I still can't believe you're the mayor of Baltimore City. You've really come a long way. When you were with me, you just wanted to sit in that ole watering hole every weekend. I see now you're a changed man."

"Well, if you can see that, why won't you give me another chance?"

"Because I know eventually you'll hit me again. You can't help it."

Rocco whined, "Paige, give me a try. I won't hit you again. I'm a changed man."

"I'm with Leon now. That wouldn't be fair to him."

Rocco grabbed her and kissed her all over her face. They embraced for a long while, and Rocco gently rubbed her back. He held her tighter and tighter. She caressed his back. They kissed. A few pecks turned into a long passionate tongue kiss. Rocco pulled her into his body. She felt the strength of his manhood against her pubis. They were making out. They didn't stop as their feet moved towards the bedroom. Once they got there, they took each other's clothes off. Paige couldn't believe this was happening. Was she about to get back with her ex-husband? The love making reminded her of when she and Rocco had first met. Nothing about it was abusive or cold like it used to be.

Should she give him another chance? Paige couldn't. She had come too far; and although she was so proud of Rocco for cleaning himself up and becoming mayor, she was in love with Leon. He helped her out of her bad situation. She would never just up and abandon him like that, but Rocco was winning her heart. After they made love, they lay in bed and talked for a while.

"How was it, Paige?"

"It was okay. It was more than okay. It made me think of when I first met you."

"See, I told you, I'm trying to change."

"I see."

"Why don't you move back in with me? I'll pay the rent, and you can save your money."

"What about Bryce?"

"What about her?"

"Do you want her too?"

"Paige, that's a sticky situation. Bryce is yours. You can bring her with you, but you'll have to take care of her."

Paige sat up in bed. "What do you mean? Bryce is your daughter, Rocco."

"She ain't no daughter of mines! That's Leon's child. Her feet big like Leon's, she got a nose like Leon, and her dark complexion is the same as him. She ain't mine. I know you'll was messing around the whole time."

"You got a guilty conscience because *you* was messing around! I didn't start seeing him until years after she was born."

"I don't believe you, Paige."

"Why don't you get a DNA test?"

"For what? I'm not paying all that money for a test when I already know the truth. That's a waste of time."

"You'll find out the truth, Rocco."

"I already know the truth."

"See, we could never have anything because you don't trust me."

"We can work on it, Paige. I'm willing to be patient and try."

"Bryce and I come together."

"That's fine. She just ain't nothing that Imma be taking care of. I fact, she needs to know that it ain't all about her. Who does she think she is? Falutin' around with all those boys like she better than everybody else? She needs to be taught a lesson!"

"What? What are you talking about? Have you been watching us?"

"No, Paige. I haven't been watching you, but I have friends in high places and all over. I can find out anything I need to know. Like I found out about your gun."

"What gun? I don't own a gun."

"No, you don't own one, but you can use it at any time. I know you can kill people, Paige, and get away with it. I know Bryce can too. It'll get passed down to her, and I intend to do something about it."

"Like what?"

"So you admit it?"

"How'd you find that out? I never told you."

"I work for the government now, and I am privy to lots of top-notch information." He lunged at Paige. "Why didn't you just tell me?"

Paige pulled back. "I've never told anyone. There's no need. I never planned on using it. I just move along in my life like it doesn't exist. It's a hoax. Who can kill someone and get away with it?"

"Did you tell Bryce?"

"I told you I didn't tell anyone."

"Well, make sure you don't let her know. If she finds out about it, she'll try to use it. I know she will."

"You think so?"

"Of course. She's crazy like that. I told you she thinks she's better than everyone else."

"Well, I'll make sure she doesn't use it. You're lighter than her, and you should be able to use it before she does. That's the law."

"See, that's why I love you, Paige. You're always on my side. It's you and me against the world."

"I got you. Don't worry about Bryce. I got her too."

Paige was sucked in by Rocco's success. She knew she didn't want him back, but now she was stuck in the middle. She still loved him and wanted to take up for him. She wanted to have his back, and she would from now on now that she had his insight about her daughter. Things were making sense to Paige now about Bryce. Before she was an enigma. Paige was curious about what her ex-husband said and looked into it.

When she got home, she saw her daughter through a different lense now. Bryce was doing well in school. She had a job and played basketball. That was a lot of responsibility for a fourteen-year-old, but Bryce seemed to handle it with grace. Her GPA was a 3.8; and at the catering place, she was promoted to head waitress. She was first string on the basketball team and had plenty of friends. She was doing well, so Paige let her be, but she was watching her, waiting for an opening.

Over a little time, Rocco had won Paige over, and that's what he wanted. He was jealous of Bryce, and his goal was to destroy her. When she was a child, she was not a threat; but as she grew and blossomed into a young woman, Rocco was afraid that someone would tell her about the gun. People knew, and people talked. Bryce knew that Rocco used to hit her mother. Would she want to take revenge on Rocco for hurting Paige? Could Bryce kill Rocco and get away with it? He constructed a plan. He knew he had to be subtle, though. Any startling and Bryce might go off. She did have a bad temper, and Rocco was well aware. He had to be cautious.

The first step in his plan was to exert influence over Bryce's life. He needed her to know that he was in charge, so he would get friendly with her teachers, coaches, bosses, and co-workers. Being the mayor helped. People would welcome him into places where he probably shouldn't have been. Bryce could feel the pinch. She just didn't know where it was coming from.

Bryce's world gradually changed. On one hand, she was some star. Everyone wanted to know her and be close to her. But she was a pariah. No one wanted to be her boyfriend or get too deeply invested. She was a liability. It was as if something bad would happen to them for getting too close. She was an inviting lake of frozen ice. Everyone wanted to skate across but were afraid to fall through.

Rocco's plan was slowly working. His influence over her life made Bryce unsure because she didn't know what was going on. Friends handled her with a ten-foot pole and were not true. She was all alone even as an only child.

Then it happened. At the beginning of Bryce's junior year, they went in. Her mother came to her high school without her knowing and talked to the teacher of her favorite subject, which was English. Paige explained to the teacher that Bryce was getting too much attention at home and in other areas of her life. She wanted the teacher to "tone it down" to balance out Bryce's life and teach her a lesson. Normally, the teacher would dote on Bryce because she was one of her favorite students, but this day she ignored her. When Bryce spoke up to ask a question, the teacher yelled at her. Bryce was humiliated. She wanted to crawl under her desk. After that day, she stopped going to English class. She would just hang out in the lunchroom. Eventually, she stopped going to school altogether. Paige had turned on her at home. To get good grades and be a favored student meant the world to Bryce. It was where she got her validation; so when her English teacher took it away that day, she didn't know how to handle it. She felt like this was the beginning of the end. She almost dropped out of school.

Bryce fell into a mild depression. She would spend her days asleep at home while Paige was at work. The first indication that something was wrong to Bryce was when her mother would come home early and ignore her. She wouldn't ask why Bryce was not at school. She wouldn't want to know why she was always in the bed asleep. She seemed not to care. That affected Bryce even more because she wanted her mother to say, "What are you doing? Why aren't you in school? What's wrong?" To Bryce to say those things would have been showing love, care, and concern. However, she didn't show her those things. Bryce was confused about the matter. She didn't know what was going on.

She mustered up enough strength to go to work in the afternoons, though. She would work from around nine to five Monday through Friday. Nothing could stop her money grind. That's the only way she knew that she wasn't falling too deep into this depression. She had something to keep her going, something to sustain her. About two days a week, though, she would pull herself together to go to school. Her friends would fill her in on the homework and tests coming up and what to study for, but they would also ask questions like "Where have you been?" or "What have you been doing?" Bryce didn't have a serious answer, but that made her feel good. That let her know that they cared.

This skipping school went on all throughout her senior year. Somehow Bryce made it through. She chose not to go to her senior prom because she couldn't find a date. She stopped playing basketball because for the first time in her young career she wasn't first string. Sitting on the bench watching lackluster players get all the time didn't make sense to Bryce. It wasn't just her either. There were girls on the team she grew up playing with who were better than her. They got benched too. It didn't make sense; When she confronted her coach about it, all he said was that it was a confidence-building thing. The older players got time because they were leaving, and they needed the experience. The younger players could wait their turn. She didn't think that was fair. If you got skills, you shouldn't be on the bench period. She couldn't wrap her head around it.

Senior year was a real struggle. The high school she went to had a rule that if you missed over sixty days you were automatically expelled. Bryce knew she missed over sixty days, but somehow they let her hang in there. Maybe someone wasn't doing their job and she just fell through the cracks. Whatever happened (or didn't happen), it was a blessing. She was thankful then and years later.

One day Bryce came to school, and the dean called her to his office. Her mother was sitting with this stoic look on her face. Bryce was sure she was getting kicked out, but she wasn't. The dean just wanted to know what was going on and he wanted to see if Paige knew what was going on. She knew, but she didn't care. The dean was determined to get to the bottom of it.

"Ma'am, are you aware that your child has not been attending school regularly? We're concerned because we know this is not in her character. Is there something you want to share with us?"

Paige was nonchalant. "Something like what?"

"What do you think I'm talking about, ma'am? Her truancy!"

"Some days when I get off early, she's home in the bed asleep."

"Okay, and?"

"I don't know why, but she is."

"You never asked her any questions as to why she wasn't in school?"

"What kind of questions?"

The dean was irritated. "Ma'am, do you even care about this child? She is missing school, you know about it, and don't seem concerned! What is going on?"

Bryce turned around and looked at her mother. Paige didn't have an answer. She was embarrassed. Paige got up and walked out of the room. Bryce apologized for her mother and made up excuses.

"Dean Turner, I'm sorry for missing so much school. I've just had a hard time waking up some days, so I'll just stay in bed. That's why I've been missing school. That's the only reason I promise."

"I'm no doctor, but that sounds like a mental health issue to me. Are you depressed about something? Are you and your mother getting along? Do you have friends? Is there anything out of the ordinary going on that you want to talk about?"

"No. I think I just need some coffee in the mornings, that's all."

"Coffee, huh?"

"Yes, sir. That's all."

"Okay, try that. I don't know what's going on, but your mother obviously has some issues. Do you think you all can work them out?"

"I'll try."

"Do you think you can come to school a little more often so you can get that diploma in June?"

Bryce smiled. "Yeah, I think I can do that."

"Good. I want you to be invested in your future. You may not realize it now, but everything you do today will affect you tomorrow, okay?"

"Yes, sir."

"Thank you for coming in. See you tomorrow."

"Okay."

Bryce got up and went into the hallway to look for her mother, but she was gone. Bryce couldn't believe that she just left her there like that. Bryce wanted to talk to her mom and find out what was going on, but maybe it was better left alone, so she just went back to class. From then on, Bryce tried to do better; but eventually, she just fell into her old habits. She came to school every day for about three weeks straight. Then she skipped again.

This year she had English with a different teacher, but this time Bryce had her guard up. She expected no special attention, and she did all her assignments as expected and turned them in on time. Her GPA in English was back up. This last year, though, the students would have to write a term paper. The term paper was being calculated as one-third of the total grade, which meant if you didn't turn one in, you would automatically fail even if your average was 100 percent.

That's what happened to Bryce. Her average was about 98. But when she skipped school again, she fell behind and missed the deadline. Not turning in a paper meant she would fail English. English was a basic requirement for a state diploma. For the first time in her school career, she would have to go to summer school.

Bryce was scared. She had never been to summer school before. Summer school had a bad reputation. Some said that only bullies and gang members went to summer school. Bryce didn't feel like getting into any fights. She just wanted to earn her diploma and get out of there. To her surprise, though, she met very interesting people.

CHAPTER 9

A lot of the people she met were into music like her: rappers, singers, dancers, and producers. On the weekends, she would meet up with them and go to different studios all over Baltimore. What a time! Bryce knew she was good because every time she would rap people would ask to link up with her later. Then she'd meet more people in different crews and organizations, though she could never seem to get anywhere. It was as if people would invite her in and then leave her hanging. They would be impressed by her talents, but something would always stop them from committing. That didn't stop Bryce from trying, though.

She would basically go from studio to studio, from one crew to another, meeting all these people, racking up all these points, but never scoring. She always felt like something was wrong. She didn't know what to do. She was too young to just give up, but the way people responded to her made her hopeful never the less, so she went on.

Rocco went on too. He went on being the mayor and seeking to ruin his child's life although he wasn't claiming her. He maintained a distant relationship with Paige. It was purely sexual, but it was enough to win her over and make her turn on her daughter. She was in cahoots with Rocco. They saw eye to eye. They agreed that they didn't understand Bryce's choice of friends and how fast she was growing up. They wanted her to slow down, and they would help her from a distance. Rocco and Paige talked often, and he would always convince her to creep around Bryce's life screwing things up just like she did at her high school in her English class. No one knew Bryce the way Paige did. She knew exactly how to get to her without confronting her directly; and this became a way of life for Paige, Rocco, and Bryce.

Rocco did well as the mayor. The people loved him. He was welcome anywhere in the city. When people saw him coming, they would smile and open up, congratulating him on his accomplishments and asking questions about what he planned to do. Rocco would sit there and entertain the conversations. He was honest about his plans; and if he wasn't sure about something, he wouldn't lie. He would just say he wasn't sure. People respected that as they got to know him. If only they knew about the havoc he was wreaking in his child's life.

As time went on, Rocco got comfortable and slipped back into his old ways. He would frequent up scale bars talking to the people there and drinking heavily. He got used to living this "rock star" life. He couldn't imagine himself without it. He became another person, and Paige got caught up in his star power. She was dominated by it led by it. She knew no other way. She never forgot or even forgave him for the abuse, but she did defend him. She even took up for him when he got into some trouble.

Rocco was at a bar one night when he ran into a Republican heckler from a convention he spoke at a year prior. He recognized the man and in his drunken stupor wanted to get him back for almost making him look bad at the convention. They got into it.

"Hey, I know you. You had everything to say at the convention during the election. Whatchu got to say now?"

"Hey, nothin'. You're just an uppity nigger! I still don't know how you beat Chapin in that election! You must have rigged it!"

"How a black man gonna rig an election? Only your kind does stuff like that. Git outta here with that bullshit!"

"I'll show you some bullshit!"

"What you gonna do about it?"

"What you think I'm gonna do about it?"

"Why don't you come over here and show me you so big and bad?"
"I'll show you something all right!"

Then the heckler pulled out a gun and pointed it at Rocco. Rocco lunged towards the man, seeking to grab the gun. Since Rocco was drunk, he stumbled; and the gun went off. Then it fell on the floor. Apparently, the heckler was drunk too. The two men became entangled on the floor. Sloppily, they wrestled back and forth. It seemed personal as if they both forgot about the gun. The other patrons seemed to ignore the two drunk men and went on drinking. A few left. Then there was another gun shot. Rocco pulled himself up on a nearby chair. The heckler stayed on the floor. Concerned, the bar tender went over to the heckler and turned him over to see if he was still breathing. There was a pool of blood on the floor. The bar tender called 911. By the time the paramedics arrived, Rocco was gone. When they saw it was a gun shot, they called the police. Witnesses at the scene identified Rocco as the shooter. The police conducted a full investigation.

When Rocco got home, the first thing he did was call Paige. He told her what happened. He said he was afraid because he thought he might have killed him. Paige told him not to worry just yet. She had a card to play. She told Rocco again about the gun. She explained that Bryce was his daughter, so coverage of the gun could be extended to him. Rocco wasn't too sure, but he said he would try it. He asked Paige to accompany him to city hall. She obliged. She met Rocco at his house. She knocked on the door, and no one answered. She waited for about five minutes; and just as she was about to turn around and leave, she heard the door crack. She turned around and Rocco was hiding behind the door. All she could see was his eyes peering through the door's slit.
"Yes."

"Rocco, stop playing and open the door. We got work to do."
"I'm not playing. Come in."

Rocco stood behind the door and opened it just enough for Paige to walk through. She crossed the threshold and looked around for clues as to why Rocco was acting like this. She turned to address him and saw he was standing behind the door with nothing on. He closed the door. They both froze, standing there, just staring at each other.

"Rocco, where are your clothes?"

"Paige, I missed you."

"And this is how you show me?"

Rocco crept towards his ex-wife and reached out for her. "Come here."

"No . . . now stop playing. We gotta get to city hall and talk to some people before they try to arrest you. Do you want to go to jail?"

Rocco slipped his hands around Paige's waist and kissed her gently. He pulled her close as she allowed him to kiss her. Then she pulled away. "Come on now, we gotta go."

Rocco persisted with a slight force. Paige eventually gave in. She just kept saying, "Come on, Rocco, we gotta go."

Soon they were entangled in each other's arms, making out passionately against the front door. They slid down the door and ended up on the floor. There, they made love again. They became one until Rocco was finished and left Paige there on the floor. She got up and straightened out the wrinkles in her dress as Rocco showered and got dressed. He put on his favorite gray suit with his blue-and-silver tie. He and Paige looked like they were going to the prom. His suit matched her dress on purpose. He wanted them to look like a couple a unified force and they were.

They held hands as they approached city hall. On the way there, they talked about who they would see and what they would say. They talked to the president on a conference call. At city hall, Rocco was the mayor, so he was the chief operating officer there. Everything revolved around him. There was really no need to talk to someone under him. They got the president on the line, and salutations were in order. Rocco introduced Paige as "his partner." She thought that was suspicious and hoped he didn't think that they were getting back together, but she said nothing to keep up appearances. Rocco asked the president if he knew anything about this gun. He briefly explained what it was and where it came from. The president said he knew nothing of the sort, but he would investigate and try to find out. The president hung up the phone, promising to call them back in about an hour when he discovered more information. The president had everyone from NASA to the FBI to the CIA investigating. They all came back with answers. By the time the hour was up, the president had a full report. He called Rocco back to fill him in.

"Mayor Rocco, what is your real name? I feel funny calling you Rocco."

"Oh no, don't worry about it. My real name is Timothy Parran, but Rocco is the name I ran my campaign with. That's what everyone calls me, and that's what I go by. Mayor Rocco is just fine, thank you."

"Oh, okay, well, I have a full report for you compiled by the CIA, the FBI, and NASA."

"Okay, great, let's hear it!"

"Well, it appears that back in the early 1800s Paige had a great-grandmother three times removed named Irma. Irma saved the then-president's life and was rewarded with a license to kill when she murdered her husband. This license, or gun as you call it, was said to have been passed down to all the women in her family. It has only been used a few times because reportedly it's not something that your family talks about. Most women in your family don't even know they have it and are afraid to use it anyway."

"Well Mr. President let me interrupt you. I've seemed to have gotten myself into a pinch, and I may need to use this gun. Do you think that since my daughter is an heir, I can use it in her name?"

"Well, gee, I don't know how that's supposed to work. I'll have to find out."

"Can you find out soon? I may be facing charges."

"What happened?"

"I got into an altercation at a bar with a heckler from about a year ago. He ended up getting shot, and I think he may be hurt badly. I left before the police got there, but I'm almost certain that they're looking for me. Before I get into too much trouble or before this hits the press, I need to know what my options are."

"Stay by your phone. I'll see what I can do to help you."

Just then, the police burst into the office and told Paige and Rocco to freeze. The officer in charge demanded that Rocco put the phone down and put his hands in the air. Rocco tried to finish his conversation; but with guns drawn, the officer said, "Put the phone down now!" Afraid that he might be shot, Rocco just hung up on the president. The officer made both get down on the ground spread eagle.

As they complied, Rocco tried to explain that if the officers could hold off from arresting him for about an hour, he was waiting on an important phone call that could prevent him from being arrested. The officer in charge laughed. He wanted to know what could be so important that it would prevent him from being arrested for the murder of a man where several witnesses said he did it. The officer told Rocco he was going down as he put the hand cuffs on his wrists.

A female officer cuffed Paige. She wanted to know why she was being arrested when she wasn't even there. The female officer just said, "Come along, ma'am. You can ask questions later when you talk to your lawyer." Paige fussed as she put the cuffs on and the whole way out the door. The officers were careful to keep Paige and Rocco separate, so they took her first. They put them in two squad cars. Rocco and Paige could see each other's eyes through the windows of the squad cars. They made love with their eyes for a moment. Then Rocco mouthed the words "I love you" as a tear fell from Paige's left eye. Then her car pulled off. Just like that, she was gone and they saw each other no more. The phone in his office rang, but no one was there to answer.

Back at the police barracks, Paige requested a phone call. Her request was not granted immediately, but eventually she was allowed a five-minute call. She remembered the number from the office and called the president's direct line. A secretary answered and said she could take a message because the president was not there. She said he had just left about twenty minutes prior. Paige asked where he went and if he would be coming back soon. The secretary said that was privileged information and that she would relay the message. Paige told her exactly where she was and that he should call there to find her.

An officer approached Paige from behind and snatched the phone from her hand and hung it up. Paige maintained her composure because she had said everything she had intended to. Her call was not in vain although the officer was rude. Paige said, "You could have just told me to hang it up!" The officer grabbed her by the arm and shoved her back into the tiny cell she came from. Once everyone left, Paige put her face into the palms of her hands and cried profusely. She didn't know why because she knew she was innocent. Paige just felt like everything was coming to a head. It was overwhelming and becoming too much to bear.

She fell asleep on the plastic mat that lay on a metal bed in her cell. She awoke to the jingling of keys and the loud clank of the lock being turned on her cell. The metal bars creaked open, and in walked an older man of average height. She rubbed her blurry eyes to see the person. She assumed he was a lawyer or public defender. When her eyes finally cleared, she could see he was dressed in dungarees and a cotton white shirt. Usually accompanied by the secret service, he came alone today. He greeted Paige with a firm handshake and a wry smile.

He began, "Hello, Paige. It's nice to meet you in person. We spoke yesterday on the phone, remember?"

"Yes. I remember. How are you?" Paige tried to stand up, but the president refused her energy and sat next to her on her bed.

"Let me apologize for your arrest. I looked into it, and it was unfounded. They only arrested you as an accomplice because you were there with your ex-husband. You'll be released shortly."

"And what about Rocco? Will he be released too?"

"Yes, but his situation is a little more complicated than yours. His release will take some time, but eventually, he will be let go."

Paige smiled long and wide. "Do you know how long it will take?"

"I'm not exactly sure, but you need to know that this meeting and everything being said here is classified information. You cannot tell anyone that I was here, what I said to you or anything about this gun. It is for your purposes only, and the way this works is that since Rocco is not a direct heir of the gun, we need to prove that he was using it on your behalf to justify him using it."

"Oh well, Mr. President, I assure you that that is exactly what took place."

"How can you be sure? You weren't there."

"Well, Rocco, told me that the heckler threatened my life. Rocco got upset. They tussled for the gun, and it went off. Rocco was only fighting with the man to protect me. That's how it all started."

The president looked suspicious. "Are you sure?"

"Absolutely. I am willing to testify to it if I have to."

"No. That won't be necessary. I believe you. I just need to document what has happened."

"Okay."

The president thanked Paige for her time and wished her well by saying good luck. He then excused himself and left. Paige cried again; but this time, they were tears of joy. She cried herself to sleep; and when she awoke, a guard was at the doorway of her cell, telling her to get ready to leave. The guard escorted Paige through several hallways and into the admittance suite. She gave her the clothes she had on when she got arrested. Paige got dressed in a hurry. She wanted to contact Rocco to see if he had heard the good news, but he was no where to be found. Paige figured that he must be still locked up, so she investigated by calling the men's jail. The woman who answered the phone said that he was there but he was getting released today. Paige said thank you and quickly hung up.

She wanted to surprise Rocco and meet him at the gate of the jail when he got out. She got there just in time. Rocco was walking out as she pulled up. They hugged like the old lovers they were. Paige drove Rocco to his house, and they chopped it up in the car enthusiastically. The first thing Paige asked Rocco was if he knew that he would be exonerated. He laughed heartily, "Baby girl, I knew it would go through! Bryce is still a child, and I'm a grown man with credentials. The mayor of Baltimore City is intelligent, wise, rich, accomplished, and free! I run this shit now! It's mine!"

"But what about Bryce? What if she wants to use it?"

"She can't. Not anymore. It's mine. If she wants to do anything, she'll have to go through me. That's my final word."

"You're right, Rocco. It's rightfully yours anyway. You deserve it more than she does. You're right. She's just a child. We'll see to it that she never finds out about it anyway. Then we won't have to worry about it."

"I'm not worried about it. We have to see to it that she doesn't get anywhere either. Other people know about this, Paige. It's a secret, true, but you know people talk. People put two and two together and come up with answers. You never know. Someone might let Bryce know something one day. Then we'll be in trouble. She'll turn on us, so we have to make sure she doesn't reach the same status that I have."

"You're right, Rocco. She's smart. In the future, she could pose a real threat to our well-being. We must begin now."

"Paige, I don't know if I can trust you. That's your child, and I know you care about her."

"No, Rocco. I care about you. Bryce is strong. She'll be okay, but she has to be stopped. Her future is very bright. If she finds out, she would be upset. She would come back and destroy us both."

"Right. So this is war now. You know what we have to do. The first step is making sure she doesn't find out. The second step is seeing that she gets used to not making it."

"How do we do that?"

"I'll continue to exert my influence. The people of authority in her life must know that we are in control."

"Okay."

"We have to also let them know to keep quiet as they help us in our efforts to keep her under our thumb."

"Okay. When and where do we start?"

"Today. I want you to go to her basketball coach and make sure she doesn't get any more playing time. If she's gonna be on the team, she has to be on the bench, not a starter like she has been in the past."

"Okay. I'm on it. Anything else?"

"That's it for now, but I'll let you know. We're in this together, Paige. Remember that I need your help. We need each other. Don't forget that, all right?"

"I got you, Rocco."

They embraced, and Paige tried to pull away to leave, but Rocco wouldn't let her. He overtook her and kissed her hard as he pulled her towards the bed. Once they got there, he threw her on the bed and took what he wanted. Paige was in too deep. She felt obligated to help Rocco and do whatever he wanted, and that included having sex with him. She couldn't refuse. She never had the chance to. He simply would not allow it. He was in control now, and that's what he wanted all along.

Paige could have been in control or at least exercised some power and protection for her child, but she was not aware and did not see it that way.

Leon was her man, but Rocco was *her* protector. Leon could not compare to the massive shadow of Rocco's influence that served as an umbrella over Paige's family. Paige was caught up in his persona and had fallen back in love with him. The only thing that kept her from leaving Leon and getting back with Rocco was his aggressive nature. Paige did know that abuse was wrong, although she did not know how to stop it. She didn't want to succumb completely, so she played her position and fell in that way. Bryce lived with Paige, but she was now officially out of the picture.

Now Paige had to figure out how to get in good with Bryce's basketball coach. Normally, she didn't go to Bryce's games especially since she had quit during her sophomore year. She would always find some excuse like she had to work or tend to some church business. Today, however, she showed up with bells on, ready to root on Bryce's return to the team. Paige took a seat near the front row. She cheered for Bryce's teammates and cautioned Bryce to get the ball. Bryce didn't even realized she was there.

When the summer league game was over, Paige approached Bryce to tell her she had a good game. She asked Bryce to introduce her to her coach. Bryce obliged. The coach said he was glad to meet Paige finally and gave her a brief report of everything Bryce had been doing that year. He also said he was proud of her and wanted her to work on jump shot at home or at a local gym. He explained how she should spread her fingers and shoot above her head and not from her chest. He went over the details with Paige so she could practice with her sometimes. Paige said she would be happy to help her daughter improve her jump shot.

Bryce seemed a little embarrassed but went along with the dialogue as if everything was okay. Really, she was confused why her mother was taking such an interest suddenly. She went along with it anyway. At the end of their conversing, Paige asked the coach for his phone number if she needed more information on how to help Bryce with her jump shot since she knew little about basketball. The coach was happy to give her his number and thanked her for showing interest.

IRMA'S GUN

Paige asked her daughter if she needed a ride home. Bryce said sure and followed her to the car. On the way home, Bryce asked her mother why she was taking such an interest suddenly. Paige asked her if she was offended. Bryce said no, but she brought up when they went to talk to the dean at her school. She asked her mother why she didn't care about her skipping school, why she was so non chalant at the meeting with the dean, and why she changed suddenly. Paige paused before she spoke, "Bryce, I know have been a little lax in my parenting. I'm trying to change, and that's why I came to your basketball game today. You'll see the change."

"What is that supposed to mean?"

"Don't worry about it. You'll see."

Bryce stared into the windshield as her mother pulled against the curb in front of their apartment. She looked like she had seen a ghost. There was silence from the car and then into the apartment. They didn't speak for the rest of that evening.

The next day, Paige called the coach and said she needed to ask him a question, "Hey, Coach, how are you? Sorry to bother you. I just wanted to ask you a question."

"Hey, how are you, Paige? I'm glad you called. I'm not that busy. What can I help you with?"

"I wanted to talk to you about Bryce's jump shot, but I need to see you. There are some things I want you to show me that you probably can't over the phone."

"Oh, okay. Where would you like to meet?"

"Can you come to our apartment?"

"Sure. Where do you live?"

"We're in 5545 Oak Street in Northeast Baltimore near the Alameda and Belvedere."

"Oh, I know where that's at. What time do you want me to be there?"

"Can you come tomorrow while Bryce is at school?"

"Sure. I'll be there around twelve thirty. See you then."

"Thank you.'

"No problem."

Paige hung up the phone and thought about what her exact words to the coach would be. She prepared dinner as Bryce did her homework. When they ate, they ate in silence, just looking at their plates and putting food in their mouths. Bryce did the dishes, and Paige went to her room. When she returned, she had on her pajamas and told Bryce to put on hers to get ready for tomorrow's school day. Bryce said okay and went to her room. Paige turned off all the lights and retired to her room for the night.

The next day, Bryce got up thirty minutes late and was rushing around to make the last bus to take her to school. She asked her mother if she could give her a ride, and Paige said, "No. You need to learn to be more responsible. Why didn't you wake up on time?"

"Mom, I pressed the snooze button once and just over slept! Can't you just take me to school so I can make it on time? I'm trying to stop skipping, and you don't seem to want to help!"

"Don't yell at me!"

"Well, you just act like you don't care. My friends' parents don't treat them like this. It's only you."

"What do you mean it's only me?"

"I always catch rides home with my friends. Sometimes I wish I could have you pick me up and we give them a ride sometimes, but you never do it. I feel like a free loader."

"Just be happy that you have friends. Now hurry up so you can catch the last bus."

Paige went into her room and slammed the door shut. She didn't come out until she heard the front door close. Then she tidied up the apartment to prepare for her twelve thirty guest. She took a shower and made some phone calls. Then there was a knock at the door. She went to the door and waited for the second knock. Then in a pleasant voice, she said, "Who is it?" She opened the door to invite the coach in. He was smiling and looked happy to be there.

He looked around before taking a seat on the sofa. "What a lovely home you have."

Paige said, "Thank you." She brought him a glass of ice water. She sat down next to him as he sipped the water. They talked for a while small talk mostly about the weather and Rocco's plight as mayor. The coach said he liked him and what he was doing for the city. Then Paige made her move, "Well, Coach, I want you to know that I think you're doing an excellent job with the girls."

"Thank you. I try to do my best."

"But you could be doing a lot better."

"Why? What exactly do you mean?"

"Well, I'm talking mostly about Bryce. I know she gets a lot of playing time, and I know she's a good defensive player, but I think it's time for her to pipe down a little bit."

"What do you mean?"

"She doesn't need to have so much playing time. And her teammates they should know not to pass the ball to her anymore."

"Well, why do you say that?"

"Well, you know Rocco is my ex-husband."

"No. I didn't know that."

"Yes. That's Bryce's father."

"Really?"

"Yes. He's also concerned about all this extra attention that Bryce is getting."

"Well, what can I do to help?"

"She needs to be shut down and taught a lesson."

"Well, Paige, aren't you concerned about how this might affect her self-esteem? I mean, Bryce is used to getting playing time and a certain level of respect from her peers. If everything changes suddenly, she'll be crushed."

"Exactly."

"I don't follow."

"She needs to know that life is not a merry-go-round. Sometimes there will be disappointments, and she needs to learn how to handle them."

Paige got so close to the coach he could feel the weight of her breath pelting him on his cheek. As she spoke, she placed her hand on his thigh. Slowly she felt her way up to his crotch. She continued to talk as she lightly brushed her hand across his groin to inspect the size of his package.

The coach was frozen with fear. He didn't move, though. Only his head pulled back in amazement as he realized what was going on. Before he knew it, Paige was loosening his belt. He had a question, "If I comply, what's in it for me?"

"I'm about to show you."

The coach undid his belt for Paige because she was having some trouble. He slid down some to help her remove his pants down to his knees. Paige went down to taste him. She stayed there for a couple of minutes until the coach groaned with pleasure. This went on until they both were pleased and had had enough. When it was over, Paige wanted confirmation, "Was everything okay?"

"Yes. It was fine, thank you. Bryce will spend a little more time on the bench, and I'll see to it that her teammates know not to pass her the ball anymore."

"Wow. We understand each other."

"Yes, we do. I have to go now."

"Well, thank you for coming."

They both laughed at each other. They shook hands, and the coach left. Paige felt like she had accomplished something for the day. She left the house to run errands and grocery shop. When Bryce came home that day, the house was a little colder than usual. She could feel the shift in her mother's attitude. It was already lukewarm, but Bryce could tell someone had added a few ice cubes to the bath. She didn't know what was going on, but she felt the need to flee. There was no where to run, though. For now, she would just have to deal with it.

Paige went over to Rocco's to see how he was doing. She knew he was scared once he got arrested. He could have gone away for a long time behind that incident, and he knew it. She wanted to console him. She knocked at the door, and no one answered. She waited for about ten minutes. Finally, he stumbled to the door, flinging it open with one long swing. He asked what she wanted. Paige explained how she knew he was afraid and how she wanted to let him know that she was there for him and that they were in this together. Rocco cut her off and told her there was no together. He was adamant about how they had been divorced for years now. He went on about how Bryce was not his and how he had made it to the top without her and how he would continue on without her. His exact words were "I don't need you or your daughter, Paige, so why are you here?"

Tears welled up in her eyes as she held them back. With her head down, she turned and walked away. She had bent over backwards for Rocco, and now he was basically spitting in her face. She just realized how he had used her, and she felt horrible. What had she done? Could she reverse her decision? She didn't want to see him go to jail, but he didn't give a damn about her. Paige said to herself that she would just leave him alone, and she did.

When she got home, Bryce was at the kitchen table, doing homework. She told her mother she was hungry and asked if she was cooking anything. Paige told Bryce to make a sandwich with the lunch meat and cheese in the fridge. Bryce also wanted to know how Paige got her apartment. She wanted to know about all the steps she would have to take to get an apartment one day. Paige was irate. "This is my house! How dare you ask me how I got what I have! When it's your turn, you can get out there and fend for yourself just like I did!"

"Dang, Ma, I just asked a question."

"If you want to know something that bad, go figure it out. Don't be expecting someone to give you the answers all the time!"

Paige stormed out. Bryce was hurt but determined not to let it show. She gathered her things and went to her room to finish her homework. She stayed in her room for the rest of the night. Her hunger subsided, and she fell asleep with her books open on her bed. She slept all night and woke up just in time to get ready for school.

She put her books away and went into the bathroom. When she returned, she pulled the covers back on the bed and slipped in. Nestling in, she forgot about school and fell fast asleep.

When Paige got home from work, she said nothing. Bryce got up around three and went to work at her part-time job at the mall. This became her pattern again off and on. They were two ships passing in the night, coming and going, saying nothing to each other as if they didn't even live together.

CHAPTER 10

Rocco was making new strides in his mayoral campaign. He was on a mission and couldn't be stopped. He was a new man. His polling numbers were up, and everyone seemed to be on his side. Then he won again. This was his third term in office. He was unstoppable. He was absorbed in his work and forgot all about Paige and Bryce. He knew that he could have gone to jail for a long time for killing that heckler in the bar that night good thing for the gun. You would think that he would want to claim Bryce and get back with Paige now that their wealth of heredity had saved his life. He did realize how lucky he was. The press almost got hold of the news of the scuffle in the bar. Everything was halted. Rocco was let out of jail. The newspapers and television were called off, and his campaign went on. Within days, everything was swept under the rug, and Rocco was free to go without question.

He even found a new girlfriend. She was twenty years his junior and as lovely as could be. She was a teacher at a high school in the city, and they met when Rocco was campaigning. They only dated for about a month before becoming an item. They were seen everywhere together and were the talk of the town. Dating columns discussed their love, and they held hands whenever Rocco spoke to an audience. Paige would call occasionally to see how he was doing, but Rocco never accepted her phone calls. He had forgotten about her. Soon, within a year, he was engaged to his girlfriend. She became pregnant with what Rocco was telling everyone was his first child. The pregnancy went well; and in the fall, she had a girl. While talking to a reporter on the evening news, Rocco said, "We decided to name her Bryce. Although Bryce is a little boyish, we know this is a rough-and-tumble world that we live in, and if they think a boy is coming, they might be a little more welcoming. When they find out she's a girl, they'll be surprised, but baby, they'll be ready when she gets there! I promise you!" Then he and his wife laughed heartily as the interview ended and a commercial came on.

Paige was watching in tears. She didn't realize it until just then, but she still loved Rocco. With all the ignoring and abusing and using her then throwing her away like a piece of trash, she still loved him. Bryce was at work and basically oblivious to all that was going on. Growing up without a father was something she didn't think about.

Bryce had gotten used to the absence of a male figure and replaced him with "big brothers" and male friends who looked out for her. Paige thought she was in a gang and going down the wrong path; but actually, considering her circumstances, she was headed the right way. She was learning how to respect herself from the music she was listening to and her big brothers. These big brothers were normally young men a few years older than Bryce whom she would talk to on the phone every day. They would give her advice about other young men from their perspective. They would look out for her and keep her safe by telling her the truths that others would not expose.

With all the lack of safety not having a father and now not having a mother provided, Bryce was actually safe anyway. She chose good friends who kept her out of trouble. She knew Rocco was her father, but she also knew or picked up on his not wanting her, so she forgot about him as he forgot about her. Life simply went on. She felt like she had enough love in her life to sustain her even without the support of her mother.

As Paige watched the newscast and cried, she listened intently. She heard Rocco and his new wife say that their little girl's name was Bryce too. She wondered where he got that idea from. Paige had never felt so low. Not only did he use her, but now he was building a life on her back. She was his slave. What a slap in the face. The worst part was that they had a connection that could not be denied.

Whatever happened in life, Paige would always have a reason to butt back into Rocco's life. Bryce was a card she could always play to get back at Rocco, but she never did. That was just not in her heart. Now with his new wife, she was subjected to the abuse from a distance. She didn't know which hurt the worst: his hitting her, her being quietly made a fool of from a distance and not doing anything about it. She was a victim all over again and could tell no one. If she did, they would say she was trying to bring a good man down.

Things between Leon and Paige were souring. He wasn't coming around as much, and the attention he used to lavish on Paige was dwindling. Paige would never meddle in his business, but she was wondering if he was talking to his former best friend. She noticed that as she got closer to Rocco around the time of his alleged offense, Leon became more distant. It was as if he could sense she had feelings for Rocco that were resurfacing. She never talked about Rocco, but Leon seemed to know everything, so she figured he was talking to someone. She punished herself by saying that's what she got for dating the best friend of her ex-husband. Maybe she should finally leave him alone and find someone else. That made sense, but it was more complicated than that. Paige was the woman who enjoyed being in a settled relationship. The hard part was finding one, and even harder than that was letting go of something that you've maintained for years. She knew Leon, and he knew her. They were comfortable, but lately, Leon was becoming more and more uncomfortable. Paige was in a lonely place.

She thought that maybe God was punishing her for the way she had treated her daughter. Paige knew she was wrong, but she and Rocco saw eye to eye about lot of things. They were alike in a lot of ways. Whose fault was it he fell in love with someone else? Paige could only do what she knew how to do, and that was to be black and be a woman. Everything else was second, so she kept on the path she was on. Eventually, she and Leon grew apart and went their separate ways. Sometimes he would come over, she would cook, they would have sex, and he would leave. They were just going through the motions. They wouldn't even talk the way they used to. Paige was sure that Rocco and Leon had made amends, so she let him go slowly.

Sometimes Paige would try to cozy up to Bryce out of guilt for not being a whole mother to her. Bryce was getting older now and developing a mind of her own. Whenever Paige would try to get closer, Bryce would buck back at her. It was as if she didn't need her anymore. She didn't have her when she needed her, and so she learned to get along without her. Now that Paige wanted to make things right because *she* had no one, Bryce had moved on. Her seventeenth birthday was approaching, and she was a senior in high school. She was already planning to move out. She had a decent job at Nordstrom in the children's shoe department and was making good money, enough to support herself riding solo. Paige was not ready to let go. She was used to having Bryce around, and it was easy to control what was going on in her life while they lived together. What would she do after she moved out? Bryce had learned to be independent without even realizing it, and now she was about to take it to the next level.

On her eighteenth birthday, Bryce looked at apartments. She found one a few blocks from the apartment she grew up in. She felt at home in the neighborhood because she grew up there and was already familiar with her surroundings. When she looked at the one-bedroom apartment, she thought that all together it was small, but she liked it. It was cozy and just enough for her; and for $375 a month, it was right up her alley. So she filled out an application.

When the application came back, Bryce was denied because her credit score was not high enough. At eighteen, she had no credit cards or credit history. They told her she would need a co signer. Asking her mother to co sign for an apartment would defeat the purpose of her moving out. She pleaded with the woman who took her application, requesting if there was an alternative to getting a co signer. She said there was one more option. Bryce could pay a triple security deposit, but she had no money saved up. She told the lady thank you and said she would be back.

She went home and thought about her options. She talked to some of her friends, and one of them suggested that she go to a bank and take a loan. The friend said she had a good job and had been there for a year plus she didn't need a massive amount of cash. She just needed enough for the security deposit. She could handle the rent and utilities on her own. No one had ever taught Bryce about how to handle or budget her money. She was good at making it but didn't know how to manage it. She saved nothing. She would just pay the small bills she had and spend the rest on herself, clothes, hair, nails, and nights out with friends. If ever she got into a financial bind, she'd be in trouble; but she never anticipated that.

The next Monday she went to her bank and asked for a loan. The loan officer turned her down flat. She said she was too young and had no collateral and no co signer. Bryce had run into the same problem she had with the apartment. But Bryce was a salesperson. She told the lady that all she needed was $600. She was sure she could raise the rest on her own. The loan officer perked up, "Is that all you need?"

Bryce knew she was in. "Yes, ma'am. That's it. I can handle the rest on my own."

The loan officer said she would see what she could do. She talked to her manager and came back to tell Bryce she would reply to her within a week. Bryce was courteous and thanked her again before leaving. She was so excited. With a good job, she should be able to get a mere $600, right? Why not?

A week went by, and the loan officer left a message for her to come in and meet with her. Bryce didn't even call back. She just showed up at the scheduled time. The officer extended her hand and said, "Congratulations. You made it. You got your $600!" Bryce almost hit the ceiling. She thanked her again and signed the paper work. The lady wrote her a check for $600, and Bryce went directly to the teller to deposit it into her checking account. With her next check, she would have enough to move in. She went home to call the leasing office to make arrangements, hoping no one had rented the apartment that she wanted. They hadn't. It was hers.

CHAPTER 11

Bryce was so inexperienced. She didn't pack or prepare to move. When she ordered a moving truck, the day they came, she rushed to jam everything into big green trash bags. The movers had to disassemble her bedroom furniture and move the large items into the truck. The movers couldn't believe she didn't even pack. They did their best to move her anyway. They didn't care. They were getting paid by the hour. When Paige figured out what was going on, she came into Bryce's room to watch.

Once Bryce got a moment, Paige made eye contact and made a peace offering. She handed Bryce a pink book. It was the Bible. She looked Bryce in the eye and said, "God will be with you wherever you go. Remember that." Bryce thanked her mother for the Bible and gave her a hug. Paige left her alone to finish moving. Bryce gathered up the last of her belongings. She rode with the movers in the front seat. Once she got there, all embarrassment from not being ready was gone. She was too overwhelmed with her new life and hardly noticed how much of a novice she was at moving.

She got out and let the movers do their jobs. She didn't even help. She just got out and walked around her new apartment. She could tell they were in a hurry to get out of there. She asked them to assemble her bedroom furniture. The leader gave her an evil look. She promised to tip him and his crew. He said okay, and they put her bedroom together for her. Now she was all set. All she had to do was unpack. No more mommy dearest meddling in her affairs. She was independent. This was her apartment, her life. She paid the rent. She called the shots. Before the movers left, Bryce paid them in cash and gave each of the three a $20 bill. They were happy with that and left her alone. She sat out on the balcony to enjoy the view. She called all her friends to let them know she had her own place. She went to the post office to put in a change of address and went to the grocery store to buy groceries. No party, no house warming she was just happy to have her own. If ignorance is bliss, Bryce was the all-not-knowing, but she didn't even care. She was out of Paige's house and out from under her thumb.

She went to work with renewed confidence. It helped her sales. She was working overtime and making plenty of commission. Her customer book was overflowing with names, addresses, and credit card numbers. Her business was booming. Then came trouble. Bryce was doing so well that her manager was talking about making her a buyer for that department. Bryce had done nothing like that before but would take a chance and try it. If her manager had confidence in her she could have confidence in herself, so she entertained the idea. Then Karla came in.

Karla was the manager replacing the woman who ran the whole department. She had come all the way from a store in Alaska. Who knows what propelled her to end up in Baltimore, but there she was. She was a great salesperson but a force for the other salespeople to reckon with. She was vicious and cared about no one but herself. That is never a sign of a good leader.

Karla would steal sales from other salespeople knowing a manager makes way more than the others and commission is not a priority. She didn't care. She was a money hound and eventually ran every salesperson out of the department. They scattered like roaches. A couple of them went to maintenance. The rest went to other departments. Bryce left the company altogether. She was so frustrated she didn't want to deal with that store any more. Thus began her career as a waitress.

"Hello, Karla. It's nice to finally meet you."

IRMA'S GUN

"Hey, Rocco. Thanks for inviting me to lunch. You're more handsome in person than the picture I saw of you. Your wife is a lucky lady."

"Thank you. Have a seat. Let's get right down to business. I have a small problem that needs to be taken care of."

"Oh really?"

"Yes. Her name is Bryce. My ex-wife seems to think that she is my daughter, but I know better. She is slowly ruining my life."

"Why? What do you mean?"

"I can't escape this girl. I mean, she is everywhere. Some years ago, I did her a favor, and now instead of being grateful, she wants to do me in. She's jealous and wants to ruin me."

"Well, what has she done?"

"Last year, for example, she sent a heckler at a bar my way. I was sitting there minding my business when this drunk guy walks in and starts badgering me. It got so bad that we ended up fighting. He pulls out a gun and tries to shoot me. By the grace of God, I end up with the gun and wind up killing him, but I could have died myself!"

"Wow . . . what a story. Are you okay?"

"I'm fine, thanks. I did some investigating and found out that this Bryce was behind it. She wants revenge because she thinks that I'm her father and that I don't want her, but I'm not her father!"

"Did you ever get a DNA test?"

"No, that's not necessary because it's not even possible that I could have fathered a child around that time."

"I see."

"She needs to be dealt with before she ruins me! I need your help please."

"Rocco, you are in a really unfortunate situation. I'm so sorry for you, and yes, I will help you. What do you want me to do?"

"I know you're a manager at that store in Alaska, and I want you to relocate to Baltimore for a while. Bryce is doing really well there and needs to be derailed. Can you look out for me?"

"Absolutely. Do you want me to fire her?"

"No. She's very sensitive. Just encourage her to leave on her own. I don't want her to know that I'm behind this. I don't want her to get any funny ideas about anything. I don't want her to know that she is being ousted. I want her to think that she made the decision on her own. Do you know what I mean?"

"Rocco, I've got you. I'll work my magic and get her out of there, okay?"

"Thank you, Karla."

"You're welcome."

CHAPTER 12

Bryce's first year alone seemed wonderful. Being an only child, she enjoyed living alone and having her own. There was no one looking over her shoulder telling her what to do. She was paying her rent and other bills. She didn't have a car; so she didn't have to worry about a car payment, insurance, gas, or car maintenance. Becoming a waitress was a god send. She made cash money every day that she went to work. That made it easier to budget her money. If ever she came up short on the rent or some other bill, she could just pick up a shift or two and make up the difference. There was no waiting for a check for two weeks or planning out a month's worth of commission.

She did miss her last job, though. The people there were great, and the benefits were extraordinary. Bryce regretted allowing someone to push her off a good opportunity. Looking back, she always felt like she should have stayed like everyone else and simply went to another department. She always wondered what would have happened if she would have stayed and fought instead of fleeing. Oh well, she ran into another good opportunity anyways, so maybe it was for the best.

She was walking down at the Inner Harbor when she saw a sign that said Now Hiring. It was posted at a restaurant called Seafood City. She went in, filled out an application, and got an interview on the spot.

She was hired just like that. There are advantages to being young and looking for a job. People know that you are energetic, impressionable, and willing to learn. They always want to hire young people, so it's always easy to find a job. Bryce had the basics of serving down already because her first job at fourteen was at a catering place. She was high strung and ready to go, so a fast-paced environment like a restaurant downtown was right up her alley. For a twenty-year-old, she made good money.

At home was another story, though. Still there was no furniture. The bedroom was complete. There were burgundy drapes, lamps, and throw rugs. A closet full of clothes and shoes. It was just like living with Paige in her room there. That's all she felt she needed, so she never aspired to save for living room furniture or a dinette set. That was an omen, though, because whenever she had male company over, there was no where to go or sit besides the bedroom. It was a complete set up, and she didn't even realize it. That's probably why her relationships never lasted too long, and she never had to worry about anyone robbing her because she had nothing. There was a wooden floor and model television in the living room; but besides that, Bryce had nothing to take. Maybe it was a blessing in disguise. Her domain never invited trouble no matter who she invited over.

Bryce would only work at Seafood City during the summer months. When it was hot, business was booming because the Inner Harbor was near the water. When it got cold, Bryce would look for work elsewhere; but she would always return to Seafood City. She would make so much money in the summer she could save some to last her through hard times in the winter. She did this for about four years until one summer there was a new manager suddenly. Bryce knew she hated him right away. He showed favoritism toward the white servers with the schedule and seating arrangements. Whenever he worked, Bryce could count on her money being slighted.

Then one day she got fed up. It was a beautiful day, and no one showed up for work except Bryce and one other server. It was a weekday, so no one counted on business getting out of hand. The new manager told the two waitresses to just alternate instead of making up a seating chart. He said that would be the fairest way to do things. Bryce was all for it. She just knew she would make some money that night even though it would be slow.

Graciously, she let the other server go first. Bryce went next, and they went back and forth. Everything was working out until Bryce was patiently waiting for someone to come in because it was her turn. Then a party of about twenty grown men walked in. Bryce got excited and went to set up her tables. After she got everything ready, the new manager told Bryce thank you and gave the party to the other girl. Bryce went off. Didn't he know that she had eight years of serving experience to this girl's one? Didn't he know it was Bryce's turn?

Bryce couldn't take it anymore and just walked out. That was it no more Seafood City. She was establishing a pattern, and so was Rocco. Rocco would nudge her into quitting, and she would run for the hills. Afterward, she would always wonder what would have happened if she would have stayed to fight. Young and wide-eyed, Bryce would just move on, trying hard to forget about another bad experience. She knew there was racism out in the world. She knew she was a brown-skinned black girl in a white man's world, but she couldn't resist the feeling that something was chasing her. She just didn't know why or what it was.

Once Bryce got wind of her pad being basically just a sex room, she wanted to change things. It never occurred to her to get some furniture for the whole apartment. She just became more selective in who she brought home. She would talk on the phone longer. She would date and go places other than her home or her friend's home, and then she met Kay Kay. Kay Kay was a cab driver who picked her up to take her to work one day when she was running late. Bryce hopped in the back seat and looked up. From precisely the right angle in the back seat, the driver looked just like LL Cool J, and Bryce told him so. He snickered and said, "Oh, you think so?" and a conversation began. By the time she got to work, she had Kay Kay's phone number.

Bryce let a week go by before she called him; and when she did, a woman answered the phone. She asked for Kay Kay, and the lady handed him the phone. They talked mostly small talk, nothing too heavy. Then Bryce said she had to get off the phone. These talks went on for about a month, and one day Bryce asked who the woman who always answered the phone was. Kay Kay said it was his roommate. Bryce said oh and never questioned it again.

One day she invited him over.

She pulled two chairs onto the balcony, and they sat there and talked some more. As the sun set over the balcony, Bryce said she was getting tired and had to work the next day. Although she enjoyed talking to Kay Kay and she enjoyed his company, she knew she had to play this game if she was ever to have anything that lasted. So she excused herself.

The next time Kay Kay came over, he wasn't as cordial. He kissed her. They went from the balcony to the bedroom. Slowly, he undressed Bryce and then laid her out on her bed. He kissed her more and then did things to her that no one had ever done before. The kisses were placed all over her neck and down her body until he reached her southern region. He kissed her there too. She breathed deeply and sighed. He kissed her thighs and down her legs. Then he sucked on her toes. She begged him not to, but he did it anyway. Then they made love. Bryce fell fast asleep, and he crept out of her apartment only to call her the next day and apologize for leaving her that way.

Bryce was not upset and understood. She told him he could come over anytime although she did not mean he could come over uninvited. He made a habit of it. That's when she discovered that he lived in the same apartment complex, only walking distance away. Kay Kay would bring fresh fruit salads and feed her while rubbing her feet. She knew he was a few years older than her, but she had never been romanced that way before. She fell in love. Then one day they were talking on the balcony again, and Kay Kay told her he was married.

"Married! But you're here all the time. Most of the time, you spend the night. When do you spend time with your wife?"

"She's a nurse. She works at night. So she never misses me when I'm with you at night."

Bryce paused. "We can't be together if you're married. I would have never had sex with you if I would have known that."

"I know. That's why I didn't tell you."

IRMA'S GUN

"Kay Kay, that's not fair. It's my choice, not yours. You should have told me and let *me* decide."

"Bryce, I really like you and wanted to be with you. I didn't want you to miss the opportunity to let me love you. Have you ever had anyone treat you the way I did?"

"No."

"See what I mean? If I would have told you, you would have missed out. Just let me love you and enjoy the moment. If ever you feel uncomfortable, I'll leave. All you have to do is say so, okay?"

She paused again. "Okay."

Their love affair lasted about six months. Kay Kay always wanted to have unprotected sex, but Bryce did know enough to protect herself. She always made him use a condom; and if it broke, they also used foam as a back up. Bryce did not want to have a baby by a married man. Then one day Kay Kay brought his photo album over. He was showing her all his pictures and explaining who these people were. Then Bryce came across some people who looked familiar. She asked Kay Kay who they were, and he said friends of the mayor.

Bryce knew Rocco was her father, but she also knew that he did not want her, so she said nothing to Kay Kay about that, but he seemed to already know. She thought it was a coincidence that Kay Kay knew people that she knew, but she never made an issue of it or thought about it further.

Bryce's apartment became Kay Kay's hang spot. He would introduce her to his cousins and his cousins' friends. They would come over to smoke weed and play cards and drink. At one gathering Kay Kay and Bryce were sitting on the balcony talking while the others were inside playing spades. At the time Paige was driving a big blue van, and it came racing around the corner just below the balcony where they were sitting. Kay Kay laughed and jumped up. "I gotta go!" He went inside with big smile on his face. "Party's over, you'll. We leaving!"

Everyone rushed out. Within seconds Bryce's apartment was empty. Bryce hated when Paige would come over unannounced. Now Paige and Kay Kay had never been in the apartment simultaneously. Bryce never introduced them. She never even talked about her mother when

Kay Kay was around. So how did he know that was her? How did he know that was her van driving around the corner? Bryce was puzzled.

Then there was a knock at the door. It was Paige. Bryce unlocked the door, and Paige didn't wait for Bryce to open it. She just rushed in. Paige saw the empty beer bottles and cards on the table. "What, you just had a party?"

"No, Ma. No party, just some friends over. Why didn't you call first?"

"I have to make an announcement before I come over?"

"Yes. This is my apartment. I pay rent here, and I would appreciate it if you would call before you come over."

"You show up to *my place* unannounced."

"I used to live there."

"But you don't anymore."

"Ma, that's different."

"How? I pay the bills there."

"Just next time call before you come over."

"Whatever."

A few weeks later Kay Kay came over unannounced and was acting strange. He started an argument with her. They never argued. Bryce felt like he was trying to exit their relationship because he was basically making up and assuming things. With tears in her eyes, Bryce stood up to confront him.

They got into a physical confrontation. Then Kay Kay pulled out a knife. Bryce froze. This had never happened before, so she didn't know how to react. Kay Kay took advantage of the opportunity and told her to get on her knees. He stood behind her and put the blade to her throat. With the other hand, he pulled a handful of her hair upward. Bryce thought he would cut her throat for sure. Tears streamed down her face as she begged him not to. He was mumbling things and cussing at her. He seemed to not hear her pleas. Then suddenly, he stopped. He just put the knife away and left her there on the floor. The door was still open when Bryce got off her knees to stand. She wiped her face and slowly closed the door. She wondered what brought on the attack, but it didn't matter. It was over.

IRMA'S GUN

    She thought about what she would do if he showed up unannounced again. She didn't want to get a gun, and she didn't think to call the police. Instead, she chose a new knife set with a large butcher knife included. She thought about contacting Rocco to see if he knew anything about Kay Kay or why he would resort to these antics. Then she thought about it again and realized that it was not a good idea. She knew Rocco didn't like her and would most likely have a fit if she ever approached him about something like this. Bryce decided to just let it go, hoping Kay Kay would never come back. Good riddance, he was married anyway.

CHAPTER 13

Bryce looked into and focused on her other interests and hobbies. Besides making money, she loved music. She had plenty of friends into it: producers, singers, rappers, managers, and dancers. She had been doing it for years and knew everyone in the city who was into it. She had one friend who was a DJ named Darron. He would always introduce her to his musical friends and take her around to different studios. Once, he introduced her to another DJ who had made a beat for a promo at a radio station. They were looking for a rapper to rap over the promo for a new show that came on at midnight on Fridays. Darron suggested Bryce, so they gave her the information to be in the promo and told her to include it. She wrote it on the spot and recorded it. They all agreed that it sounded good, so they sent it to the DJs on the radio show to listen to.

That night they opened their show with the promo that Bryce recorded with Darron. They all listened to it together from the studio. It was perfect. The hook stated the name of the show and that it was at midnight. Bryce was elated. She just knew what she had recorded would be opening up their show every week. Then with the stroke of a pen, they changed the time of the show so the promo couldn't be played anymore because it didn't make sense. Bryce was disappointed but not crushed. She had always felt like someone behind the scenes caused that to happen, but there was no way to prove it. As usual, she just moved on.

Bryce wasn't sure if she was losing her mind or not. Strange things kept happening. Everyone around her was encouraging and helpful, "Bryce, you can do it! Keep going. Don't stop." She always felt like she had the green light from all her peers, but she could get nothing accomplished. She'd do and do, and everyone seemed happy with her; but when crunch time came, something would always screw things up.

At first, it was never Bryce's fault. She was always a victim of circumstance. However over time, Bryce expected things to go wrong and therefore would cause them to go wrong herself. It's hard to *stay* optimistic when things always go left, and you can get nothing accomplished, but she tried anyway.

Bryce needed some spirit lifting, so she called her girlfriend Sheila. They would talk on the phone for hours about nothing. She told Sheila about what was going on with her failing music career and her troubles back and forth at work. Sheila suggested that they go out to a club. She picked Bryce up around eleven on a Friday night. They were headed to a place called Teeka's on Greenmount Avenue. Once they were inside, the first thing they did was sit at the bar. Bryce had never been to a bar before and didn't know what to order, so Sheila ordered her a shot of Hennessy and a mixed drink.

Bryce was twisted. A side of her came out that Sheila had never seen before. The two danced and mingled all night. Then Bryce ran into Kay Kay. They just stared at each other for a few seconds, then turned, and acted like strangers not speaking. That is how Bryce knew it was definitely over. Sheila didn't notice a thing. She had never met Mike before, and Bryce didn't entertain telling her who he was. She was through.

Sheila drove Bryce home and dropped her off. Bryce stumbled up the walkway and fumbled with the keys before finally getting into her apartment. She went straight to the bathroom to pee. Then she collapsed on the bed in her dress and fell fast asleep. Saturday morning she woke up feeling refreshed. A night on the town did her some good, and knowing that Kay Kay was not coming back made her feel like there was a new beginning.

She cleaned up her place and made two over hard eggs with cheese, four strips of bacon, and a bowl of grits. Then she called into work to see if they needed help for the evening shift. Her boss said yes, so she prepared herself to go in by doing some laundry.

When she got to her winter job, things seemed a bit off. The servers were not as friendly as they usually were. When she went to her "cage" in the back, everything was gone. The servers had robbed her. There were no dishes, no glasses, no napkins nothing. So she had to search the restaurant for necessities to get ready for her shift as a room service girl at the hotel. The task was daunting since it was busy, but somehow she accomplished it. Once she was ready, she took orders.

Then Troy sauntered into the cage. "Hey, Brycey, it's busy tonight so be on the look out. You ain't gon have shit tonight. There are a lot of high-profile people coming in tonight, and some of them might stay at the hotel. So be on your *P*s and *Q*s. Plus, those mystery shopper people will be lurking, so do everything by the book. Don't cut no corners! Aiigght?" Bryce thanked him for the heads up and got straight to work.

Everything he said turned out to be true because Bryce ran into several celebrities that night. She tried to play it cool and just act like they were regular people (which they were) so she wouldn't get nervous and drop anything on anybody. She did a good job and made some good tips that night. Then the owner made his way to her cage. "Good evening, Bryce. I see you're working hard tonight. You always do. Next weekend we'll have a new girl coming in, and I want you to train her. She'll be doing room service and occasional banquets like you. Show her the ropes please. Thank you."

Bryce agreed and kept it moving. She was up to her eyeballs in orders. She went into the dining room out front to look for some napkins for her carts, and guess who was sitting at a table in the dining room. It was Rocco and his entourage. Bryce grabbed a handful of napkins and darted back into her cage in the back. She couldn't believe he was here. Did he know that she worked there? Was he looking for her, or was this just a coincidence? She didn't tell a soul that her father was out front, and she hoped that he didn't see her. Then the manager came to the back snapping all kinds of orders to Bryce knowing how swamped she was. He didn't seem to care. Bryce did her best, but he was confusing her. Just as she would get into a zone, he would appear and bark orders as if she was sitting there doing nothing. It all fell to pieces within minutes, and Bryce was in what they call the weeds. She didn't know her top from her bottom and was racing around like a chicken with its head cut off.

When it was over, napkins, food, and dishes were everywhere. The cage was a mess, and no one seemed to care. Bryce stopped for the first time that whole night and caught her breath. The manager was right there to witness it. "What are you doing? You don't see this mess everywhere, and you're just standing here?"

"I was"

"You were what? Taking a minute to do what? They say you do a good job, but tonight has not been evidence of that. Clean this place up!"

"But I was going to. I've been running since I got here. I was just catching my breath. I"

"No excuses, ma'am. Get to work."

He left, and Bryce was hot. She didn't even have the chance to explain herself. She felt disrespected. It's like the manager had left her with a heap of responsibility and hard feelings. She didn't like it, but she couldn't do anything. She cleaned up as fast as she could. All she wanted to do was go home. When everything was done, she checked her credit card receipts and counted her cash tips. This was a phenomenal night. This was the most she had ever made in one night working anywhere. Her mood suddenly changed, and Troy reappeared.

"Hey, sweetness, you made out tonight, didn't you? The last server just tipped me out. I made out like a fat rat myself. Let's celebrate."

"What do you want to do?"

"Come over to my place. You know where I live. Imma give you some money for a cab, and I want you to get a bottle of champagne. Stop by the liquor store on the corner and get some along with some condoms. Here are my keys. I gotta stay and clean up. I'll meet you there, okay?"

"Okay. You trust me that much?"

"What you think?"

Bryce smiled and accepted the keys. She finished up and was on her way to Troy's house. She put on her heavy coat and pulled the hood up over her ears and went outside to hail a cab. She must have been standing there for an hour watching cab after cab go by when she finally realized that she must have looked like a man with that huge coat on. Nothing was showing but her eyes.

The next time she saw a cab approaching, something told her to take off her hood. The wind tousled her hair some, and her earrings glistened a bit. The cab almost hit her trying to stop. They thought she was a man. Now she knew how black men felt trying to catch cab.

She told him to drop her off at the liquor store on the corner of North Avenue and St. Paul Streets. She got the champagne and condoms like Troy told her to and walked a few blocks up to his place. She put the champagne in the fridge and made herself at home. She got tired waiting for him, so she took her shoes off and lay across his bed and fell asleep.

Later Troy came in and woke her up by kissing her on the lips. They fell into a long passionate kiss, and Troy placed himself on top of her. They embraced and kissed more as he grinded against her with their clothes still on. Then Troy asked her if she wanted some champagne. She said yes, and he retrieved it from the fridge and brought it into the bedroom.

"Thirsty?"

"You know I am."

"You want a lot or a little bit?"

"I want you."

"You can have that too, but right now I'm asking about champagne."

"A lot. My throat's dry."

Troy unwrapped the top and twisted off the cap as it popped and flew across the room. A swirl of smoke came out of the bottle, and he poured some into a plastic flute until the bubbles reached the top of the glass. He waited patiently for the fizz to flatten and poured more and then handed it to Bryce. She said thank you and waited for him to pour one for himself. Then he held his arm up in front of her and waited for her to put her arm through his. With their arms twisted together, they made a verbal toast and took a sip. They untwisted their arms and discussed work for a while.

Troy told Bryce she should watch her back more. He said she was too easy going and free. He wanted her to look for the signs of back stabbing in her co-workers. Bryce said that besides the usual bullshit, she didn't feel like she had anything to worry about. Troy told her she was wrong. She thanked him for having her back and said she would try to be more careful, and then they made love.

The next Saturday morning Bryce was scheduled to come in, which was unusual because it was always slow on Saturday mornings. When she arrived, a white girl named Amber was there. Amber introduced herself and told Bryce this was her first day and that she was told that Bryce was supposed to train her. Bryce remembered what her manager had told her the week before and understood why she was there now. She guessed that a Saturday morning was a good time to train someone, so there she was.

She told Amber she had only been working there for a couple of months and that she did banquets whenever they had them. She gave her a synopsis of her work history and told her she was twenty-five. Amber said she was only eighteen and this was her first job. After a little more small talk and breaking the ice, Bryce showed her the ropes. They continued to talk, and Amber mentioned that she was getting paid $25 an hour for banquets and minimum wage plus tips for room service. Bryce was only getting paid $3.15 an hour for room service and $15 an hour for banquets. She was hurt but didn't feel the sting of it until much later. She didn't tell Amber how much she was getting paid. She just let her assume that her wages were the same.

Bryce worked hard to train Amber although she acted like she already knew what she was doing. She had to teach her the fundamentals and the rules of room service. Bryce didn't think that was fair because she knew she was more experienced than Amber was but oh well. She figured she would outlast her anyways since she had no clue about what she was doing.

Bryce didn't let this bother her although she knew it wasn't right. She trained Amber for a whole week and then turned her loose by herself. Whenever she would mess up, the management would come back to Bryce and ask why she didn't teach her this or that. Bryce would defend herself, but they would always hold Bryce responsible for Amber's short comings. Bryce liked working there and didn't like all the negative attention that training Amber had brought her way, but she didn't complain and dealt with it the best way she knew how. She feared losing her job if she pressed the issue, so she just kept her mouth shut. This went on for about a month and a half. Still, Bryce said nothing.

Then one morning Bryce woke up with a terrible headache. She felt nauseated and had to throw up. The stress of being used as a scapegoat at work was getting to her. She needed the money because the rent was due, so she just took some Tylenol for her headache and pushed on. When she got to work, she had to throw up again. She couldn't imagine running around in the hotel going from room to room with vomit on her breath and feeling nauseated. She told her manager she wasn't feeling well and asked if she could be excused. He said he would call Amber in but Bryce would have to wait until she got there. Bryce agreed and held on.

She went home and took a nap. When she awoke, she felt better and took the rest of the day to run errands and make some business phone calls. One of her calls was an appointment with her gynecologist. She was long overdue and had missed a period, but she thought nothing of it. When the day of her appointment came, she was on time and didn't have many questions. To her, this was just a routine visit. She went through the motions and said little. Her doctor told her she would be in touch to give her the results of the lab tests, and Bryce said thank you. In two weeks, her doctor called her to let her know that she was pregnant. Bryce gasped. She had no venereal diseases or any cancers. Her doctor recommended that she come in for prenatal visits if she was going to keep the baby. Bryce agreed. She was ecstatic.

The first thing she did was call Troy. He was not officially her boyfriend. They were just messing around, but she did like him because he respected her and treated her well. Whenever they went out to eat, he always paid; and he was always sure to satisfy her and himself when they had sex. He was a great lover and a great friend, but Bryce enjoyed things the way they were and didn't want to complicate things. She let them be.

"Troy, I'm pregnant."

"Are you sure it's mine?"

"Yes, I'm sure. You're the only one I've been with."

"How far along are you?"

"Six weeks."

"Oh, okay, well, are you going to keep it?"

"Do you want me to?"

"It's your decision."

"Yes, I'm going to keep it. I think you'll be a great father. You've been good to me, and I think you'll be good with the baby. Are you excited?"

"I don't know."

"What do you mean you don't know?"

"I don't know. Let me think about it."

"Okay. I'll call you later."

"Bye."

Troy was mostly quiet and in deep thought on the phone, but Bryce didn't pass judgment. She had decided to keep her baby, and any help that Troy offered would be icing on the cake. She didn't know what to make of his dispassionate attitude but was ready to take on the challenge. This would be her first child, and all she could do was imagine how the baby would look, what she would name the baby, and how she would care for it. Her thoughts did not include Troy because she knew he didn't want to be tied down, but she figured he would still be a good father from a distance. She told no one else though because she knew she was still deciding.

A week went by, and she called her mother to tell her the good news. Paige's reaction was tepid, but Bryce still wanted her mother's support.

Paige was quieter than Troy was. Bryce asked her if she was ready to be a grandmother. She wanted Paige to be happy, but Paige was on the fence.

Bryce thought that was strange. Most first-time grandmothers are jumping for joy. Maybe a baby made Paige feel like she was getting old. Or maybe she thought Bryce wasn't ready. She didn't even have a living room set. Bryce told her cousin Tammy, and her cousin told her not to be afraid. She said when you have a small child you'll be surprised how people will help you. Things will figure themselves out, and Tammy thought Bryce would make a great mother. Bryce was inspired.

She called Troy back to let him in on the progress she had made with Paige and Tammy. She was grateful for his friendship, and that's all she wanted from him. She didn't anticipate taking him to court for child support or being his girlfriend or wife. She just wanted him to be the father to her child that Rocco never was to her. She felt like he was up to the task, and she was proud of him already. When he picked up the phone and heard her voice, he was livid.

"What the fuck are you calling me for?"

"What? What's wrong with you?"

"Don't ask me for shit! I'm not your man!"

"I thought you said you wouldn't mind if I had the baby?."

"I never said that! Your ass is crazy! It's not mines anyway!"

"Troy, I don't want anything from you. All I want is you to be a father to your child and spend some time with your child."

Troy cut her off. "I can't be a father to something that's not mines! Get lost and don't call me no more!"

Troy hung up on her, and that was the end. Bryce thought they had something beautiful going although he was not technically her boyfriend. He had always respected and cared for her. She didn't understand. What made him change his mind so suddenly? He didn't have kids, so maybe he didn't want to be burdened with the responsibility. Bryce thought they were friends. She thought they could co-parent and make it work. Apparently she scared him by telling him she was pregnant. She was so hurt. All she could think about was repeating the cycle of having a child without a father. She knew how it felt to grow up with a father who didn't love her. Now she was about to do the same thing to her child.

Right then, she knew she couldn't go through with it. She was still young, and who knows what the future would bring? She knew one day she would meet someone better than Troy anyway, someone who would want children with Bryce and would want to be a good father. She threw in the towel. She would have an abortion.

CHAPTER 14

Her doctor told her she would need to come in for an exam before having the abortion to make sure everything was okay. She said that some women may not be "eligible" for an abortion. Bryce went to see her. She waited for an hour, which was not unusual at this clinic. It was located downtown in the heart of the city and served women from all over Baltimore. Bryce waited patiently. When her name was called, Bryce walked in with confidence and followed all instructions. They took her weight and asked her a whole list of questions. They wanted to know when her last period was and the actual day she conceived. Bryce didn't keep a calendar and couldn't remember actual dates, so she improvised using work days and other appointments as markers to remember when certain things happened. She tried to be accurate. Then there was the pelvic exam.

Bryce undressed and put on a paper gown and covered her bottom half with a white sheet of paper. Bryce could feel the cold from the table through the blanket she was sitting on. The doctor came in and introduced herself then told her to lie back and put her feet into the stirrups. She hated this. It felt just like a regular pap smear and the same exam she had every six months. She was so glad when it was over. The doctor left and said someone would be in to talk to her.

IRMA'S GUN

Bryce got dressed and waited. Another woman came in and sat down. She too introduced herself and explained that the doctor gave her the information from the exam. She was here to analyze the results. The first thing she said was that Bryce was eligible for an abortion, but she made light by saying it was close. Bryce wanted to know what she meant by that. She showed Bryce a chart that looked like the spin wheel in the game of Twister. It had little numbers on it that represented the weeks of her pregnancy. The lady showed her where she was.

Bryce said no, she was here and pointed to a different area on the chart. The only person Bryce was sleeping with was Tony, and they had sex sporadically, so she knew exactly when she conceived. The woman told Bryce she was certain that she was almost twelve weeks. Bryce knew she wasn't that far along. The woman asked, "How can you be so sure?"

Bryce told her frankly, "Because I know when I had sex. I've only been sleeping with one person."

The woman wanted to know if she was sure. Bryce was insulted. She felt like another number instead of a person, like she had to come in there and lie to this woman about who she had slept with. Then Bryce thought, what if this lady told her that she couldn't have the abortion because she was too far along when Bryce knew she wasn't? She was instantly angry and wanted to leave. Bryce clammed up to hasten her visit. She shrugged it off and left.

The first person she called after she made her decision was Paige. She wasn't surprised at all even after Bryce announced that she wanted her child. That took Bryce aback. Paige didn't ask any questions or give her a speech about wanting to be a grandmother. Her only reply was "When are you going to do it?"

Bryce said she didn't know just yet and that she would get more facts from her doctor and get back to her. The next person she called was her doctor at the clinic. The clinic gave her an appointment to abort and told her she would need to have someone drive her home. She thought about calling Sheila first, but they had fallen out. She never even told her she was pregnant. Bryce called Paige back.

"Mom, I need you to drive me to the clinic on the twenty-third of March and stay there with me while I get the abortion. I can't be alone. I don't want to be alone. Will you be able to?"

Paige told her she could do it, and they set up a time for her to pick Bryce up that day. For a moment, Bryce felt like they were a family again. What circumstances to be reunited over. After the way her mother treated her, she was surprised that she would be there for her. It all felt so strange. Bryce wondered why but didn't make an issue of it.

Then the twenty-third came. Paige was on time and beeped the horn for Bryce to come out. Bryce locked the door and slowly walked to the car. Paige was sitting there looking stoic. Her head was held high, and she said nothing. She just pulled off and drove her daughter to the clinic. She asked her if she wanted her to be in the room with her. Bryce said no. She would be fine by herself, so Paige waited outside in the lobby.

Bryce felt like her mother was proud of her for getting an abortion. She wished at that moment more than anything that she would just talk to her, but Paige was from the old school. She didn't believe in being open and honest with her child. She believed that certain truths should be kept hidden. Bryce believed that you should educate your child about the hardships of life so they don't have to go through them. That's what parenting is all about. Paige was just the opposite.

The beginning of the abortion was just like a pelvic exam until the practitioner showed Bryce the needle to be inserted into her uterus. Bryce almost had a heart attack. She wished she had been put to sleep. When the needle went in, she felt a pinch. Then all her insides went numb. She sat there for a while, waiting for the numbing agent to work completely, but the worst part was the actual act of it. It felt like someone was taking a vacuum cleaner to her vagina and sucking everything out.

It took forever. All she could imagine was what her child was going through. Could they feel any pain? Occasionally, the vacuum would get stuck, and Bryce would hear a clump or two going through the tube. She wiped the tears from the sides of her face and inside her ears. She felt horrible and never wanted to go through this again. She promised herself she wouldn't no matter what.

When it was over, the clinic gave her sanitary napkins to wear and told her to change every hour until the bleeding subsided. They gave her some pain medication and sent her on her way. Paige was waiting patiently in the lobby. There was complete silence. No "Are you okay? What was it like? Did it hurt? How do you feel?" Nothing. Bryce imagined that her mother had an abortion when she was younger and was reliving the experience. She had a habit of doing that. Bryce would explain away things she couldn't understand or that didn't make sense. She had a vivid imagination. It made her feel better to know why things occurred; but sometimes in life, you never know why things happen the way they do. You just have to accept them.

Paige dropped her off and drove away directly. What a cold exit. Any other time, she would want to come in and explore Bryce's apartment. She came over unannounced like she was curious about Bryce's life when really she just wanted to pry. Bryce wondered why her mother was this way and wished she was different. She would pay attention to her friends' mothers and how they treated their children. That's how Bryce realized something was wrong. At first, she just thought Paige was a typical black mother with an attitude. She would write off all her short comings as just "issues; but when her friends' parents would come to school for them or take up for them in other ways, Bryce wondered why Paige never did that for her. You never know that your surroundings are faulty until someone or something makes you aware of it.

As Bryce grew older, she became more and more aware of what was wrong; and she was wise enough to know that she couldn't change anyone. All she could do now was try to change what would happen to her and *her* children. She knew she could change the future, not the past.

It seemed like Bryce's past was haunting her, though. She took a few days off from work to recuperate. When she went back, everything was different. Attitudes had shifted, and the pedestal she had been placed on for all her hard work was no longer there. It seemed everything was a real struggle now. Bryce could no longer simply demand her respect and get it. She had to fight for it, and sometimes even that was not enough.

She was taking a break in the cage when her manager came in. He wanted to know why she was sitting down. Before she could tell him she was taking her break, he fired her. She was upset but not surprised. She gathered her things and left with her pride in her back pocket.

It had happened again but why? Was this sheer racism? What was she doing wrong? It was becoming a pattern. She would be welcomed with open arms, establish her respect, and do well for a while. Then just like that, everything would be gone through no fault of her own. All she could do now was try to avoid getting depressed.

CHAPTER 15

Rocco was sitting on the beach in the Bahamas with his wife. They were at a hotel, enjoying the scenery. Many children were playing, and Rocco's wife told him she wanted another baby. He figured that she was just inspired by the beautiful day, so he shrugged it off and told her to wait a little while to give it more thought. If this was just a whim, it should go away with time.

After sitting there for a few hours, they ate lunch at a nearby café. Rocco told her they would be meeting friends of his. After picking out something to wear for himself, he went into his wife's closet and found an off the shoulder peach dress. He laid it on the bed and placed gold heels underneath the bed. He even picked out a few pieces of jewelry: three gold bracelets, a gold watch, gold earrings and an ankle bracelet to match. His wife got out of the shower heading for the closet when she realized her outfit was laid out for her already.

"Oh, thank you, baby. You are so considerate. Now I don't have to worry about what I'm going to wear."

"You know I gotta keep you looking good."

"Ooohhh, and you do it so well."

They kissed. "Now get dressed and put some of that sweet-smelling lotion on. I want you to really wow my friends."

"Oh, so I'm just an arm piece, huh?"

"No, don't be silly. You know you're more than that, but you also know that some people judge you by the company you keep."

"So I'm your company?"

"You know what I mean. You're my wife, and I need my friends to know that my life is together and complete. You understand."

"Of course, I do. Do you need me to do anything else, honey?"

"Just look good for me like you always do. That's all I need you to do."

"Done. By the way, are you still taking those pills the doctor gave you?"

"What pills?"

"What do you mean what pills? The ones the doctor prescribed for your bipolar disorder."

"You really think I have that mess?"

"Well, how else would you explain the sleepless nights and moodiness?"

"I'm fine. You know I have a heavy work load, and sometimes I get all wrapped up in it. You know that. Stop acting dumb."

"I'm not acting dumb. You're in denial."

Rocco slapped her. "Deny that."

"Rocco! All I'm doing is being honest with you. The way you treat me sometimes, it's evident that something's wrong. One minute you're sweet as pie. The next, you're hitting me like I stole something. It's crazy."

"You're crazy."

"Do you remember what your doctor said? The lithium will control your mood swings, and the Prozac will keep you from getting depressed. Don't you want to feel good and even keeled all the time, not just every once in a while? I know you haven't slept well in months. Just give it a try and see what happens."

Rocco paused. "I don't like the side effects, babe."

"Well, you have to ask yourself if you want to get better and have a little dry mouth and muscle soreness or if you want to suffer with fresh breath and be able to work out whenever you want. Your mental health is important, babe. Plus, those side effects can be remedied. I got you that special mouthwash for the dry mouth, and you can take those shots for the muscle soreness. It's a bit inconvenient, but in the long run, it's worth it."

"Yeah, that's what you keep telling me."

"You know I'm right. You're just being stubborn."

"I'm being real."

"But you have to come down and treat this thing. I'm here for you. I'll help you."

"You're always there for me."

"That's why I'm your wife, Rocco. Now will you take your meds?"

"Where they at?"

Rocco got dressed and waited in the den for his wife to finish getting dressed herself. Rocco put some ice in a plastic bag and wrapped a wash cloth around it. He gently placed it on the side of his wife's face where he had slapped her, "This will make the swelling go down." After about ten minutes, she smeared on her makeup. Then as a couple, they went downstairs to the café to meet Rocco's friends.

Everyone had on linen suits and dresses. Rocco's wife thought they might be overdressed; but once she saw everyone else, she stopped feeling out of place. Everyone took their seats and settled in, making light of the nice day and how long it had been since they saw one another. Greetings and introductions were exchanged.

Then they got down to business. Rocco started by saying his next term as mayor was at stake. Everyone sat up to take notice, sipping on their glasses of wine and cocktails. They were very interested and told Rocco to go into some depth about his dilemma. He was eager to. He started off by asking if they were familiar with Bryce and how his ex-wife, Paige, was claiming that she was his daughter. No one seemed to know about this, so Rocco educated them.

"It all started when I was married to Paige. I found out she was cheating on me with my best friend. When she got pregnant, she tried to say the baby was mine, but I knew it was his. That's why we got a divorce. I guess it was for the best because after it all it made me a better man. I got myself together and became mayor for the first time. Then when she saw how successful I was without her, she tried to come back, but I wasn't having it. She kept trying to push this little girl on me, but I just couldn't accept her, knowing she was my best friend's child. I know she is telling Bryce that I'm her father because she wants her to be connected to someone like me. I know how Paige is. She's spiteful. I know she's putting all sorts of ideas in Bryce's head about getting revenge for not having a father because Leon doesn't want her either and Paige is distraught about the divorce. They want to destroy me, so I have to destroy them first. I've already started watching Bryce to make sure she doesn't have anything or too many friends. I don't want to allow her to get into a position where she can come for me. It seems every time I leave her alone, she gets back on her feet. She is hyper vigilant about tearing me down."

Rocco's friends had plenty of questions. "Why don't you just get her wacked?" or "Are you paying child support?" Rocco had to explain. He wanted them on his side although deep down he knew he was wrong. He was careful to leave out details about *his* wrongdoing. He didn't want to incriminate himself.

He went on,

"I can't just kill her. Nowadays investigations are killer. I don't want anything to get traced back to me. My run as mayor is at stake. I can't go to jail. It's no place for me. Besides, I'm already forty-three. If I get twenty to life, my life will basically be over. I don't want or need that, and no, I'm not paying child support. Paige knows that to get child support, she'll have to submit to a DNA test. She doesn't want to prove that I'm *not* the father. She'd rather entertain these shenanigans that I am. I need a crew of people to support me. I can't do this alone. The task is too disheartening. I need eyes and ears on the ground. Bryce isn't making this easy, and she is a definite threat. Do I have your support?"

Rocco's friends were apprehensive. They summarized that his problems with his so-called daughter were average everyday things that a lot of men go through. They said he would be better off just ignoring her and going on with his life. If ever she tried to come after him, as the mayor, he could just go to the press and give them the same explanation he gave them. They saw it as simple. They told Rocco he was making a mountain out of a molehill, but he didn't agree. He was adamant about controlling her life and said that even if he had to do it alone he would.

His friends let him know that they loved him as a person but did not support him in this. They even told him he was wrong, but Rocco was steadfast. He wanted to crush this young life forever. He got upset and ended the meeting. His wife told him he was being hasty, and he chastised her in front of everyone. Rocco didn't realize it at the time, but that made him look bad. His friends left in a hurry. He was all alone in this, but by now, he didn't even care. He was full steam ahead.

When they got back to the hotel, he told his wife to pack their things. They were supposed to stay one more day, but Rocco was ready to go now. He threw his clothes into the suitcase, not even bothering to fold them. He called the airport and arranged to leave early, saying there was an emergency at home. It cost him some extra money, but he didn't care. With his wife, he contemplated finding someone who could kill Bryce for him. His wife suggested a person who was in and out of jail and didn't have much to live for. Rocco could convince them to off Bryce then take care of their family or something like that. He could take care of them in jail for the duration. She said it was the easiest thing to do.

Rocco feared getting caught. He said he watched crime shows about this kind of thing all the time. People would always set someone up or hire a person to kill someone, and it never failed: the person for hire would always crack under pressure and tell everything. Rocco was not having it. He'd rather continue to follow Bryce around and make her life a living hell from a distance. So that's what he did.

CHAPTER 16

Rocco was scared. He remembered that his mother always told him, "What goes around comes around. Karma is real." He believed it and had lived long enough to see it manifest. Not even his wife knew how he had used Paige and Bryce to keep himself from getting charged with murder, and now he wanted to destroy his child. He knew that to do that he had to keep in touch with Paige. He had to keep her on a string.

He did whatever he had to including sex and verbal conditioning, and it worked. Paige was a sucker for a man with power, and Rocco was the one. She was on his side even if it meant being against her daughter. She did whatever he asked her to do. She was his slave both in bed and in life, and she accepted it. There was no fighting back or rebelling. To her, there was no other way but his. She called him to tell him the good news.

"Bryce is pregnant."

"What? Why do you sound like you're in a good mood about it?"

"I am. This is a good thing. She'll be a young mother and get distracted from coming after you."

"Noooo, Paige. A child brings love and hope. I don't want her having extra family and friends. That's ammunition against me. She has to stay broken no family, no friends. That's the way I like it. You understand?"

"Yeah, I guess, but she's bent on having this baby. How can I convince her to have an abortion?"

"I'll take care of that. Who's the father, and how can I find him?"

"She mentioned someone named Tony that she worked with."

"That's all I need to know."

Rocco called the owner of the restaurant where Bryce was a room service attendant and had a meeting with him. He asked about Troy and wanted to know where he could find him. The owner gave him his address.

Rocco showed up unannounced at Troy's place with two of his security officers. He knocked gently on the door. Troy yelled through the door, "Who is it?"

Rocco said he had money for him, and Troy cracked the door to peer out into the night. Rocco said, "Can we come in for a few seconds?"

Troy removed the chain and opened the door. Rocco and his officers continued to stand.

"I'll make this brief. I want you leave my daughter alone."

"Who's your daughter?"

"Bryce, your baby momma."

"She's not my girlfriend."

"But you're about to have a baby together."

"No. Not together . . . apart."

"Do you love her?"

"We're just friends."

"Well, un friend her!"

"What? What do you mean?"

"I heard that the only reason she wants to have this baby is because you encouraged it."

"No. I didn't encourage anything. I told her I would be there for my child, but I didn't *encourage* her."

"What did you mean by *be there for your child*?"

"I just meant that I would be a father to the kid. We agreed that there would be no relationship between us. We would just be friends to coparent. You know I would be there whenever I could be but nothing pressing. The child would basically be Bryce's responsibility."

"Well, you need to let her know that you have changed your mind."

"But I haven't."

Rocco brandished a gun, and his security officers reestablished their positions. "Yes, you have."

"Oh . . . well, I don't have any children, and I don't need any!"

"That's my boy. Now you understand."

"I certainly do. Bryce needs to know that she doesn't have my support. If she has this baby, it'll be on her terms by herself . . . okay?"

"That's what I wanted to hear you say. We can leave now, gentlemen."

"Thank you for coming."

Troy gently shut the door. Rocco was satisfied and left. His goal had been accomplished. Rocco got into his car and laughed with his associates. They stopped at a local watering hole and had drinks before going home.

After Bryce had her abortion, she fell into a mild depression. She had lost her job, so she didn't have a place she had to be every day. She would stay at home and just sleep all day. Sometimes she would wonder about what her child would have looked like and how her future would have turned out with her raising a baby. There were regrets, but it was too late to badger herself about it. What was done was done, but she knew she didn't have it in her to go through with that again, so she would have to be more careful. She thought about all the birth control options she was educated about at the clinic. She promised herself she would choose and always have something on hand like she did with Kay Kay. Then she thought about it. What was the difference? Why did she take such stringent measures with Kay Kay and not with Troy? She had made up her mind she would not have a married man's baby. Did she want to have Troy's baby? She couldn't remember thinking about it. Maybe she just took getting pregnant for granted because things were going so good between them. She never anticipated him changing on her like that. It was yet another lesson to be learned.

In her depression, she never took the time to look for another job. Sometimes friends would come over; and they would talk, drink, and smoke weed. Her apartment became the meeting spot, but no one knew or even asked why she wasn't working. Bryce went on partying and sleeping all day even through the yellow eviction notices taped to her door every month.

She worried. She had been living there for three years and saw plenty of others get evicted. They would just come home one day and find all their belongings on the curb. Most of the time, people had moved on because they knew the eviction was coming. The things thrown out would be mere skeletons of the trappings of a nice apartment. Or maybe they lived like Bryce with very little. She hated seeing it around the fifth of the month because she would always wonder where the people would go. Did they move into another apartment or with family? Or were they homeless in a shelter somewhere or even worse on the streets? She would shudder thinking about it. Bryce got out of her funk and made plans to move. She went to see her grandfather in West Baltimore.

Granddaddy Sam was a small man who adored his granddaughter. She was his first grandchild. Bryce had the fondest memories of the pair walking hand in hand in Lexington Market downtown. He would pick her up and put her on his shoulder to introduce her to everyone as if she were his pet iguana. Bryce always remembered feeling so loved. Later, she appreciated his love because he set the precedent for how she expected men to treat her. As long as Bryce could remember, Granddaddy Sam never had a telephone. He said the bill collectors and strange people bothered him too much. If you wanted to contact him, you had to go see him. Bryce did just that. He was so happy to see his grandchild. They hugged, and he kissed her on the cheek. "Where you been?"

"Granddaddy I been through a lot. I lost my job, and I'm about to get evicted. Can I move in with you?"

Granddaddy Sam didn't hesitate. "Yeah, baby. I got a room. You gon pay me some rent?"

"How much you want?"

"How much can you pay?"

"Well, I don't want to stay here forever. I can pay you a couple hundred a month. Plus, I'll buy my own food. I'll save the rest of my money to get another place. I just need somewhere to go in the meantime."

"Baby, you can stay here as long as you need to."

"Thank you, Grandpa. You need anything?"

"Just that rent."

"Okay, I have to go the bank. Can I move in tomorrow?"

"Yeah, let me give you a key."

"Okay, I'll see you tomorrow."

They hugged again, and Bryce kissed *him* on the cheek this time. She was elated that she had a place to stay, and her stress level went down. Now she could pack. She went back to her apartment and prepared to move. She called a moving company and got boxes from the grocery store. Bryce was on her way.

The day she moved in, she wondered how she would move her cat. She didn't have a carrying case, so she just wrapped him in a blanket so he wouldn't be able to see. She knew he would get scared and try to run. He meowed the whole way. Once she arrived at her grandfather's house, they sat down to catch up. She hadn't talked to him in ages.

"Granddaddy, how you been? What's going on?"

"I missed you, lady. How'd you lose your job?"

"That's a long story. They basically hired this white girl to replace me. I trained her and everything."

"What? They did you like that?"

"Did they?"

"Did you like working there?"

"I did, but if they couldn't appreciate my good service, oh well, maybe it was for the best."

"If you say so. Did you start looking for another job?"

"Yeah. I put in some applications at a few restaurants."

"Anybody call you on your cell phone yet?"

"No, not yet, just waiting. This is a nice three-bedroom house, Granddaddy. How'd you find this? Was it expensive?"

"They had a sign up when I came to visit your cousin who lives down the street."

"How much is your mortgage?"

"I'm renting to own. It's only $300 a month."
"That's all?"
"Yep."
"How long is it gonna take you to buy it?"
"I don't know."
"Whatchu mean you don't know? You signed papers, didn't you?"
"Yeah."
"Well, what they say?"
"I don't know. I tried to put 'em in *your* name, but your momma wouldn't let me."
"Whatchu mean you tried to put 'em in my name?"
"Well, I ain't getting no younger. If something happens to me, I wanted it to be yours."

Bryce's face flushed. "You wanted me to have the house that you're paying for?"
"Of course, why not?"

A tear fell from her eye. "Why did she say I couldn't have it?"
"She threatened me, Bryce."
"What did she say?"
"She said I'd be hurtin' if I put your name on the deed."
"Well, what did she mean by that?"
"What do you think she meant?"
"But you're her father."
"She don't care."
"That's crazy, Granddaddy. I need a house. I can't believe she did that!"
"Well, she did. Believe it!"
"Are you hungry?"
"You gon cook tonight?"
"Yeah. Whatchu want?"
"I got some lima beans and rice in the cupboard."
"Okay, that's what I'll make. You want some cornbread too?"
"Yeah, go ahead and make some. Make it sweet like cake."
"Okay."
"You gon leave that thing here while you work?"

"What thing?"

"That cat! I can't stand cats!"

"I didn't know that, Granddaddy. I don't have any other place to keep it."

Her grandfather just walked away. "Well, I guess he'll have to stay here."

"I'm going to the store to get a box of Jiffy. You need anything?"

"No, I'm fine."

"All right."

Bryce moved the boxes in the way up to her room and went to the store. When she came back, her cat was locked in the basement. Her phone rang.

"Hello, Bryce."

"Hey, who's this?"

"It's Brian Waters. How have you been?"

"Oh, hey, Brian. Why are you calling me? I thought you got fired from the restaurant at the hotel?"

"I did. I work at Mona's now."

"Oh really. Which one?"

"The one near the Walter's Art Gallery."

"Oh, okay. I put in an application there."

"That's why I'm calling. I have your application here in my hand. Why don't you come on in?"

"Wow, for an interview?"

"No. You have the job. I already worked with you at the other restaurant. I think you'll do well here. Just come in and fill out your W2s and get a uniform."

"What? Thanks, Brian. What time do you want me to come in?"

"Come in sometime today. Get here anytime before five. You'll get your schedule too."

"Oh, that's awesome! I'll be there in about an hour."

"Okay, hun. See you then."

Brian hung up the phone, and Bryce jumped for joy. She had a job. She couldn't believe Brian was the manager somewhere else that quickly. God sure works in mysterious ways. She didn't even have to interview.

IRMA'S GUN

This experience inspired her to always do her best because you never know who's watching and who might help you later. She felt like she had friends in high places. She knew Mona's was a high-end Italian restaurant and figured that if Brian was working there she could make some good money. She was planning to move out already.

When she came back, her cat was gone. She asked her grandfather where she was, and he just shook his head and walked away. As he was going, he said the cat escaped when he opened the door. Bryce wondered if he let her out because he didn't like cats and didn't want her in the first place, but she didn't press the issue because she knew her grandfather loved her and would do nothing to purposely hurt her. If he did let the cat out, she figured he must have really hated them.

Working at Mona's was very rewarding. Bryce learned to stay later until six instead of leaving at three. All the other servers were gone by four; and customers still trickled in until dinnertime, which meant she'd have the whole restaurant to herself. She made money during the lunch shift, but after everyone left was when she made the real money. There was a woman manager below Brian nicknamed Lolli who called her "old moneybags." She enjoyed working there because the servers liked her and treated her well, and she was making plenty of money, but there was one problem: the owner. She couldn't stand Bryce.

The owner was a chef who would come in to cook and tweak the menu occasionally. One day Bryce walked in, and she chopped a pan of brownies with a meat cleaver. The closer Bryce got, the harder she chopped. Bryce asked her if she was okay, and she cussed. Bryce just stared at her for a second. The owner informed Bryce she wasn't the mayor and walked out. Bryce was puzzled. They never spoke again.

Then one day Bryce came in, and Lolli informed her that Brian had been fired. She said the owner caught him stealing a bottle of wine from the cellar. Bryce asked if he was okay, and Lolli said she wasn't sure, but he should have no problem finding another job.

Two weeks went by before they found someone to replace Brian; but when they did, things went downhill for Bryce. Her schedule was changed, and her hours were cut. They also hired another black waitress who fit the same description as Bryce. Bryce was still making money but not as much.

Since she was saving to move, she scrambled to make up the difference. She tried to stay late every day, but the new waitress would always beat her to the punch. Every day there would be a different excuse as to why Bryce couldn't stay late. She was getting angry.

One day the new waitress had something to do so she couldn't stay. A dinner server didn't show up, so they asked Bryce to stay for *that* shift. She couldn't turn down the money. By the time she got off, her bus had stopped running so she was stranded.

She called Paige and asked her to pick her up. Paige was reluctant. She had never picked Bryce up before and would not start now. Bryce had to beg. It was raining, and she didn't have an umbrella. Bryce made $300 that day. It was dark outside, and the restaurant was in a bad area. She didn't want to get robbed. After a while, Paige gave in and said she would come to get her so Bryce waited. Bryce was in the back when Lolli told her mom was at the bar waiting. Bryce gathered her things and went to the bar area. She couldn't believe what she saw.

Paige was standing there with tears in her eyes. Her head was held high. She was aloof. Bryce knew of some of the struggles she had come through and assumed that Paige was just proud of her. Mona's was a nice place, and few black people worked or frequented the place. Usually, Paige would have discouraged her from working there. She didn't believe that a young black woman could thrive in a place like this. In her day, she wouldn't be allowed to sit at the bar elbow to elbow with white people. She was surprised the bar tender asked her if he could get her something to drink.

Bryce couldn't have been more wrong. Rocco was watching her. Paige showed up because Rocco told her to go. It was the only way he knew how to control the situation that day.

That day Bryce won, and she didn't even know. Rocco was upset and didn't know how to express his feelings, but Paige knew him well and represented him. Bryce spent little time around Rocco, so she didn't know him. She didn't recognize the signs that her mother was giving her. She knew something was wrong, but she just couldn't figure it out.

IRMA'S GUN

Again, there was silence in the car on the way home. Bryce broke the monotony by telling her mother about her day. Paige was on her way to Bryce's old apartment when Bryce had to inform her she had moved in with her grandfather. There was more silence. Bryce thought of how her grandfather told her that her mother wouldn't allow her grandfather to put his house in her name. She was quiet about it, though. She didn't want to snitch on her grandfather and start trouble between the two. She talked about her cat and how he got away. Bryce told her mother how they hired a new girl who was taking her money by staying late at work. She even told her how the owner indirectly threatened her for no reason. Paige remained quiet. Bryce wondered why her mother had no comments. Eventually, she shut down and was quiet herself.

After a few minutes, Bryce was home. She asked her mother if she wanted to come in and say hi to Grandpa. Paige said no and that she would see him later. Then she drove off.

As she walked up the steps, her cat came running up onto the porch. Normally, she would rub up against Bryce's leg and greet her with happy meows. Today she didn't rub up against her. She just sat on her hind legs and cried. Bryce knew something was wrong. She stared at the cat, talking to it and telling her she missed her. She would let her back inside when she noticed that the cat had weird-looking stripes all over her. She knew the cat had been out in the streets and thought she caught the mange or something. Apparently, she knew she was sick, and that's why she wouldn't rub up against Bryce. Although she was upset about her cat being in the streets of West Baltimore, she felt good she didn't rub up against her. Bryce already had eczema. The last thing she needed was some disease from an animal itching her on her leg. Bryce knew her cat loved her and cared about her.

She went inside and brought her some food and water. She sat in a chair and watched her. The cat ate so fast Bryce thought she might choke. When she finished, Bryce was afraid she might try to thank her by rubbing up against her, but she didn't. She just turned around, meowed, and ran off into the night. Her cat was officially in the streets now, thanks to Granddaddy.

She went inside, and the first thing she did was put her money away into a small safe she kept under her bed. So far, she had saved $5,000, which was more than enough to move; but Bryce was getting comfortable. Her whole family lived on the one little street that her grandfather lived on. She suspected that's why he moved in the first place. He was such a loner. She admired that about him but wondered if he got lonely sometimes.

Bryce's grandfather was a good-looking man, and the ladies loved him. A woman always stopped by to bring him a plate or say hi. When they would see Bryce, they would always get jealous. She remembered how they would do that when he lived at his former place. Bryce was only ten, but they didn't care. They always thought she was his daughter. They'd be ready for war too, making sly comments about her right in front of her face. This would go on until they discovered she was just his granddaughter. Then suddenly, they'd be friendlier; but by then, Bryce would already be insulted. Her grandfather would pick up on the negative energy, accept the food, and then politely put them out.

CHAPTER 17

"Granddaddy, I want to talk to you."

"About what, baby?"

"I want to thank you for being gracious enough to let me stay here. I know you've been by yourself and enjoy your independence. I should be moving pretty soon because I've saved up enough to do it, but I have an old friend who's in trouble."

"What kind of trouble?"

"Well, he and his father have been arguing a lot lately. His father's an alcoholic and has been spending all his money on booze. They're in danger of getting evicted, and his father is threatening to put him out. Can he stay here with me until either he gets a place of his own or I move out?"

"Is he gonna be trouble? How long have you known him?"

"I met him when I was fifteen. No, he won't be any trouble. He doesn't drink or smoke. He isn't into anything illegal. He just needs to find a job and save some money to get his place like me."

"Okay. I trust you, but don't make a habit outta this."

"Oh Granddaddy, I love you. You're so understanding."

Bryce kissed him on the cheek and went to call Mike. Mike was a guy she had known since high school. They would talk on the phone every day and were girlfriend-boyfriend off and on for seven years. They stayed in touch, and Bryce wanted to be there for him in his time of need because he was there for her in the past.

"Hey, Mike. How you doing?"

"I'm all right. What's up?"

"You still need a place to stay?"

"Yeah, why?"

"You can come live with me and my grandfather, okay? Is that cool?"

Mike lit up, "I only need to stay for a short while. I'll pack a bag. Can I come tonight?"

"Yeah. Catch the number three downtown. Get off on Charles Street and walk over to Baltimore Street. Catch the number two all the way up and get off at Mount Olivet Lane. Call me when you get off the bus, and I'll meet you on Mount Olivet."

"Okay. Let me get myself together. I'll call you when I'm on the way."

"Okay, bye."

"Bye."

The phone rang, and it was Mike. He announced that he had just jumped off the bus after passing the graveyard like Bryce told him to do. She said she would meet him as he walked up the street.

Bryce and Mike talked almost every day. Even when they weren't going together, they remained friends. Bryce hated the thought of him beefing with his father because she knew him. When they met, she thought he didn't like her because he would always crack jokes about her. Initially she took it personally but then got used to his twisted sense of humor, and they became friends. When she discovered Mike might end up in the streets, she couldn't bear the thought of it. She saw him walking up the street, and they both smiled. They met in the street and hugged. She wanted him to know that staying with her grandfather was a temporary situation and she'd be leaving soon; but while she was there, he was welcome to stay too. Mike thanked her for her friendship.

When they got there, Bryce showed him around and offered him some dinner. She told him she didn't have a spare key for him, but either she or her grandfather would always be there. Bryce showed him her queen-sized bed and told him to draw an imaginary line down the middle. The left side was his, and the right side was hers. They had been together before, so she wondered how long this arrangement would last. He agreed to it never the less.

They talked over a plate of spaghetti. Granddaddy Sam had eaten, so it was just the two of them. He had no plans. He didn't have a job lined up. He hadn't even looked. He bounced around some ideas of going to the local community college. Bryce said nothing, but she thought that was weird. How can you prepare to get your place and one day move out when you're just going to college? How will you save money without a job? How can you be ready to move without a plan? Bryce knew something was wrong but did not question it because she had known him for so long.

Eventually, Mike signed up for classes at Catonsville Community College. As soon as he did, he informed Bryce of his schedule. She thought *that* was strange. They were only friends at the time, but he was telling her this like she was his girlfriend. The only thing she cared about as far as he was concerned was that he get himself together so he could one day move on like she was planning to do. She didn't want to pry, so she kept quiet.

It's hard to sleep in the same bed with someone that you've already been with and not eventually get tempted. They lasted about three nights before they were having sex every night. There was never talk of them getting back together. They just enjoyed each other's company. Mike even became friends with Bryce's cousins who lived on Holy Mount Lane. Some of her male cousins would come over and stay a little while. Soon they would all leave together to go different places. Bryce sometimes wondered if they were going over to girls' houses, but she never asked. She wasn't his girlfriend.

Bryce just kept working as much as possible at Mona's. Every day she would come home and put her earnings in her safe. Sometimes she wondered what would happen to Mike when she moved. Then one day she came home, and her grandfather was not there. She got a phone call from Paige saying he was in the hospital. Bryce wanted to know what was wrong. Paige said he had hepatitis with cirrhosis of the liver. Bryce wanted to know where it came from. Her mother said it came from granddaddy drinking every day. Bryce thought about it and realized that her grandfather was an alcoholic. She had never seen him drunk, but he always had a cup of something in his hand. Bryce had heard of hepatitis and thought it was curable. She figured the hospital would treat her grandfather and turn him loose. He'd be home within a week for sure. She was wrong. He died in the hospital, and she never got to say goodbye.

The night she got the news, she and Mike did not have sex. He held her as she cried. Bryce remembered her grandfather treating her like a princess. She always dreamed of sharing her children with him one day. When it became evident that that day would never come, it broke her spirit. Then she thought of how in his last days he didn't appear to be sick. He just had a nagging cough and lost his appetite. Bryce thanked God she moved in when she did because she could say she got to spend some time with him during his last days. Had she not moved in, she would have no closure. She was also thankful for Mike being there whatever his true intentions were. She could not have imagined going through this alone.

Now it was just the two of them. As the days went on, Bryce stopped crying. She wondered what Mike was doing outside of the house because he still had no job but would occasionally bring her gifts like shoes and purses. She was happy to see these gifts and did not complain but wondered why Mike was giving her things if she was not his girlfriend. Then he came to the house one night with a male friend and informed Bryce he was leaving.

She never knew what hit her. First, she lost her job at the hotel. Then she lost her apartment. Her cat followed, and her grandfather perished. Then, just when she was getting used to him, Mike left her too. Everything came tumbling down all at once. She cried herself to sleep that night wondering why.

The lady who owned the house discovered that Sam had passed away. Out of respect for him and Bryce, she stayed away for several months, never demanding rent or utilities. However, when she did come around, Bryce knew it was time to leave. Her grandfather used to fix the insides of houses for a living. This house was to be his "pet project." He gutted the entire thing. The only room finished was the kitchen; and since Bryce's name was not on the rent-to-own lease, she had no reason to stay there. In his last days, Sam complained about the terms. Bryce didn't want to get involved.

Frequenting a local bar, she ran into an old friend who said he was renting an apartment downtown and was about to move. The problem was he would have to break his lease to do so. Bryce told him she was looking for a place. He gave her the details and then asked if she wanted to move in, in his place so he wouldn't have to break his lease. The next day she went to look at it and moved in. She also looked for another job, anticipating getting fired or not making enough money at Mona's.

When moving day came, Bryce moved everything but her bedroom furniture. She wanted to leave behind her mother and everything holding her back. All she wanted was to succeed at something anything. To do so, she would have to rid herself of all that was hanging on, although she still didn't realize what was going on. She did realize that much. She took the mattress so she wouldn't have to sleep on the floor. She took the rest of her belongings, which wasn't much, and just got a guy from the neighborhood with a truck to help move her in. She felt like this was a new chapter in her life. She had a new place.

She was living in what was a nice area during the day but at night a haven for prostitutes. At night, she avoided going out. It was springtime, so the weather was warming up. The downtown area was filled with restaurants, so Bryce took one whole day to just walk throughout, filling out applications. She knew with the weather breaking she would find something. She waited for that fateful phone call; and when it came, she was ready. It was another seafood restaurant downtown called Peter's.

She went in, aced the interview, and trained the next day. She didn't bond with the other servers the way she did with the cooks in the kitchen. She made the same money she was making at Seafood City, but again, she bought no furniture.

She didn't go shopping. She would just buy groceries and experiment with cooking different dishes. She liked using her Crock pot. She could make a meal in the morning before she left and let it simmer all day while she was gone. In the evening, when she came back, she wouldn't have to expel much energy to have dinner for herself. She ate little, so she would save the bulk of the meal in plastic containers and freeze them for later.

Bryce had gotten used to living this simple lifestyle. It wouldn't be until later that she would understand how much she didn't have. It's hard to miss something you never had. She just wanted to be left alone to enjoy life, make a little money, and strive to be better. She was lonely, so she was looking for a boyfriend. She came across a prospect at work. He was a prep cook on the cold-food side. His name was Darvice. Every day they would flirt.

"Hey, pretty."

"Hey, handsome."

"You ready for your crab legs?"

"Yeah. Give 'em to me."

"It's two whole pounds. Can you handle it?"

"I don't know. Let's see."

"Come and get it."

"Boy, give me my crab legs and stop playing!"

"Imma give 'em to you all right."

The things Darvice would say and the way he treated Bryce was, on one hand, friendly and respectful but, on the other hand, borderline sexual harassment. She didn't care. She enjoyed the attention. She knew it was a bad idea to get involved with someone you work with; but one day, when no one else was around, she asked for his phone number. He smiled as he lowered his head and laughed. He was flattered. Soon after, Darvice was at her apartment sitting on her mattress.

"Why don't you have any furniture?"

"Oh, I just moved and haven't gotten the chance to go shopping for any yet."

"Oh. So what made you invite me over?"

"Well, I like talking to you on the phone but wanted to see you in person. I'd rather talk that way."

"Are you hungry?"

"No. I just ate."

"You want something to drink?"

"No. I'm fine."

"Why are you so quiet? You seem to talk more on the phone."

"You think I'm quiet?"

"Yes."

"I think I'm rather talkative."

"What? What do you mean?"

"I tell you everything. I explain myself like a psychologist or something. Oprah ain't got shit on me."

"Well, if you're so good with your words, why don't you use them with me?"

"I do."

"Really?"

"Yes. You just don't pay attention."

"You confuse me."

"I look good. I'm a nice person. People like me, and so do you."

"Well, aren't you confident?"

"Well, it's getting late. I gotta go."

"You just got here."

"Yeah, I know, but my bus is coming."

"Okay. I'll walk you to the door."

"Can I have a hug?"

Darvice was six three, and Bryce was five five. He wrapped his arms around her shoulders and pulled her close. Although their bodies were touching, he gave her a cold embrace. Bryce felt the resistance and instantly felt competitive. She thought he was such a nice guy. She just didn't understand why he was so wishy-washy. She thought he just needed some attention. If he knew she cared he would be interested, right? She gave it a shot. She continued talking on the phone, getting no where with him. She invited him over again. He declined. Feeling the depth of winter, Bryce left him alone. Her sadness deepened.

Then she came to work one day; one server was on the line, talking unusually loud and announcing that she was coming over to someone's house. She wanted to know why they kept begging her to talk to them and keep them company. She went on. Bryce understood this must have been Darvice's girlfriend. She was so embarrassed. He said nothing about a girlfriend. She didn't ask either. She guessed this is why you don't date someone at work. She had set herself up for failure because she was lonely.

CHAPTER 18

Bryce was lonely because she didn't have many friends. She was separated from her cousins and other family. She had no siblings, and she and her mother were estranged. Sometimes she would get so tired and confused. What was she doing wrong? Why couldn't she keep a job, and why couldn't she keep friends? It seemed like everyone wanted her to win. Everybody wanted to be close to her; but once they got there, they would become defensive and angry or cold and distant, but they would never leave. If things became too heated, Bryce would leave. She would be happy for the moment she got away from a bad situation; but in the end, she would be even lonelier than when she started.

She went on working. Bryce noticed that her managers would give her the biggest sections. She would have more tables than anyone else. At first, she thought, *Wow, they must have a lot of confidence in me to give me all these tables.*

However, as she worked she realized that it was hard to give good service with so many tables. Her tips suffered, and she wouldn't make much more than if she had a regular section. She would just work herself into circles with little reward. One day she got fed up and asked for a smaller section. The management acted as if she was complaining and said she was doing a good job. They didn't seem to care about her tips.

They would reduce her section by one or sometimes two tables and leave it at that. She still struggled. She felt like Superwoman.

One day she had a large section and a table of five. The table of five was problematic. They seemed a regular table at first until they ran her. Bryce brought their food, and one woman asked for extra french fries. When Bryce came back, the woman said she dropped her fork and asked for another. She brought the fork. Then she wanted more water. The woman would not give her a break. Bryce came to the table this time and asked everyone if they were okay. She wanted to know if anyone needed anything so she could bring it all at one time, but they kept making separate requests. Bryce tried to ignore her and tend to her other tables; but whenever she walked by, the woman would get her attention and ask for something else. Bryce's other tables suffered because of it too.

When it was time to hand them the bill, Bryce put automatic gratuity on their bill. The problem was you were only supposed to do that with parties of six or more. This was a party of five. From her experience, the tables that run you the most rarely tip well. Their bill was over $200. Bryce didn't want to get cheated after running around like that for them, so *she* cheated. The woman complained, and the manager asked Bryce why she put gratuity on a party of five. She tried to explain but got fired. Bryce knew she was being greedy but had worked hard and felt justified. She had to learn a lesson the hard way. When she gathered her things to leave, she saw Rocco sitting at the bar with his associates. She didn't want him to notice her, so she slipped out quietly.

Bryce thought she would soon find another job somewhere downtown because the weather was warm, but no other places called her back. She waited for a while for those calls. When they never came, she thought she would begin a new search. Nothing turned up. She got her first eviction notice and panicked. She couldn't believe this was happening again. Bryce brain stormed, and what she came up with concerned music.

She wasn't focused on it but out of desperation gave it a try. A couple of years ago, she had dealt with two producers who told her about their relationship with a local record company. The company was backed by a

IRMA'S GUN

former NFL player. He was a millionaire, so they figured he could take them to places, but it never panned out. They even let Bryce go with them to a meeting there, so she knew where it was located. Actually, it was walking distance from her apartment. She went over to the record company and knocked on the door.

A bald, short, light-skinned blackman opened the door and stared at her.

"Yes?"

"Is this still Built More records?"

"Yes. What can I help you with?"

"How you doing? My name is Bryce. I came here a couple of years ago with two friends of mine. I met you before. Do you remember me?"

"Vaguely. You look familiar, though."

"Yeah, well, I wanted to know if Mr. Pearson was looking for any new talent. I'm a rapper, and I'd like to audition for him. Does he still own Built More?"

"Yeah. We're best friends."

"Oh, okay, I didn't know that. Can I come in?"

The man opened the door farther and introduced himself as Built More's A&R person. Bryce felt like she had struck gold. She knew she was talking to the right person.

"So how long have you been the A&R here?"

"We've only been her for five years. I've been the A&R the whole time, from the beginning."

"Oh, okay, so you know about all the artists here. Do you have any currently signed?"

"Only two right now. It's an R&B group called the Couper Brothers. We also have a rap duo called Two Tigers."

"Do you have any music recorded by them?"

"Of course we do. Follow me into the studio. My name's Donald by the way."

"Okay, Donald."

Bryce sat down on a red leather sofa and got comfortable. The music came on, and she nodded. She was liking the beat. She listened intently to what the two guys were saying. Bryce wanted to get a feel for the kind of artists they signed and put out.

Right away, she had constructive criticism about what she heard but kept it to herself. She knew she wasn't the A&R. She was there looking for a deal mainly to get advance money to keep from getting evicted. A recording career wouldn't have hurt either.

"So whatchu think? You like it?"

"Yeah, it's rocking."

"I wouldn't mind doing a song with them. When are they coming out?"

"I don't know yet."

"Oh, can I record something for you to listen to?"

"Sure, go into the booth and put the headphones on. What kind of beats you like?"

"Hard. Anything with a thump to it."

"I got you."

Donald pressed two buttons, and music filtered into the headphones. Bryce rapped. She went on and on. In the booth, she was facing Donald as he sat behind the production board. He had his poker face on the whole time. Bryce watched him for a reaction. There was never any. After about seven verses, she froze. He was just playing her. She could tell he wasn't interested at all, just entertaining her company, so why would he even waste her time? Although he didn't seem genuinely interested in her music, he didn't seem interested in her either. This was as close as she had ever gotten; so if she had to play the sex card, she would have. Donald never made advances.

However, one day she came over; and Donald asked her if she wanted to go to the record pool with him. She didn't know what that was, but she said yes. They drove farther downtown and walked into a warehouse. No one was there, and Bryce got a little scared but didn't let on. She just kept talking to him. She could hear their voices echoing. Then this tall white guy with long sandy-brown dreadlocks walked in with a pile of vinyl records under his arm. The two men greeted each other, and Donald called the man Cool Breeze. Bryce said nothing and just stood there like a fly on the wall. They talked as if she wasn't even there. Their conversation was brief.

At first, Bryce was listening; but as they spoke on things she did not know of, she tuned them out. Then Donald raised his voice to ask Cool Breeze, "Is this shit for real?"

Cool Breeze heard Bryce rap one time when he was working in a record store downtown. He answered, "Yeah. She cool."

She now understood their reason for coming here. Donald wanted to get some insight on her street credibility. Did this mean that Donald would now consider signing her? Although she was initially insulted, a spark of energy came over her. She was in, or so she thought. She asked Donald to take her home instead of going back to Built More. He obliged.

Bryce didn't stop coming by, though. This was her last chance, and she knew it. Eviction was looming. Everyone at Built More was so respectful. They had her doing all kinds of light volunteer work. She would shrink wrap CDs for other artists and just sit around to chill and talk. She felt like she was making friends. She wasn't. They just didn't want to hurt her feelings.

On the day of her eviction, she panicked. She called Donald for advice. When he discovered she was getting thrown out, he became defensive and put up a wall. He didn't come out and say it, but he stopped playing the let's-be-friends game. Her hang out time was up, and so was her time at this address. Bryce went home and just sat there hoping they'd never come. There was a knock at the door. She refused to answer, and two minutes later, she heard the lock turning. Two women let themselves in. One was white, and one was black. They carried a handful of big black trash bags. Bryce and the ladies looked at each other.

The white one said, "You've been late for, like, ever. You already know why we're here."

Bryce had no plans. The ladies seemed so nice. She sold things she couldn't take with her. She offered them her microwave, Crock pot, and dishes. The pulled together handfuls of cash and bought it all. Bryce gathered what she could. The rest was put into the trash bags and thrown out on the street. Bryce descended the steps, dejected. She got to the bottom step and backed out of the door. The street she lived on was one way. People were jumping out of cars, scooping up her bags, and driving off.

Bryce held her head high, pretended she didn't know what was going on, and walked down the street. She stopped and sat down on a bench at a bus stop where she could no longer see what was going on. Is this what it felt like to be homeless? She had $132 in her pocket and no check on the way. She called her mother.

"Ma, what took you so long to answer the phone?"

"I was busy."

"I just got thrown out. Can I crash at your place until I can find something else?"

"No."

Bryce was taken aback. She paused.

"What do you mean?"

"No. You can't stay here."

She went back to the bench on the bus stop to think about it. This was not real. Here she was out in the streets with no where to go, and her mother would let it stay that way. Her heart sank. She walked over to the number three and waited for the bus on another bench. As she headed toward her mother's house, her mind was blank. She was in shock. She knocked on her mother's door once, and she answered. Bryce stood on the porch with tears in her eyes. Her mother let her in.

"What did you do with my old room?"

"That's my office now. There's a desk and fax machine in there."

"Office? For what?"

"I do taxes."

"Oh, I didn't know that."

"Yeah. There's a lot you don't know."

"Can I sleep on the couch until I get myself together?"

Paige didn't respond. She looked up into the ceiling and folded her arms. She wasn't saying anything. Then she shook her head no. Bryce cried.

"Please can I stay here? I don't have anywhere to go. I'll find another job. It won't take long to save some money and get another place. You know I won't be a problem. Why you treating me like I'm on drugs or something? You know I don't do that. I just need some time that's all. Is someone else staying here?"

"What you think?"

"Who?"

"That's none of your business."

"Who are you protecting?"

Paige got angry.

"This is my house!"

"Ma, please!"

The two argued back and forth as Bryce cried harder. The more she cried, the more her mother seemed to crack some, so Bryce didn't let up.

Finally Paige said, "You can sleep on the couch." Then she walked away. It was as if they were on the set of a movie and someone said, "Cut!"

Bryce wondered if her mother just wanted to see her beg. This was the worst day of her life. She felt so low and worthless. Her stomach churned, so she went to the bathroom and then sat on the couch again. She took her shoes off, propped the pillow from the couch under her head, and fell fast asleep. This time, she was snoring.

Bryce went on doing this for two weeks until her mother complained. Paige asked her why she was in this slump. Bryce just acted like she didn't know what she was talking about. She didn't want to get into another argument. She would have appreciated talking to her mother, but she knew she couldn't trust her. She tried to remove the thoughts of *why* from her mind. Usually, she would contemplate and investigate. What made her this way? Did she hate her daughter? Is someone else in control? Did she do this of her free will? The questions would go on and on. She simply did not know what was going on and was in too much of a funk to worry about it. She was more concerned about what was going on in front of her. She knew she had to get out of her mother's place soon, so she started hunting for a job again.

This time, after some rest, she was more aggressive. She would put in applications and wait a couple of days and then call them instead of waiting for them to call her. Then someone *did* call. Bryce got an interview with the telephone company. She got the job and informed her mother she would be moving out in approximately three months.

She took her hourly rate and multiplied it times forty, then multiplied that times four weeks, and then multiplied that times three months. Her calculations left her at about $7,500. That was more than enough for a deposit and first month's rent plus some furniture and whatever she might need to get started. The only thing she couldn't afford was a car, but she didn't worry. She would just work with what she had.

For her first day, she bought a few skirts and blouses to wear in this new corporate environment. She also bought one pair of navy-blue shoes that would match everything else she purchased. Now she was ready to earn and save to move out. She forgot about what happened at her last residence. That was all behind her now.

She waited for the forty-four and transferred to the number eight on York Road. She had to ride the number eight all the way until the end of the line to get to the telephone company. The whole trip took two hours. That's four hours of travel time every day, which is a big chunk of time out of a person's day just to get back and forth. Bryce thought it would be worth it, though.

One day she was running late and missed the number eight. She stood there on York Road, wondering when the next bus would come along. A yellow cab came barreling around the corner. She stuck out her arm, and he stopped. Maybe she wouldn't be late. When she hopped in, the driver talked to her immediately. He introduced himself as Cam and told her he was looking for a boarder. Bryce asked questions. Cam said he had a three-bedroom house he lived in with one roommate. He was looking for another. He was only charging $300 a month for rent. Quickly, she thought about it. The room for rent was furnished. He only wanted one month's rent for a deposit. There was no background check or credit check. She only had to pay in cash every month. Cam said he would write her a receipt. After work, she went to look at the house and meet his roommate.

The house was actually walking distance from Paige's apartment, so Bryce was familiar with the area. The house was clean and nicely furnished. His roommate was an African girl named Chelsea. Bryce wondered why she didn't have an African name. She talked to the girl, and she said she was born in Nigeria. That didn't make sense to Bryce, but she was polite enough not to ask questions about that. She seemed nice enough. Bryce worked for a whole month and then moved in, another new beginning. She could breathe now that she was out of her mother's house.

Her room had a queen-sized bed with a mirror built into the headboard. There were two nightstands, a dresser, and a nice-sized closet. Bryce was satisfied for now, and it was better than sleeping on Paige's couch. She got to know Chelsea, and they became friends. When Bryce moved in, Chelsea did not have a job. Her father was an African king or something. He had plenty of money and would wire her hundreds of dollars every month, and he paid her rent. When Chelsea discovered Bryce's job and how much she was making, she got inspired.

"I want to work too."

"C'mon, the hours are eight to four, Monday through Friday."

Chelsea put in an application and got hired right away. She had little experience; but with Bryce's referral, she was in there. Chelsea drove a used Volvo that her father bought for her and took the two to work every day. Bryce was relieved that she didn't have to catch the bus anymore. The two got to know each other even more because they would talk all the time in the car. They hung out and even dated two best friends.

CHAPTER 19

At work, Bryce soared and forgot all about her troubles. She would drop sales on the phone like wildfire, and a co-worker called her the quiet storm. She said Bryce would be in a corner, not making any noise, and drop like a million sales that no one would know about until they checked the monitor. She liked the job, so she would work on weekends too. She made plenty of friends.

Bryce was doing well until the telephone leads dried up. She would make a phone call to a hundred people, and ninety would say someone already called and they already said no. Sales became impossible. Then an unknown co-worker from another team would walk by Bryce's desk every day, taunting her. She would say things under her breath like

"You gon' lose,"

"This my shit," and

"Make some noise now."

Initially, Bryce wondered who she was and if she was even talking to her. Then it became apparent that she was. This mystery woman would never look Bryce in the eye. She would just say something as she walked by. Bryce became defensive and stood up with her headset on. She would look at the co-worker whenever she walked by, but there was never a direct response. There was never a verbal altercation. They never bumped into each other in the hallways. There was never a fight.

Bryce recognized the pattern again. She guessed that she was doing too well. How could she get out? She knew someone had sent this co-worker to bother her. She viewed the woman as an innocent bystander who would soon be in the way. Bryce couldn't get to who was messing up her life, so she would have to shoot the messenger. She came up with an idea. She felt like everyone already knew what was going on, so she would air her opinions about it.

There was an all-night radio show called Strictly Hip-Hop. They would always play local talent on the air. Bryce knew people who worked there, so she recorded a demo called "No Competition." In it, she humiliated the co-worker who would threaten Bryce every day. At the end, she cussed her out, but her words were meant for whoever was behind this torture. Bryce listened to the song when she finished it and was embarrassed, but she put it out anyway. She knew her stalker would eventually hear it and get the message. Maybe that would make him or her leave Bryce alone. Strictly Hip-Hop played the song on a Friday night, and Bryce was working overtime the next Saturday morning.

She and Chelsea pulled into the parking lot, and right away, Bryce noticed that the energy there was different. People were walking by one another, dapping it up and cussing. She thought that was a little in appropriate for work but said nothing. She also said nothing to Chelsea who didn't listen to rap music.

Bryce and Chelsea went in two directions. Chelsea took the stairs, and Bryce waited on the elevator. The co-worker she was talking about in the song walked up next to Bryce. It was just the two of them. The elevator doors opened, and the co-worker walked in. Bryce followed. The co- worker wanted to know. "Did you wash your ass?" Bryce was confused. She showered daily and had no hygiene issues that she knew about.

Obviously, she had heard the song. The woman wasn't a rapper like Bryce, so Bryce didn't anticipate hearing a diss record about it. She knew that was a little unfair, but so what? Putting a paper bag over someone's head and beating them in the darkness was unfair too. Bryce spoke her piece and was satisfied for the moment. She proved her point and kept this stalker at bay. Her fear subsided, but she still wanted to know what was going on.

Hanging out with Chelsea was fun. She discovered later that her roommate's boyfriend was married. She knew that was a recipe for disaster but never mentioned that to her. She remembered Kay Kay. She knew she couldn't throw stones in a glass house. She just sat back and watched her go through everything that she went through with Kay Kay. There was a difference, though. Her boyfriend didn't spend as much time with her, and she waited around a lot. When he was there, it was all about sex. Bryce witnessed no romance. And her boyfriend was aggressive. Bryce could always hear them having sex through the wall. It sounded like she was getting raped all the time. Bryce was confused. In front of Chelsea, her boyfriend was respectful. He never cursed. He never hit her, but Bryce would hear the stories about how he treated her on the low. The whole situation did not sit well with Bryce, so she kept her distance. She even stopped seeing his best friend.

Bryce had the phone number of someone else she'd met with Chelsea. His name was Mason. He didn't have a car, a job, or a girlfriend but was as sweet as could be. He sold nickel bags of weed to stay afloat. He lived with a roommate downtown on Monroe Street. Bryce would go to visit him. They would sit around and watch the game and smoke weed. Then they would have sex in his room. Bryce would always spend the night, and he would send her home in a cab in the morning. He lived right next door to a pizza shop where he worked. He was already doing favors for the owner who had big bank. The owner ran several pizza shops.

Bryce would tell Chelsea all about it. She was happy and didn't mind bragging to someone anyone. Suddenly, Mason stopped calling. Bryce wanted to know what was going on. She smelled something fishy.

She would go visit, and Mason would be quiet and unresponsive. They would watch TV but would no longer discuss what was going on. They would just sit there like two bumps on a log. Bryce was getting bored and felt like she was over staying her welcome, so she would leave.

More and more she was having to spend her money for a cab. She felt the presence of another woman.

The first person she suspected was Chelsea because she knew all about Mason through both Bryce and his best friend. Also, they lived together, so she knew all about Bryce's comings and goings. She called Mason to let him know how she was feeling and he wouldn't answer the phone. Bryce went into a jealous rage. She sat there upset with her door open. When she heard Chelsea go downstairs, she snuck into her room, looking for evidence to support her argument.

She grabbed Chelsea's phonebook first. She fumbled through the pages, looking for Mason's name and number. She couldn't find it. She rambled through the drawers of dresser, looking for answers. She listened for Chelsea coming back up the steps. The last place she checked was under her mattress nothing. Bryce got out of there before her roommate came back upstairs. She went to her room to regroup. She knew that the only thing she could do was to let it go, but she wanted to fight someone first. To do that, she had to have a reason to pick a fight with someone; or else, she would have just looked crazy. With nothing else to do, Bryce got into her bed and fell asleep again. Later, she broke up with Mason; but since she never caught him doing anything wrong, she remained his friend.

They would talk sometimes. A few months later, she went to visit him just to see how he was doing. Honestly, she missed him. She called first. He said it was okay to stop by; but when she got there, another female was sitting in his living room. Bryce thought she was over him and that they were just friends. She wasn't. She left and never came back but stayed in touch with the owner of the pizza shop. Whenever she was feeling lonely, she would stop there to get a free slice of pizza; but after seeing that girl there, she never went back to Mason's apartment.

The leads at work were drying up fast. Suddenly, it became so hard to make a sale. In her short time there, Bryce had seen people get fired for not making sales. She worried. She didn't want to get fired again. She would rather quit than let that happen, and that's what occurred. She went a whole month with poor sales, and the guidelines clearly stated that a six-week period with sales below a certain percentage were grounds for termination. Bryce left.

She got a newspaper and started her search for a job all over again. She had a driver's license but no car. There were a lot of ads for drivers, truck drivers, limo drivers, delivery drivers, and the list went on and on. Maybe she should try that. She circled an ad for something called Sedan Service. She called to inquire about what it was exactly. She was told that it was a cab without a meter. The customers were charged a dollar per mile. The base fee was $5, and they were charged waiting time if they made a stop.

It sounded like a new adventure, so she checked it out. She filled out an application. The manager looked it over and then called some guy named Lenny over. He instructed Lenny to show Bryce the ropes. Lenny told her to follow him. They got into a burgundy car, and Lenny explained some things to Bryce. Then off they went.

Lenny started picking up people and answering Bryce's questions. It seemed easy enough. The most attractive part of the deal was that Bryce would get to keep the car every twenty-four hours, so she would have something to ride around in too. She went off by herself later that night. Her first night she made around $100.

The most disappointing part of the job was the car they gave her. It was the worst car on the lot. The exhaust pipe in the back was hanging and would drag on the ground whenever she went over a speed bump. The paint was chipped, and there were dents in the back bumper and on the left side. Bryce didn't care. She wanted to get away, and she wanted to make money. She jumped in and drove off.

Her schedule was flexible. She could drive whenever she wanted to as long as she paid her nut. A nut was the cab rental fee for the day. Hers was $75 a day. Sunday was free. Bryce kept the sedan seven days a week. One thing she noticed was how the names of the streets in the county would mimic the names of the streets in the city. Once she got an address and looked it up in her map, she had to make sure she was looking at the city map instead of the county map.

One night she was feeling a little tired. It was about 3:00 a.m., and she was about to get off. The dispatcher told her to pick up at 3705

Sun Bloom Avenue. She found the address on her map and headed out on York Road. She drove for a while and promised herself this would be her last pick up. Her stomach was growling too. The map gave her a cross street. When she got there, she looked for Sun Bloom Avenue but couldn't find it. She tried calling dispatch. Apparently, she was out of her call range because no one was answering. Bryce thought they were just busy, so she went to a gas station and bought a bottle of water and a container of chicken salad to eat while she waited for dispatch to answer. She parked her sedan in the gas station parking lot, turned off her headlights, and took a break. Dispatch never answered. She didn't want to wait too long, and the chicken salad was nasty, so she closed the container and drove off to find the address again. She forgot to turn her headlights on.

She made a right turn out of the gas station parking lot and waited at the red light. She took a sip of her water and noticed a police officer staring at her from his car. Bryce paused and looked away. She drove farther up the street and couldn't shake the cop car. He didn't have his lights on, but she got nervous anyway. She pulled off the road and waited until he passed by, so she made another left-hand turn into an empty parking lot. There was a lamp post at the top of the parking lot. Bryce had a habit of checking all mirrors when driving. She looked into her rearview mirror and saw the cop following her into the parking lot. He was looking over his shoulder. Bryce panicked and threw her sedan into park. The cop smashed right into the back of her sedan. She looked into her rearview mirror again, and the police officer was embarrassed. Bryce's back was as tense as ever; but she just sat there in shock, wondering what had just happened.

The officer jumped out of his car, frantically apologizing. Bryce was a little out of it. He asked if she was okay. She said yes and wanted to leave, but the officer insisted that she wait until another car came. It wasn't long before another officer drove up, asking questions. Bryce answered the questions the best she could and then asked to leave again. The second cop told her to stay put because an ambulance was on the way. Bryce insisted she was not hurt, but the second cop yelled at her and said, "No ma'am. You need to go the hospital." She waited. He took pictures of the inside and outside of the sedan with Bryce still in it.

An ambulance arrived, and they put Bryce's head and neck in a brace and carefully removed her from the vehicle. She didn't understand what all the fuss was about but went along with it anyway.

When she got to the hospital, she was checked for broken bones. She had none but did have a black eye from the air bag hitting her. Bryce looked in the mirror and opened her mouth wide twice. The bruise under her eye didn't hurt, so she figured she was okay. She went back to sit on the hospital bed. The doctor came in and went over all the tests. Bryce was all right. She just had some soreness in her back from muscle tension. The doctor gave her a prescription for a muscle relaxer called Flexeril and said she could go.

It was about 5:00 a.m., and she wondered if she could make it home. She was so tired. Then she remembered that she had to call a cab, so she did.

Bryce drove from 4:00 p.m. to 4:00 a.m. mostly. The majority of the call area for sedan service was what most people would call the hood. She had to buy a map and always made sure her radio was working. She met a lot of interesting people. One was a guy named Chippy. He had two chipped front teeth. At first, she thought he was a drug dealer; but as she got to know him, she understood that he was a stick up kid. He would rob the drug dealers and anyone who had access to cash.

He and Bryce took a liking to each other, and she became his personal driver. She would pick him and his cousin up and take them all over, sometimes waiting while they went into places. They always took care of her and treated her to something to eat when they got hungry.

They got closer, and Bryce hung out with them. She would even invite them over to the house where she was staying to chill. Chippy always carried a pistol on his person. One day he showed it to Bryce. She was surprised that he could conceal a gun that big in his waistband. He called it his enforcer. He said that's what he used to get what he wanted and needed. He also said he was never into hurting people unless there was no other option.

IRMA'S GUN

Bryce wasn't afraid of Chippy. He was a gentle giant, but she wondered why he brandished his gun. She didn't ask to see it, and they weren't talking about weapons or anything. She thought he was trying to let her know that if anything crazy happened he would protect her. So Bryce let go of any fear associated with him showing her his gun and continued to see him as a friend.

Chippy taught Bryce a lot about the streets. When she would drive him to places, they would be on tight side streets and run into traffic where someone had to yield. Chippy taught her how to stand her ground. One time they were in the car together, and he made her sit there until the other car backed up. They had to be sitting there for at least five minutes. Finally, the other car backed up. He showed her how not to fear anyone and how a real person would always recognize you for who you are. There would not be twenty-one questions about your character or what you would do. They would already know. He also said a real friend would never leave you under any circumstances. Bryce tried to remember that.

For a long time, they never had sex or did anything intimate; but when they did, he gave her $500. He said he would give her that amount every time he saw her. Bryce was flattered. No man had ever given her that much money at one time. A week went by, and she went to pick him up. They talked little in the car, and he said he wanted to go over to her place, so she took him there. Once they got inside, he said, "Remember that $500 I gave you? Well, I need it back." Bryce was insulted and fussed until he put his hand on his gun. He didn't pull it out. He just rested his hand there. She gave him back the money, and he left. He didn't ask for a ride or anything. She guessed that he just walked home or caught the bus.

Then he invited her to a comedy show. Bryce thought it would be just the two of them; but when she went to pick him up, he was with someone he was calling his little sister. Chippy introduced her as Corey. Bryce instantly felt connected. *Wow, she's a girl with a boy's name too.*

Bryce voiced her opinion about what they had in common, but Corey just looked at her. She said little the whole night, so Bryce figured she was just young and felt out of place. She was dressed to the nines, though. Chippy mentioned that he had bought her a new outfit because she had nothing to wear to the show. Bryce thought nothing of it.

Throughout the night, Chippy was not indiscriminate about his affections. He showed them equal attention. Bryce thought of asking him if he was a Muslim, but she didn't. Chippy was acting real funny that night too. He wasn't being himself. Occasionally, Corey would walk in front of Bryce, and she noticed how big her butt was. Again Bryce said nothing, but she thought to herself, *I wouldn't be surprised if he was fucking that girl.* She never asked him about it because she only saw Corey one other time.

The next thing Bryce knew, Chippy's cousin was calling her to say that someone had shot Chippy. Bryce wanted answers. His cousin said he was on his way home when he caught a sedan. He never made it home. The police found his body on the side of the street in front of where he lived. They said it looked like someone had shot him and pushed him out of a moving car and then just drove off. Bryce instantly thought he was trying to rob someone and got caught up. His cousin wasn't with him, so he wasn't sure. Bryce didn't ask about a funeral or a wake or anything. She never got complete closure about his death.

After a while, she missed him, so she went to visit his cousin. They talked and laughed for hours, mostly about Chippy. His cousin rolled a blunt and shared it with Bryce. Bryce knew she wasn't a real smoker but tried it anyway. She could feel Chippy's spirit in the room, and she could feel the protection he gave her when he was alive being extended through his cousin. She let her guard down. She inhaled one long time and coughed some. About ten seconds went by. Everything sounded like it was going into a tunnel under water, and Bryce felt a weird feeling come over her whole body. She had smoked several times before but never felt like this. Chippy's cousin was just sitting on his dresser, staring at her. Bryce got up and walked fast towards the door. Chippy's cousin didn't stop her. He opened his bedroom door and let her out.

That was the highest Bryce had ever been, and she didn't enjoy feeling that way. She was out of control. She drove away in the sedan and never looked back or called him again. When she got halfway up the street, her heart was beating fast. She thought she was going to die, so she got out of the car to walk up the street. She didn't know where she was going. She just knew she didn't want to die alone in that car. When she saw people, she asked for help, "Can you help me? I think I'm about to die. I don't know why I feel this way. I need help." No one said anything. They just stared at her. Bryce kept walking. She ran into Wendy's. She went inside and ate chicken nuggets to help herself feel better. When she finished one order, she got another, trying hard to eat away the high.

Finally, she realized it wasn't working, so she just walked back down the street to find the sedan. She had made it that far, so she guessed she would not die after all. Bryce drove home and went to sleep again. She didn't call Chippy's cousin anymore.

The next day Bryce was downstairs and wanted to go outside on the porch to enjoy some of the nice weather. She looked through the thin curtains and saw an unfamiliar car sitting in front of the house. She pulled back the curtain but didn't want the three men sitting in the car to see her. They were vehemently discussing something and pointing at the house. Chippy had just gotten murdered the day before. Bryce remembered how she used to drive them everywhere and hang out with him in his neighborhood. She had met a lot of his friends that way. Chippy was always the go-between. He would introduce Bryce to someone and then later explain a brief history of the person and how Bryce should act and treat them to remain safe and in good favor. Bryce took it all in. It was obvious how much people loved Chippy. He did a lot of bad things, but the good outweighed the bad. She wondered if these three unknown men had come to kill her, thinking that Bryce had set Chippy up. Well, she would not walk up to the car and ask. They stayed there for a few minutes more and then drove off.

Her phone rang. It was Chippy's cousin. He wanted to know what she was doing. She found it strange that he called right after the three men drove off. She felt like she was in danger. Someone was going to kill her because Chippy got killed. She got herself together to move down south to her grandma's house for a while. She called her to see if it was okay.

"Hello?"

"Grandma?"

"Yeah, honey. I'm okay."

"What? I didn't ask you if you were okay."

"But I am, honey. Whatchu want?"

"Can I come to stay with you for a while?"

"Oh yeeaah, honey. C'mon."

"You sure?"

"Yeah, honey, you can stay here."

"Okay. I'll call you when I'm on my way."

"Okay."

Bryce packed what she could in a hurry. She left the things she couldn't take in boxes in the basement in a closet. She would come back for the rest of it later. She knew Charles would probably throw it out, but she didn't care. She had to get going. Bryce called a cab and piled her belongings into it. The driver was complaining because he couldn't see out of his rearview mirror. Bryce ignored him and asked to go the bus station.

When they arrived, Bryce realized she had too much stuff with her. She had about six big boxes and two suitcases and a carry-on bag. She asked the driver to help her get everything into the bus terminal, and he did. She gave him a $10 tip, and he thanked her.

After getting her ticket, she took a seat. A little embarrassed from all her belongings being neatly stacked next to her seat, she was quiet and read a nearby magazine. When she heard the overhead call for her bus, she jumped up to find the person driving the bus. Once she located the person, she wanted to know how she would get all her belongings onto the bus. The driver lifted a hatch on the side of the bus and told her to get her stuff. Bryce went inside and asked a couple of men sitting nearby to help her. They did. The boxes were heavy; and when they were all loaded into the bus, Bryce imagined the bus turning over because she had too much stuff in the side. She knew this idea was ridiculous, but she felt guilty. She felt like people were staring at her.

The trip to South Carolina was a long one. She had made this trip several times in a car, and it had taken her six hours. On the bus, it was more like fourteen hours. Bryce was exhausted. When she unloaded her things from the bus, she called a cab. The people in South Carolina weren't staring like the people in Baltimore. They paid Bryce no mind. She liked it that way. She felt like she was at home away from home. Her cab pulled up; and the driver got out immediately, spoke to Bryce, and put her things in the cab. She didn't lift a finger. He asked her where she wanted to go, and Bryce gave him her grandmother's address. He asked questions about how to get there, but Bryce was confused. She knew her way around the neighborhood where her grandmother lived but outside of that she was lost. She described some landmarks in her grandmother's area. The cab driver said he was familiar and turned the meter on.

When she got there, her grandmother was waiting on the porch.

"Hey, honey, what took you so long?"

"I'm carrying a lot of stuff with me, Grandma. I had to load and unload it all a few times, but I'm here now. How are you?"

"I'm doing good, honey. How you? You looking plump."

"What's that supposed to mean?"

"You been eating good, honey... that's all."

"That's what I'm supposed to do."

"But don't do it too much."

"Okay, Grandma. Whatever you say. Let me in."

"C'mon on, honey. You know where the bunk beds are. Go and put your stuff in there."

"Love you, Granny."

Bryce kissed her on the cheek and went inside with a box in her hand. Soon she had all her bags and boxes inside the back bedroom. She felt at home because this is where she always slept when she stayed with her grandmother. She sat on the bottom bunk bed to reminisce. She went all the way back to being seven years old. Her grandmother woke her up earlier than usual and told her to get ready for church. She dug through her suitcase and found a baby-blue dress with white trim. She washed up and put on her sandals with it. She remembered feeling a little awkward because she had stockings on. When her grandmother saw what she had on, she told her to take off the stockings. She said it was too hot. Bryce was confused. Her grandmother was from the old school. She had always taught her to wear stockings with a dress. She said all proper ladies did this. She remembered trying to question her grandmother, and she cut her off every time. It was like she knew what she would say and didn't want to hear it.

When Bryce got to church, her grandmother went off with the choir; and Bryce went to children's Bible study. Bryce noticed right away that all the other little girls had on dresses with either stockings or knee-high socks. A little girl sitting next to her even asked her where her socks were and why she had her legs out. Bryce just remembered being embarrassed and looking at the floor without an answer. She wanted to cry but held back tears.

Bryce lay back on the bunk bed and put her hands behind her head and starred at the wires underneath the top bunk bed. She guessed that this piece of furniture must have been in her grandmother's possession since she had school-aged children. Bryce could see the rust along the sides of the top bunk bed's guardrail. It was like looking at the rings on the inside of a tree trunk. Bryce didn't unpack anything. She opened two boxes to see what was inside but basically left everything alone until she needed something. She was living out of her suitcases and boxes.

Bryce had a few dollars left but knew she would need a job. The next day she went looking. She filled out applications at every gas station, convenience store, and restaurant within walking distance of her grandmother's house; and Bryce was aggressive. She would only hand her completed application to a manager or owner. She knew how to introduce herself and inquire about a position so that whomever was hiring would remember her.

She had gotten jobs this way before; but this time, it wasn't working. No one called her back. Everyone she talked to had a strong Southern drawl. She could sense *they sensed* that she was different because she sounded different. And here she was a young black girl from up north who was down South trying to get a job. They probably thought she was going to be a trouble maker.

CHAPTER 20

One day she was doing her laundry when she read a free circular in the laundromat. She turned to the help-wanted section. All the jobs she read about required education and experience. She had none. Then she came across an ad that read:

Dancers Needed
No experience required
Excellent pay
Apply in person

Bryce loved to dance. Whatever they needed her to do, she was capable. She went in right away, prepared to show off her dance moves. When she got there, only three girls were ahead of her. Bryce thought there would be a group interview, but they did it individually. There were two connected rooms at a business park with white plastic chairs lining the walls. Bryce wondered what kind of dance she would have to do. When they called her in, she put on a big smile to hide the fact that she was nervous. She stood in the middle of the floor and waited. Three men looked her over. Then one told her to take her shirt off. Bryce asked no questions. She needed a job. She pulled her shirt over her head and neatly folded it and then placed it on a chair. She stood there again, still smiling. The same man said, "Take your bra off."

Bryce still asked no questions. She slid the straps off of her shoulders, turned the bra around so the clasp was in the front, and undid her bra. She let it fall to the floor. She was still smiling.

The three men looked around at one another and nodded. "Okay, you got the job. Be here Friday night around seven. Bring something skimpy to dance in and some heels." Bryce thanked them and picked her bra up off the floor. The men walked into the other room. Bryce was all by herself again. She put her bra and her clothes back on. She had never done anything like this before. She wondered what it would be like. She remembered looking down on girls who were exotic dancers and thinking, *Why would they do something like that, expose their bodies and dance half naked for complete strangers?* Now she understood. She was just trying to survive; and if this is what she had to do, then so be it.

When she got back to her grandmother's place, she didn't dare tell her what she was about to do. She thought about it some more and wanted to know one last time if there was an alternative. She thought about this guy she'd met walking to the store named Leech. His real name was Leithanderfeld, but everyone called him Leech for short.

Bryce knew that he sold weed and cocaine in the neighborhood. Maybe she could help him and make some money doing that, so she started hanging out with him. She asked him if he could show her how to sell weed. Since her grandmother had lived around the corner for so long, Leech and his crew knew her, and that let them know that Bryce was not a cop or someone they should not trust.

Leech introduced her to his crew. Everyone was so nice. She would spend the entire night hanging out at the trap house watching the fellas sell drugs and drink, but they never let her participate. During the day, Leech would make house calls to his regular customers, and he would let Bryce go with him. Leech's customers would be apprehensive. They would look at Bryce, then look at Leech, and then tell him to come back later. Leech had to reassure them that it was okay.

Reluctantly, they would let the couple in and buy what they wanted. He showed her how to bag the weed, and the rest was basic common sense. She thought he would introduce her to the person he got his weed from, but he said he would just give her some of his and she could sell that. Bryce tried for a while, but she had no clientele. What was she supposed to do, go up to people asking them if they wanted a nickel or a dime bag? She was barely making enough money to eat every day, so she depended more on dancing. She told none of the fellas what she was doing there.

At the club, there were a lot of girls and they all looked like they were broke, so Bryce fit right in. She discovered later that the closest place to buy the appropriate gear for the job was at a mall thirty miles away in Columbia, South Carolina. Other than that, it was lingerie and six-inch heels from Payless. She felt right at home, although this was a weird step for her. Bryce was focused. All she wanted to do was make money.

She saw a lot of things and had a lot of new adventures while working at the club. It was definitely a new experience. No one actually taught Bryce how to give a lap dance or how to entertain. There were no rules. She just watched the other girls and then did what she felt.

Watching the other girls was entertaining enough. One girl, a veteran stripper, used to get completely naked and have sex on the dance floor. Bryce thought that was unprofessional but understood that this was not the corporate office she was used to working in. She witnessed girls giving blow jobs on the dance floor. The manager said these actions were forbidden; but when he wasn't around, everyone scrambled to do what they wanted. The goal was always to make extra money, and the girls would watch each other's backs. Bryce would pick up countless bottoms thrown into the middle of the floor from girls, wanting to make more by letting customers pull out on a lap dance. The rule was supposed to be that your top would come off but the bottoms always stayed on.

Over time Bryce learned to respect the girls she once looked down on from a distance. She was one of them now. However, a few girls didn't even care about getting money. They just wanted to fuck. This disturbed Bryce. They would give a lap dance for countless songs and walk away without getting paid and not say anything to anyone. They would have sex or do whatever, mainly for the attention or the feeling of it. Bryce only cared because this made her job more difficult.

Performing after a girl who wasn't about getting her money affected Bryce's pockets. The men at the club would assume that since they got free lap dances from the previous girl that Bryce should do it too. She would have to fight to get paid sometimes. With certain customers, she learned to get paid up front. They would be reluctant; but she learned that after fighting for it, they respected her and would acquiesce. She was not only learning how to strip but was also learning about another element she at that point had only heard about in rap songs.

There were two girls there who were a little older although they didn't look it. They would travel with the manager to other clubs and dance. They always got the best spots and always got to pick their music first. Bryce watched them more than anyone else. She did her make up and got her nails done with wild designs. Instead of just folding her outfits up and sticking them in a black tote, she learned to separate them in large Zip loc bags. She would talk to the girls to discover where they were getting their outfits and shoes from. They always mentioned some far away place that Bryce could not get to. She asked the manager if he could organize a trip to the mall in Columbia, South Carolina, so she could purchase some things. He said he would think about it, but it never materialized even though he would complain about the lingerie and shoes some of the girls were wearing.

Bryce kept track of how much she was making. She calculated her expenses for the week and for the month. Her grandmother didn't ask for any rent, so Bryce only had to feed herself and purchase toiletries. Her grandmother was rarely home and cooked little, so Bryce didn't either. She was spending about $20 a day in food or about $140 a week. She only worked at the club three days a week and was only making $120 a week. She noticed that no matter what happened, she never made over $40 a night. Business at the club was slow; and since it was a new club, she figured business would eventually pick up. Bryce waited. Nothing ever happened.

At the time, she wasn't aware of the small fortunes that other girls made at the more popular and more established clubs. When she noticed

IRMA'S GUN

she was only averaging $40 a night, she knew she could eat that up in a regular restaurant like Fridays, Applebee's, Phillips, etc. She wasn't well versed in these atmospheres but knew something was wrong. Her threshold had been reached, and she could not surpass it. She knew it was time to move on.

She came in late one night, and a pad lock had been placed on her grandmother's door, so her key was useless. She waited on the porch in the cold all night. There was a thermometer on the wall outside. It read two below zero. Bryce thought, *That can't be right.* After being curled up in the fetal position in a chair for hours, she knew what she read was correct. She almost froze to death. At around 6:00 a.m., she heard the lock on the door clicking. Her grandmother unlocked the door. Bryce jumped up and opened it to come inside. She didn't say a word to her grandmother. She just went straight to her bedroom and curled up under a blanket both to get warm and to get the sleep she couldn't get outside in the cold on the porch. Her grandmother said nothing to her either. She heard the back door slam as her grandmother pounced down the steps to slop the hogs and begin her day.

Then she got a call from her cousin Liz who lived on the other side of town. She sounded upset and told Bryce she was in trouble.

"What? What do you mean I need to move?"

"Your grandmother is tripping, girl. She about to put you out."

"Why? Did she find out where I work?"

"I don't know but you about to be homeless. Come over here and stay with me and Sandra for a while."

"You'll don't have an extra room."

"You can sleep with me or sleep on the sofa, whatever you choose."

"I won't be in the way?"

"No. But we got a contract with the government to live here, so you can only stay for a little while. We don't want any rent or anything, and you can save your money up so you can get another place. Be over today in time for dinner."

"Your sure?"

"I'm positive. Your grandmother ain't playing."

"Okay. I'll see you later on today."

"Bye, baby. See you later."

Bryce put her stuff together and called a cab. Liz didn't have a job. She just stayed home all day entertaining her friends and sipping on clear liquor, so Bryce didn't bother calling her to let her know she was on the way.

When she got there, her cousin Liz was most hospitable. She helped her put her things away and offered her some dinner. Bryce ate like a starved hostage, and no one said a word. They just watched with a slight grin on their faces as if they were happy to have her there.

After dinner, Bryce tried to help Liz clean up the kitchen; but she wouldn't allow it. All she could do was scrape her plate clean into the trash and set the dish on the counter for Liz to wash. She felt bad but didn't let on. She wanted to help and be a part of the family.

At bedtime, Liz brought her two clean sheets and a thin blanket. Bryce unfolded them and spread them across the couch to make a bed for herself. Her great-grandmother stayed there too. She had Alzheimer's and did a lot of weird things that Bryce didn't understand like smearing feces all over the bathroom whenever she went or wetting her pants or cussing Bryce out for no reason. Bryce had never been around someone with Alzheimer's before, so she was confused about it, and it kind of hurt her feelings. Her great-grandmother was her grandfather's mother, and she had plenty of vivid memories of growing up spending time with her, but this woman today was a different person.

Samantha told Bryce what to expect, but Bryce didn't care. This person played hide-and-seek with her when she was little. This person defended her when outsiders would come over and ask questions. This was the woman she loved for raising her grandfather to be a good man, so she tried to talk to her anyway. She knew what Alzheimer's was but didn't believe it.

Bryce asked her great-grandmother if she remembered her son. Her great-grandmother paused and then smacked her hands together as if she were dusting them off. Her great-grandmother leaned her head from side to side, keeping a familiar rhythm, and patted her feet on the floor to the same time. The only other person Bryce ever saw do this was her grandfather. Apparently, she had some recollection. Maybe at this time her Alzheimer's was in its early stages. Bryce felt like she was being protected from something.

Directly across the street lived another cousin with the same name, Liz, but she was a little older. Bryce was still looking for another job but maintained her spot at the club with meager earnings because that's all she had. Her second cousin Liz had a son who owned a gas station with a convenience store. He heard that she needed a job and got her a position as a cashier. The pay wasn't much, but it was better than nothing, and Bryce could begin to save her money. Trying to get ahead, Bryce kept her position at the club too. She went back and forth between the two places for about three months, saving her money. Samantha was a Jehovah's Witness, so she was opposed to Bryce coming in during early morning hours. She could only imagine what she was doing out in the streets to get money to move. Between three and four o'clock in the morning, she would go to the house across the street, sleep on the couch until sunrise, then go back across the street where her belongings were. She was just hanging on by a string.

Working at the gas station was easy enough. She only had to ring up items, give change, and operate the gas pumps from a motherboard behind the counter. Being in the South, she expected the white people she came in contact with to be mean and nasty. She was pleasantly surprised. She was nice to them, and they were nice in return. Not one person threw his or her change on the counter. They always put it in her hand once she extended it. She met a guy named Alan while she was working one day. He was tall and lean, light brown, and very handsome. He looked young but had bags under his eyes like he hadn't slept in days. He and Bryce hit it off, vibing right away. They exchanged phone numbers. He invited her to his apartment to hang out, and this became a regular thing.

New Year's was right around the corner. It was 1999, and Bryce didn't want to ring the new year for the new millennium alone. She told Alan she didn't have plans, and right away he said she could spend New Years's with him and his roommate. She was delighted because she didn't have to ask he offered. To her, this meant they were friends.

On New Year's Eve, he picked her up and drove her to his place. They stopped by the liquor store to get some Mad Dog 20/20 and cheap champagne. He asked her what flavor she wanted. She pointed to the red one. He got a big bottle of it for the both of them. When they got back to his apartment, there was no party, no other invited guests, no decorations, no food, no party favors just Alan, his roommate, and Bryce. They talked and watched TV and played some music. At midnight they watched the ball drop and listened to the fireworks and gunfire erupt outside. Alan hardly touched the Mad Dog 20/20, so Bryce helped herself to it. Before she knew it, she had drunk the whole bottle. It was fruity tasting, so she didn't notice until it was too late. She was a little buzzed, but she didn't even feel drunk. Bryce thought she must have been a born alcoholic. Apparently, it was in her blood. She had heard that her father was a heavy drinker. This scared Bryce, so she vowed to stay away from it.

Finally, she did save enough money to move. She thought that in two weeks she would announce that she was moving; but before she could do that, Liz came to her one day and told her she had to move. She felt like she was being rushed because she was about to move anyway. It was as if someone was counting her money; and when she had enough, she was being rushed out. She felt like she was being watched again.

There was a one-bedroom apartment in town with her name on it. She went to look at it, put a deposit down, and moved in the next day. Bryce felt like she was on the run, but what could she do? Again, she had no furniture. She got the heat turned on, and a neighbor gave her a dark-green sleeping bag. Bryce thanked him but wanted to know how he knew she had no furniture. She never invited him over. Maybe the landlord was running his mouth. Who knows?

Bryce's apartment was nice for being on a median strip. At her back door were train tracks. During the night, the train would pass through slowly, making much screeching and loud banging noises that would wake Bryce up. She would just curl up inside her sleeping bag and pull it up over her head. This lasted about three more months until Bryce had had enough. She realized that she wasn't trying to furnish her apartment. She was just sleeping there, paying the rent and eating out of cans. This was no way to live, and she knew it. Things weren't getting any better. All she was doing was running from one place to another, but she didn't know how to make it stop. The thought of living like this depressed her, so she moved back to Baltimore where she could at least find a job. She was making just enough money to pay her rent, so she skipped out on one month's rent using the money for a bus ticket back to Baltimore. She rolled her green sleeping bag up and gave it back to her neighbor. He thanked her, told her good luck, and gave her a hug. Then it was back to Baltimore.

When she arrived, she went straight to her cousin Shawna's house. She knew she was always welcome there. She already had enough money to get a place but just needed to find one. Shawna let her see the newspaper and told Bryce to keep the want ads. Bryce circled several ads for places but only checked out one. It was a house split into two apartments. An elderly gentleman was living upstairs already. Bryce would have the basement. The apartment had carpet and was clean but was dirt cheap. Wondering why, she inquired about all responsibilities coming with the apartment since it was in a house on the corner and had a lawn out front and in the back.

Bryce would have to purchase her lawn mower and keep the grass mowed. She would also have to purchase her refrigerator. Those were small things to deal with; so instead of looking any further, she signed the paperwork and moved in. Shawna was elated for her.

While perusing the want ads, she spotted another driving job. There weren't many details, so she went to the address in the paper to find out about it. It was a cab company. She had done this before, so she figured it would be easy and it was. She only had to pick up and drop off passengers all night. This time, she kept the car for only twelve hours at a time, so her nut was $20 less than before.

A few months went by, and Bryce was doing well. She had saved money and was paying her bills on time. She even bought her first car. It was a 1985 gold Ford Tempo. She bought it for $600.

She felt stagnant, so she went to school. She applied to the state university. She was making enough money to pay for books and fees but couldn't afford the tuition, so she applied for financial aid. She got a little more than she needed, so she was in business.

Her favorite hip-hop show was in the radio station on campus, so she wanted a spot on their show. She went there to talk to a few people, and they let her do the hip-hop news. During the day, she volunteered at the radio station during the smooth-jazz segment. Bryce was getting her life together and going places with no more interruptions. She continued on looking for an eventual degree in communications.

Then it happened again. First, she came back from classes one day, and there was a large hole in the driver-side window. Someone had cut it out. Bryce thought maybe someone had punched the hole in her window, but there was no shattered glass anywhere. She looked around at the other parked cars for damage. There was none. Only her window had a huge hole in it. She looked around to see if there were any cameras anywhere. There were none. She decided that calling the police would be a waste of time, so she drove to the base at the cab company to see if her favorite mechanic could fix her window. He instructed her to go to Crazy Ray's, which was a lot full of abandoned cars where people would remove and pay for parts. She found a window, and her mechanic replaced it for her. The whole thing only cost her about $50. It just took a little time to find the window and then have it replaced.

Then she was in English 101 one day, and the teacher instructed everyone to turn their chairs and desks around to create small groups. They would discuss a book they were reading called *Their Eyes Were Watching God* by Zora Neale Hurston. Bryce was excited. She had heard Oprah say this was her favorite book. She felt like she was getting a little piece of the real world here in her English class. She had her head down looking through her book. When she looked up, she noticed a young woman she had never seen in class before. She was stunning. She stood about five feet eight and had long curly black hair. She looked like someone out of a *Vogue* magazine. Bryce couldn't help but stare at her. The professor noticed Bryce gawking and was noticeably upset. Bryce was in big trouble.

From that moment on, the professor made serious efforts to fail Bryce. She didn't understand. What did she do besides notice a beautiful woman? Bryce thought the girl had something going on with the professor and the professor got jealous because Bryce noticed the student. Bryce didn't care. She just wanted a decent grade and to move on, but the professor kept giving Bryce Ds. She would turn in all her assignments on time and completed to the letter. She knew she at the very least deserved a C for what may have been average work but a D was below average and only one letter above failing. She went to the professor's desk after class to find out the problem.

"Hello, Professor. How are you?"

"I'm fine thanks. What can I help you with?"

"I just wanted to know why you keep giving me Ds.? Do you have an example of what you consider A work?"

The professor pointed to the woman that Bryce was staring at that day and said, "This is an example of A work."

It was evident now that all this harsh grading was just a personal blow because Bryce got caught staring at the wrong person. She wanted to drop the class, but it was too late.

All these negative events put a damper on Bryce's attitude toward her schooling, but she didn't let that get her down. She still had her volunteer work where she was learning about her major and the news spot on Strictly Hip-Hop to look forward to. Then one day she went into the radio station, and her mentor turned her around because she said something horrific had happened in New York. It was September the 11th.

Going to school during the day and driving the cab on the weekends was wearing Bryce down. Every Monday she was late to her algebra class because she would get off at 4:00 a.m., get home by 4:30 a.m., and have to be up and in class by 8:00 a.m. She would get a couple hours' sleep only but after driving all night needed more. Bryce would be groggy and never make it on time but miraculously the teacher never penalized her for this.

CHAPTER 21

Driving at night was getting dangerous too. One night Bryce got robbed at gunpoint. She picked up a young man from a house party. He approached the cab with his shirt in his hand. Right away, she knew something was wrong. She thought that maybe she shouldn't let him in at least until he put his shirt on. But it was a warm summer night; and because of having eight uncles and so many male friends, Bryce had a soft spot in her heart for black men. She never minded picking them up off the street when they flagged the cab down, and tonight was no exception. She unlocked the doors. He seemed friendly enough.

"How you doing?"

"I'm all right. Can you put your shirt on please?"

"I'm good like this."

Bryce pulled off. When she got to the end of the street, she asked him where he was going.

"4709 Patterson Park."

She wrote it down on her manifest and pulled off again heading towards South Baltimore.

"You know I got a gun on me."

Bryce thought about putting him out again; but with a gun in the mix, would that be problematic? She continued to drive.

IRMA'S GUN

"You wanna listen to some music?"

She turned the radio up as much as she could but still wanted him to hear her conversation.

"Who's your favorite rapper?"

There was silence. Something was wrong. Bryce blasted the radio, trying to listen for any clicking noises. She drove more erratically and faster to the destination. She turned onto North Avenue and barreled to the end. As she prepared to turn right on any through street, her passenger shouted, "Turn left here!" Bryce obliged and almost hit a lamp post making the turn. All the lights on this street were out. Bryce thought she would die.

"This ain't Patterson Park!"

"Yes, it is. You know where you at?"

"Patterson Park is farther that way."

"It begins here, lady."

Bryce checked her manifest for the address. She searched the numbers on the houses for 4709. She stopped at the address and waited. Nothing happened, so she turned around to see this huge silver gun pointed at her stomach. Her passenger was calm.

"You know what it is. Give me all your money."

Bryce reached into the pockets on her cargo shorts, handing over a fists full of crumpled-up money. He scrambled to stuff the pockets in his sweat pants with the bills.

When Bryce had given him all her money, again, there was silence. They both waited. He never stopped pointing the gun at her stomach. Bryce got scared, and her voice changed.

"Okay. You got all my money now go. Just get out!"

As he continued to hold his gun, her passenger waited. Bryce got upset.

"Get out! Get out of my cab! Here! Take my phone! Just get out!"

He accepted the phone as a peace offering and slowly exited the vehicle. Bryce watched him stagger up to the house and put his key in the door and go inside. She was livid, speeding off and away from the scene. When she got about a block away, she radioed in to inform her dispatcher she had gotten robbed. Dispatch said she would have a police officer come over to meet her. She asked for Bryce's location. Bryce waited there alone under a street lamp for about twenty minutes.

Finally, a police car casually pulled up and stopped when their windows lined up.

"Are you okay?"

"Yes. This guy just robbed me."

"Do you have a description?"

"I have his address."

"You know where he lives?"

"Yes. He robbed me in front of his house and then went inside."

The officer tried not to laugh.

"What's his address?"

"4709 Patterson Park. He was about five feet eight, light brown skin with a short hair cut, and no shirt. He didn't have any tattoos. You want me to show you where he lives?"

"No, ma'am. That's right down the street. I'll be back."

The officer drove down to the address, and Bryce followed. She couldn't believe he had the audacity to rob her right in front of his house. She was ready to point him out. Bryce waited while the officer went up to the house and knocked on the door. An elderly woman came out and had an attitude.

"May I help you?"

"Yes, ma'am. Does a young man about five eight, light brown, with a short hair cut live here?"

The woman got upset.

"NO! Don't nobody live here but me!"

"Are you sure?"

"I don't know what you're talking about! I live here alone!"

"Okay, thank you."

The officer walked over to Bryce and said, "No one by that description lives there."

Bryce argued, "I just saw him put his key in the door and go inside. Why would he have a key if he didn't live there?"

"The lady at the door said she lives alone."

IRMA'S GUN

Bryce didn't want to hear another word. She just sped off and went back to work. She had lost her phone and about $60. She needed to make her money back, but the dispatcher refused to give her any more work for the night and told her to go home. Reluctantly, Bryce did that. She was so upset.

The next day she went into the base to pay her nut and had to report she had been robbed. Her supervisor asked a few questions and typed information into his computer and then printed something for Bryce to sign. He told her that her cab rental had been waived for that day. Bryce brightened up. "Thank you."

"Are you okay?"

"Yes. Just a little upset, but I'll be all right."

"Did he hurt you?"

"No."

"How much did he get?"

"Sixty dollars."

Her supervisor cringed, "Oh, man, why'd you give him so much?"

"I didn't have a choice. I just reached in my pockets and gave him what I had."

"That's a lot, Bryce."

"I know. I couldn't help it, though."

"You want a cab for today?"

"Yes."

"Okay, you got it."

Bryce got behind the wheel and went back to work. She promised herself that if another person tried to get in without a shirt she would refuse them service. After that, she felt a little uneasy. She was more cautious about who she picked up; and whenever she picked up young black men, she would always ask for her money up front. At first, she thought they might be offended; but to her surprise, they were just happy that someone picked them up. One hundred percent of the time, they would pay her up front when she asked and patiently wait for their change when reaching their destination.

When she got to the yard late one night, only one cab was left. The mechanic said she could have it, and Bryce jumped at it. He said it needed some work but would be okay to drive for the night. She drove around, picking up people for several hours, and noticed that the gears would slip. The cab stalled whenever she'd try to press the gas. Bryce didn't care. She guessed this was the work it needed and would return the cab promptly after she'd made her $100. The night wore on, and Bryce was tired from being in school all day. She was fighting nodding off behind the wheel. She pulled over to count her money. She had $89. She was beat but needed one more fare. She picked up this white guy from a bar on Greenmount Avenue. She asked him where he was going; and instead of giving her a destination, he said he would just instruct her on how to get there. Bryce didn't like that. She wanted to know where she was going, so she asked for an address, and he said he didn't have one. He was cooperative, though, so she didn't feel the need to put him out.

They proceeded to Greenmount. He said he needed to stop at a nearby 7-Eleven on Thirty-Third Street. You couldn't turn directly onto Thirty-Third, so he told her to go around via a side street. He went into the 7-Eleven to buy a pack of cigarettes. It had just rained, and the ground was still wet. Bryce tried to turn back onto Thirty-Third, but the passenger insisted she go across Thirty-Third to take a short cut. Bryce obliged. As she approached the small intersection, her cab stalled. She was stuck dead in the street. She looked up, and a car was coming straight at her. Bryce pushed the gas pedal again and again. Nothing happened. The other car sped up and was headed directly for Bryce. The car got close enough that she could see into it.

It was Rocco staring at Bryce like he wanted to kill her. There was nothing she could do. She covered her face and dug her chin into her chest as the car plummeted into the cab. Her passenger was laughing and snickering with joy. She heard his door open, and he jumped out and slammed it.

When Bryce looked up, she was facing the opposite direction. The cab had been hit so hard that it spun around in the street. Bryce opened her eyes to see the air bag opened and, covering the wheel, all crumpled up and deflated. Smoke was everywhere. She was out of it from the impact of the accident. She sat there for a moment to gather herself.

IRMA'S GUN

Then like an angel out of heaven, a police officer appeared. He had on a yellow raincoat and said nothing to Bryce. He just wrote down her tag number and the tag number of Rocco's car and took pictures. When she looked up again, Rocco was standing right next to the cab with his back turned to her and talking to the officer. The officer requested his driver's license, and Rocco handed it to him. Next he asked Rocco to walk a straight line, and he couldn't. He was pissy drunk. The officer gave him a breathalyzer and continued to record everything. Finally, he asked Bryce if she was okay. She said she was and with his permission drove off and back to the base. Before she left, the officer gave her a piece of paper where he pointed out a number for a police report. She thanked him and left.

Bryce drove back to the base with a blank mind. Although she saw Rocco's face, it didn't register that he'd hit her until she got home. That night she got into her bed, pulled the covers up over her head, and cried. She was terrified. Why was Rocco doing this to her? There was nothing she could do about it. On her lunch break the next day, she went down to Dundalk to a gun shop to see about purchasing one. The man behind the counter asked her how serious she was about purchasing a hand gun. Bryce said very, so he told her to begin by doing the required background check. It took her about twenty minutes to fill out. She felt like it asked a lot of unnecessary questions but answered them anyway. The clerk said the background check would take several days. Bryce perused the shop and came back when they called her to do so.

She had no idea what she was looking for. All she knew was that she wanted a gun that would not fail her. A shooting range behind the shop was connected to it. Since she didn't know what she wanted, the clerk suggested that she try firing a few guns to see which ones felt the most comfortable.

Bryce agreed and stepped behind the counter to enter the shooting range. She was given a pair of headphones, three guns, and three boxes of ammunition. The first gun was a 38 caliber. It was too hard to load. Bryce anticipated getting into a bind and getting stuck trying to load her gun, so she put that one away. The next one was way too big. She knew she would have no way of concealing it or keeping it in a purse.

The last one was a 45-caliber Ruger. It was sleek and just the right size. She tried shooting it. It shot smoothly, but the shells backfired right at her. One of them got caught in her glasses and burned the outside of her eyelid. She didn't care, though. She just kept shooting. Bryce was sold. She wanted a Ruger. She went back inside the shop to ask more questions about the 45 Ruger. The clerk said it was $400. Bryce knew she didn't have that much but would try to save for it. She told the clerk she'd be back in two weeks.

When she returned, the clerk remembered her and asked right away if she still wanted the Ruger. Surprised that he remembered her, she said yes but she didn't have enough money. She only had half. Bryce asked if he had a smaller version of the gun she'd shot two weeks before that. He informed her that the only 45 Ruger he had was the one she'd shot before. However, there was an option to the 45. He had a generic 45 for only $200. Bryce jumped at the opportunity and asked to see it. He placed it on the counter. She just stared at it for a second. It wasn't as pretty as the Ruger; but for $200, it would have to do. She picked it up. It was cumbersome but not as big as the other gun she had shot at the range. The clerk asked if she'd like to shoot it. Bryce said no. She wanted to buy it. The clerk had made a sale.

The guy at the gun store let Bryce know that it was against the law to carry the gun around. She would need a special permit for that. He told her that to transport it home it would have to remain unloaded and preferably in the truck of her car. Bryce agreed. When she got it home, she just stared at the case and didn't open it. She couldn't believe she'd gotten a gun. A looming fear was in the back of her mind. She wanted to know what was wrong. Why couldn't she do anything? Why couldn't she keep a job? Why did her mother hate her so much, and what could she do to remedy the situation? All she wanted to do was succeed at something anything. She also wanted to protect herself from danger. This gun would help her do that. Bryce carried her gun with her to work. She kept it loaded with the safety on and tucked it in the waistband of her pants. It gave her a security she didn't have before. That $200 was the best money she had ever spent.

IRMA'S GUN

Bryce went on working as hard as she could, going to school, driving the cab on the weekends, and volunteering at her school's radio station. One Saturday night, she was in her cab on Mulberry Street making a left turn onto Carey Street to pick up a fare. Just then, she saw Rocco cruise around the corner looking angry and drunk as ever. He threw his hand out of the window showing off a bright gold wedding band on the appropriate finger. He was silent and scowling at her. Two other men were in the car with him, and they were both looking in the opposite direction.

Rocco cut Bryce off because he wanted her to see him. She stared. What did this mean? And why was Rocco driving around Baltimore City at 2:00 a.m. acting crazy like this? She let him finish his antics and watched him drive off.

She thought about it later and got scared again. It was the same feeling she had when her passenger had told her he had a gun. She knew she was in danger but could do nothing about it. So what was she supposed to do now? Wait for Rocco to appear again and maybe do something terrible to her? She called her mother to ask for help. If anyone was an expert on Rocco, her mother was.

"Hey, Ma, it's me, Bryce."

"Hey, whatchu want?"

"Have you seen Rocco lately?"

"You mean the mayor, Rocco?"

"Yes."

"No. I haven't seen him. Why do you ask?"

"Because I saw him last night at work and he was acting strange."

"What was he doing?"

"He cut me off and acted like he wanted me to see his wedding band. It was like he was trying to tell me something without using words."

"Rocco doesn't have that much interest in you."

"Then why did he do that?"

"I don't know. He might have been drunk."

"Ma, I'm scared."

"You should be."

She couldn't believe the conversation she was having with her mother. She just sat there for a minute, letting it all sink in. She was in danger. Her mother knew and didn't care. To Bryce, that meant that her mother was an accomplice. Bryce didn't know where Rocco stayed and thought of going downtown to city hall to see what he wanted. Then she thought that might be a trap. There was too much security and too many cameras there.

Bryce didn't want to invite that trouble. Although they were no longer married, Rocco and her mother were still close that she knew. She would not wait around for something bad to happen to her. If she couldn't get Rocco, she would get the next best thing: her mother.

"Bryce, have you been taking care of yourself?"

"Yes, Ma. I always do."

"Why don't you come over to do your laundry tomorrow?"

"I can go to the laundromat. That's what I usually do."

"You know I have a washer and dryer. Just come over and bring your clothes. I haven't seen you in a while."

"Is this a date?"

"If you want it to be."

The next day Bryce brought her clothes over to her mother's place. She put them in the trunk of the cab and carried them around with her as she worked. As usual, she had her Ruger in her waist band. Once it slowed down, she went to see her mother. Bryce knocked on the door, and Paige made her wait for, like, ever. Finally, she came to the door. She said nothing. She just opened the door wide to let her daughter in.

They caught up on missed time, and Paige offered Bryce a sandwich. When she opened her refrigerator, Bryce asked if everything she saw wrapped up in aluminum foil were leftovers. Paige said yes but that she was saving them for later. Since Paige lived alone, Bryce wondered why she was saving them but left it alone. She ate her bologna and cheese sandwich and was happy with that. Then Bryce changed their conversation back to Rocco. She was tired of playing games, so she took a more direct approach and accused her mother of protecting Rocco when she knew he was abusive and didn't care about her or Bryce. Paige backed her daughter into a corner and got in her face.

IRMA'S GUN

"Don't forget it was me and Rocco who created you. Without us, you're nothing."

"What? I don't need either one of ya'll!"

"Then why are you here!?"

"Because you invited me!"

"I hadn't seen you in a while, that's all."

"You really don't care, do you?"

"What do you mean I don't care? I'm your mother."

"What's that supposed to mean? Having a mother is not an automatic means of getting love and understanding. It's not just a title. You have to do something. You have to actually care. You're supposed to protect me, and Rocco is supposed to protect us. The both of ya'll are screwed up and"

"Bryce don't talk to me like that."

"Like what!?"

"Like you're grown."

"But I am grown! I have my place, my life. I'm over twenty-five now! Why can't you accept that?"

"Why can't you accept that I'm the one in control here? Rocco's the mayor. He controls the city that you live in. You have to learn to live with that!"

Paige got in Bryce's face, and they argued until the argument turned into a fist fight. Paige was no match for her daughter especially when Bryce was angry. Then Bryce pulled out her gun and shot her mother in the stomach. Paige ran for the front door, and Bryce shot her four more times in the back. When Paige got to the door, she turned around and laughed at Bryce as she slid down the door to the floor. Bryce shot again but froze. She couldn't believe her mother was laughing at her. As she got shot, Paige never asked her child why. She never said, "I'm your mother!" or "Is this how you repay me?" She just took the shots like a soldier. It confused Bryce; and instead of finishing her, she stopped shooting. With a sudden burst of energy, Paige jumped up and ran out the door. It was like something out of a movie.

Bryce tried to comprehend what had just happened. Her first instinct was to call 911.

"911, what's your emergency?"

"I just shot my mother."

"Okay, where is she now?"

"Outside in the hallway."

"Is she still breathing?"

"I don't know. I'm afraid to go outside and see."

"What's your address?"

"I don't know. I'm in the Dunville apartment complex off Liberty Road."

"The paramedics are on the way. Are you injured in any way?"

"No."

"Stay on the line until they get there."

"Okay."

Bryce said nothing else to the 911 operator. She knew she had said too much already, but she was out of it. The worst part was that she had no feelings about what she just did. She knew she was defending herself, but she knew it wouldn't look that way to the judge or jury. Bryce was going to jail, and she knew it. What had she done? All she could do was reflect while she waited for the paramedics. She thought about her childhood and how everyone in it had always expected so much from her. Everyone always made her feel like she was special and destined for something great. She had no clue what it was but just knew it was out there for her and now this. Had she just thwarted her destiny? She wanted to cry but could not.

There was a knock at the door. Bryce told the 911 operator that the paramedics were at the door. She said okay, wished her well, and hung up the phone. There was another knock, but this time it was louder, "Police! Come out with your hands up!" Bryce unlocked the door and a man yelled at her, "Place your hands outside the door!" Bryce followed the instructions. He repeated the same thing this time with more vigor. Bryce got scared and pressed both hands on the outside of the door. "Show me your hands!" Her hands had been outside the door for several seconds now. What else did he want her to do? She didn't want to get shot. Then four officers rushed in, pinning Bryce to the ground as one of them retrieved the gun from the floor. "Okay, I've got it!"

The other officers searched for shell casings and took pictures of the crime scene. Bryce was stoic. They handcuffed her and made her kneel and then sit on her legs. A female officer came in and searched her person before taking her to the squad car. She placed her hand on Bryce's head as she gently put her in the back seat. Bryce sat there for about twenty minutes. Then a blonde-haired officer got in the driver's seat and headed for the precinct.

It was quiet in the car. Bryce watched the officer drive and tried to figure out where they were going. She was not familiar with the area. She noticed that sometimes he seemed to jump a little and check out his rear view mirror to see if Bryce was still there. He feared her even though she had handcuffs on. When they arrived at the precinct, he helped her out of the back seat and directed her to a small cell on the inside. He removed her cuffs and left her there for a while. Another female officer came in and told Bryce that she needed her clothes. She replaced them with a gray sweat suit. She watched Bryce take off her clothes. Then she pulled some periwinkle-colored socks out of a brown paper bag and carefully put each one on Bryce's feet.

Bryce didn't know what to think. Here this white woman was on one knee tending to her socks and feet as if she cared for Bryce. This was a new experience for her. Bryce told her thank you and was grateful nevertheless. For a moment, she felt special again. The officer neatly folded Bryce's clothes and put them in a gigantic brown paper bag then left her there alone. Moments later, another officer came in and took Bryce to a long silver railing where a chair waited. He handcuffed one of her wrists to the railing. It was so uncomfortable there. She wondered why they just didn't leave her in the holding cell. She felt like she was being tortured. Then the officer came back with four brown paper boxes. He asked Bryce if she was hungry.

"What is it?"

He opened one box and said, "Ham." He opened another and said, "Turkey."

Bryce motioned towards the ham. He handed her the box, and she picked through it, unwrapping the sandwich and tearing through the naked meat, cheese, and bread with her teeth. She finagled the straw into the juice box and sipped slowly. She didn't have an appetite but didn't know when she would get to eat again, so she stuffed the sandwich down. She imagined the officer would come back, un cuff her wrist, and let her go home but that never happened. Bryce sat in that uncomfortable chair for four hours. Then an officer came in uncuffed her and took her to a big yellow bus outside where she was transported to jail to await a trial. Her bail was a million dollars.

CHAPTER 22

When she arrived at the jail, there were two tiers; and each tier had several pods. They put Bryce into a pod where she was the only black woman. She stayed there for two weeks and got to know her counterparts. Most of them were there on petty charges like prostitution or minor drug possession. She looked through the gate and noticed that all the black women were lumped together in an adjacent pod. When she asked why, one girl said, "Oh, that's high bail-no bail." Bryce wondered why she wasn't over there but never said anything. In the morning, a CO gave her an indigent bag. It contained a toothbrush, a small bar of soap, a tiny stick of clear deodorant, a shorty pencil, two pieces of paper, an envelope, and one stamp.

Bryce took a shower and put some of the clear deodorant on. It didn't work. Her armpits were sweaty and got musty, so she took another shower. This would only last for about two hours. It got to the point where she was taking six showers a day. A white girl offered to buy Bryce some deodorant from commissary, but Bryce refused. She didn't want the girl to get the wrong idea. The same girl helped Bryce take her braids out so she could perm her new growth. Bryce's extensions were silky Indian hair. The white girl asked her what she wanted her to do with the hair. Bryce just told her to throw it away, so she put it in a clear trash bag as she took it out. The next day Bryce saw two black girls walk by with the hair she had thrown away braided into the front of their hair.

Bryce made a few phone calls, but no one would answer the phone. She decided to write a letter to her bank explaining her ordeal and requesting some money from her savings account in the form of a money order. It worked. A week later, she received a money order from her bank for $200. She was in business. She bought some deodorant, some snacks, and a book of stamps. Upon further conversation with her inmates, she discovered that 90 percent of the women in this pod had hepatitis. Now she knew hepatitis wasn't readily contagious, but she was still concerned. Bryce's mind wandered to an extreme. What if she got into a fight and cut herself and one of her inmates bled on her or into her cut? She would be infected. She knew the chances of that happening were slim, but she was still concerned.

She wrote a letter to the jail's warden asking why she was even in this pod and if there was something he could do to place her else where. To her surprise, the warden came to visit her. Bryce stated her case, and he assured her that she had nothing to worry about. Bryce pleaded with him, and he said he would see what he could do. In the morning she was moved into protective custody (or PC). Bryce had a cell all to herself. She was in heaven. She could sleep all day if she wanted to and not be bothered by the clamor of being in jail.

A few days later, she was moved to another pod on another tier. Bryce made friends fast. She met a tall dark-skinned woman who called herself Brother-man. Brother-man looked after Bryce and taught her how to play pinochle. She also got her into the spades games in the evening. Bryce told Brother-man how beautiful her velvety, chocolate brown skin was and she seemed to fall in love. She said no one had ever told her that before. The two started spending more and more time together, and the other girls seemed to get jealous. They appreciated Brother-man being for all of them, and they didn't mind sharing; but when they saw that she had an affinity for Bryce, it slowly caused problems. There was a tall white woman on that tier they called Big

Momma. She was an open dyke and seemed to be friends with Brotherman until she started spending all of her time with Bryce.

Then Big Momma began bossing Bryce around just to let her know who was in charge. Big Momma had what looked like bruises and cysts all over her body. It was rumored that she was HIV positive, but she still had a little weight on her, so she did not appear to be in the final stages of it. One day Bryce stood her ground because she was tired of Big Momma bossing her around. They were about to fight when Bryce asked the CO standing guard to put her on PC again. She obliged, and off Bryce went, escaping the clutches of Big Momma.

The only thing Bryce didn't like about being on PC was that the guards down there were not concerned about getting inmates showers on a regular basis. Bryce was lucky to shower once or twice a week, but she didn't care because she was all alone. During meal times, there was an opening in the grill of her cell. One day Bryce was asleep, and the inmates serving lunch that day left her tray in her window. Bryce awoke to the clamor of mealtime and turned over to see this skinny white woman chomping on her cheeseburger and french fries. Bryce went ballistic.

"What da fuck! Is that my shit?"

The woman just sat there directly in front of Bryce's cell, eating the cheeseburger, seemingly to taunt her. Bryce cussed and fussed and hit her cell door in angst. She threatened the woman and said if she ever came across her again it was on. The woman never said a word. She just stood there and kept on eating. The guard came over to see what the problem was. Bryce explained, and the guard laughed as she told her to calm down. She brought Bryce another tray, but Bryce was too upset to eat her favorite meal.

Another two weeks later, a guard woke Bryce up and told her to get ready for a trip. This was her first time going through this, so she had no idea where she was going. When she asked, the guard said it was confidential. Bryce got scared. She thought she was going to prison. But how could they do that when she hadn't even had a trial yet? She put her periwinkle-blue pants on over her shorts and put on her shirt to match over her sports bra. She already had on the socks that the officer from the precinct had given her, and she slipped into her plastic neon-orange slides. The guard came into the cell and handcuffed her and then connected the handcuffs to the chain that was wrapped around her waist. She was escorted to the same big yellow bus that brought her there. The ride seemed to take forever. They traveled up York Road so far, that nothing looked familiar.

When she got out she was taken to an office inside of an office. She waited there for about ten minutes until she was called in. An extremely tall white man in his fifties with reddish-blonde hair and glasses sat behind the desk and smiled at Bryce as if they had met before. She was confused. He was very friendly, and Bryce was glad she had not showered in a week. He asked random questions.

"Hello. I'm Dr. Bloomingdale. I want to ask you a few questions."

"You don't look like a doctor."

"I'm the lead psychiatrist for the court in Baltimore County."

"I don't need a psychiatrist."

"How do you know?"

"I've never seen one before."

"Tell me about your childhood. Do you have brothers and sisters?"

"No. I'm an only child."

"What about your parents? Were they present in your life growing up?"

"Just my mom. I only met my dad once."

"And how do you feel about that?"

"I don't feel any kind of way. I don't know him."

"And what about your mom? Are you close?"

"No."

"What makes you say that?"

"We've never been close. She treats me like a step child."

"Give me some examples of what you mean."

"Well, she's just never there for me. I didn't realize it until recently, but it's like she wants to see me fail all the time. The other people I know their mothers don't treat them like that."

"How do other people's mothers treat them?"

"Like they care. For example, when I was in school, my friends might get into trouble, and their parents would be there the next day to rectify the situation. My mother never came to school for me, didn't matter if it was good or bad. It's like I was always on auto pilot even when I was little."

"And how do you feel about that?"

"I'm hurt. I love her, but she doesn't love me."

"Did you have any friends?"

"Yes, plenty."

"So why did you shoot your mother?"

"I don't want to incriminate myself."

"I understand."

"So is there anything wrong with me?"

"No. You seem fine to me."

"So why am I here?"

"This is a preliminary screening to see if you have a mental illness."

"Where am I going now?"

"Back to the jail to await your trial."

"Oh, okay."

An officer came in and took Bryce back to the bus where she went back to jail. She was puzzled and wondered what that was all about. When she got back to her cell, she ate dinner and went to sleep. Bryce just knew that eventually she would be put back into population; but to her surprise, they let her stay on PC for about a month.

During that time, her public defender came to see her. He informed her of when her court date was and told her that her presence in court was unnecessary. Bryce got upset. She wanted her day in court. She wanted to tell the judge that the only reason she shot her mother was because she was afraid for her life. If she didn't shoot her mother, someone may have shot her or worse. To her, it was self-defense but the public defender told her the judge would not see it that way. Her mother was running from her, and she shot her in the back. He said most likely she would get twenty years in prison. He was sure that the best thing for her to do was to end up at a state mental facility.

Bryce was quiet. All this talk of prison and mental facilities was new to her. Her public defender assured her that he would represent her well. He told her to watch her mail for a response from the judge within ten days after her court date. Bryce was oblivious to everything. She didn't wait for anything. She just kept on living day by day in jail. Then a guard came one day with a clear trash bag and told her to pack her things. She didn't even think about anything. She just followed the instructions she was given.

She wound up in another interview. This time, it was with two white women. They were smiling at her just like the psychiatrist at the last meeting. Bryce was offended. Here, she was about to spend a good portion of her life locked up; and everyone was happy to see her, white people.

They took turns asking her a bunch of questions she didn't have the answers to. When *she* asked questions, they seemed impressed and more than happy to answer her. But they seemed to give her the information they wanted her to have instead of giving her direct answers. They left her alone for a while. Then some nurses came and said she was going to intake.

"What, back to jail?"

"No. You're being admitted here."

"Where am I?"

"This is Clayborn Mental Facility. You'll be a patient here indefinitely."

The two black women made Bryce take off her clothes and take a shower. They gave her a solution to put in her hair and told her to leave it in for two minutes and then rinse it out. After she'd dried off, they gave her a pair of navy-blue pants and a stripped shirt to put on along with some navy-blue deck shoes. They never asked her what size she wore. Somehow they already knew.

When she got to the ward, Bryce was not prepared for what she was about to be a part of. Everyone was sitting in the day room watching TV. No one seemed to notice her walk in. A man sitting next to her was talking to himself.

Then a fight broke out. A young girl named Stacy walked up behind another girl who was sitting down watching TV and sucker punched her for no reason. They instantly got into it. The two rolled around and pulled each other's hair until security was called and pulled them apart. Stacy was cussing and fussing all the way to a padded room in the back of the ward where she was given a long needle with some kind of medication in it and told to quiet down. She stayed there for thirty minutes. Then they let her out and told her to stay away from the girl she had hit.

Was that it? What if that girl sucker punched Bryce? What if Bryce got into a fight? Was this *their* PC? You get a needle and go to the quiet room? That's the consequence? That meant that anyone could get hurt at anytime. Bryce was scared all over again. She had jumped out of the frying pan and into the fire.

She called Jerman Henry. Every number she had was stored in her cell phone, so she didn't have any memorized. She went to the desk and requested a telephone book. There were only two Jerman Henrys listed. She called them both, hoping to hear from her old friend. The first one was the right number. She hadn't talked to him since they broke up eight years ago. She figured he would be the best person to talk to at that moment because she knew he had become a social worker. She was right. He was working at a place similar to Clayborn Mental Facility and offered Bryce some insight.

"Is this Jerman?"

"Bryce?"

"Yeah, it's me."

"How'd you get my number?"

"I looked it up in the phone book."

"The phone book?"

"Yeah. Jerman, I'm in some trouble. I need your help."

"What kind of trouble?"

"I shot my mother, and now I'm at Clayborn Mental Facility. Do you know what that is?"

"Yeah. I almost ended up working there before, but I found another job. I work at the children's center now."

"Are you still a social worker?"

"Yeah. How'd you end up in there?"

"I shot my mother."

"*Really?*"

"Jerman, I'm scared. I'm gonna be in here with these crazy people for twenty years."

"Relax. You won't be there for no twenty years. You just gotta let them get to know you. Once the doctors feel comfortable, they'll let you out."

"What do I have to say?"

"Just be yourself. Let them know you're remorseful and that you won't do it again when they let you out."

"Okay. Oh, am I glad I talked to you. I was so scared."

"You'll be okay."

"I miss you."

"You don't miss me y. You're just lonely."

"I do miss you. I haven't spoken to you in years."

"Exactly. When people get locked up, they'll say anything to get some attention from the outside. It's human nature."

"How do you know?"

"I do this for a living, Bryce. Plus, I know you, remember?"

"So you don't think I care?"

"I'm not saying that. I'm just saying you're in a bad place right now and feeling needy. Don't worry, it's normal."

"Can you come visit me? I wanna see you."

"I gotta make sure it's all right first."

"Who do you have to ask?"

"Your social worker. Get her name and number. If she says it's okay, then I'll come see you."

"I love you, Jerman."

"Yeah, whatever. Call me later."

"Okay, bye."

Bryce was at ease now. She felt confident that she could do a few years here. She hadn't been there long; but already, she could tell it wasn't nearly as bad as prison would have been. She felt blessed. Maybe God or a guardian angel was looking out for her.

In the morning, a doctor came over to Bryce in the day room and said she needed to talk to her in the conference room. She told Bryce her name and explained that she had been diagnosed with delusional disorder. She went over the medications Bryce would be taking and told her to feel free to always ask questions. She wanted her to go to what they called medication group to learn all about the benefits and side effects of her medications.

Bryce wanted to know what delusional disorder was. The doctor said that Bryce's explanation of why she shot her mother was fictitious. Apparently, they didn't believe that Bryce's mother was out to get her. The doctor said, "She raised you and took care of you. She never abused you or brought you any harm, so why would you shoot her?" She told her that seeing Rocco while she was driving the cab was a figment of her imagination.

Bryce said, "I know who I saw."

The doctor told her she was tired from driving too many hours and at night. Besides her mental illness, that caused her to have a break and the psychosis developed, and she started to see things.

Bryce just stared at this woman. She knew who Rocco was and what he looked like. She knew he was no good and up to no good. She knew it was him. She also knew that she wanted to get out of there as soon, as possible so she decided to just go along with it. Fighting a doctor was most likely going to keep her in that facility longer than necessary.

She acquiesced, "Yeah, I think you're right. I was kinda tired. I don't know who I saw for real."

The doctor leaned toward Bryce and told her this was the first step in her recovery. She recommended that she go to as many groups as possible to gain insight into her mental illness. Bryce wanted to know how long she would be there. The doctor said it all depended on her but informed her that the average stay of a patient was seven to ten years. Then she said it was uncommon to see people leave in two or three years, and then again some would spend the rest of their lives there.

That scared Bryce, but she assumed that forever was the exception and not the rule. She could do two or three years for shooting her mother no problem. She wanted to get focused and begin the work necessary to one day leave, so she stopped asking questions and studied.

When Jerman came to visit, he surprised Bryce by bringing his best friend. The three of them used to rap and make cassette tapes together. They weren't a group or anything. They would just ham it up and record. In the visit, they laughed about when they used to hang out. For a minute, Bryce forgot all about where she was at. She thanked her friends for coming to see her, and they promised to come back for another visit.

The wards were co-ed. Bryce didn't understand it. They had rules about no touching, no sex, etc; but when you lock up males and females together in close proximity, someone is bound to try his or her hand. Some people got into relationships and had boyfriends or girlfriends. Bryce had suitors but was determined not to be interested. She viewed that as torture, to be locked up with someone you had feelings for and could only talk to them all day. Over time, she had heard about people sneaking into the laundry room together or the kitchen area to cop a quick feel. There would only be a matter of minutes before staff would walk by, so they had to plan it out and be quick. Bryce thought it was too much trouble. Plus, if you got caught, it would be reported to your treatment team and could possibly cause your stay there to be longer than necessary. To her, it wasn't worth the gamble.

Clayborn had a minimum-security side and a maximum-security side. Both sides had several wards that patients would be moved throughout as he or she progressed. In the hospital center, there was a gym, a chapel, a canteen, an art room, and a clinic. Everything was done in-house. If you got sick, you went to the clinic. They never sent you out to the emergency room unless it was a matter of life or death or you needed some kind of surgery. You could order snacks, stamps, stationery, coffee, etc., from the canteen and play basketball, soccer, volleyball, or exercise in the gym. They also had recreational groups to go to like Zumba, chess, bowling, music, or a store where other patients made you a hot chocolate or coffee like it was Starbucks. There, you could sit and watch a movie while you sipped your drink and also try on and get free clothes that were donated by outside sources.

Clayborn was a far cry from prison. The administration and staff actually cared about the patients' well-being. The social atmosphere was way different than any jail or prison. If someone made you feel uncomfortable, you could always tell a superior and squash it before it got out of hand. But Clayborn surely had its share of tragedies and fatalities. Although there were metal detectors everywhere and security to pat you down when moving from one place to another, just like prison, if someone really wanted to get at you, they could get you. In the time that Bryce was there, she had heard stories about people getting strangled or pummeled to death. And with mental illness, you never know what's on someone's mind. You could be attacked for no reason at anytime.

For example, there was this guy named David who was friends with Bryce. David was a real flirt. He would hit on all the women, staff, and patients alike but he didn't mean any harm. Most of the time, he was very respectful and knew when and where to draw the line. David grew up in the streets of DC and lived by a certain code, even in the hospital. He didn't separate himself just to survive here. He operated the same way he would as if he were at home. David had a connection who would bring him molly and e-pills. He would share with a friend or two. That friend or two would share with their friends, and soon word got out that he was the go- to for the stuff. David had no problem getting it in. He was cool with the security guard who brought packages in, so no one questioned when he would receive more than one box in a month's time. Soon he was supplying the whole ward. David never wanted for anything. He had all the snacks, coffee, stamps, phone cards, and ramen that anyone could ever want.

David slept in a dorm with two other males. One of his roommates' names was John. John was a conservative white guy who was very protective over his female friend Dietrich. Dietrich was friends with all the guys, but she was a little naive. John saw this in her and wanted to protect her. He became like a father figure to her. One day Dietrich innocently told him that she'd gotten some molly from David. Right away, John was concerned. Drug abuse was a part of Dietrich's diagnoseis, and he didn't want to see her spiral downward. John went to the doctor.

"Doc, I got some information you might want to know about."

"Oh really? Come into my office, John."

"David gave Dietrich some pills a few days ago. You know she's getting over a drug problem. He obviously doesn't care about her if he's giving her pills. What can you do to make it stop?"

"Pills? What kind of pills?"

"Something called molly."

"Where is he getting it from?"

"I don't know, but I know he has them."

"Where does he keep them?"

"Probably in his room."

"Have you ever seen the pills?"

"No."

"You just heard from Dietrich?"

"Yes. She has no reason to lie to me."

"Are Dietrich and David an item?"

"No."

"Do you like Dietrich?"

"Yes. She's like a sister to me, though."

"Do you plan on staying in touch with her when you get out?"

"Yes."

"Do you want more than a platonic relationship with her?"

"Well, I never thought about that, but I do care about her."

"I can see that. Well, John, thank you for telling me this. I'll look into it."

The next day there was a shake down on the ward. There were twenty-seven beds on the ward. Security found pills in mattresses, tucked into ceiling panels, zipped into couch cushions, and attached on the persons of thirteen patients. The ward was in an up roar. Because of the nature of this environment the doctor could not crucify someone based solely on one person's opinion. He needed evidence and documentation to support whatever action he was going to take. He decided to question each patient about what security found. When the doctor's investigation was over, he didn't know how the pills got in but several people gave the doctor David's name. The doctor felt like this was enough evidence to send David back, so he called him into the conference room.

"David, we have reason to believe that you are the one who has been distributing pills on the ward. Is this true?"

"No. What pills?"

"Don't play games with me, David. Four different people gave me your name. They all said the same thing. You gave them ecstasy and molly. Where did you get it from?"

"I don't know what you're talking about."

"Pack your things. You're going back to maximum security tomorrow."

"How you gonna send me back when you can't prove anything?"

"I just told you. Several people gave the same account of you giving them drugs. We cannot allow this to go on here. You must go back."

David stormed out of the room and went to pack his things. As he gathered and organized his belongings, his other roommate Paul walked in.

"Man, what's going on? They found pills everywhere. Everybody's about to get fucked up!"

"Who's going back?"

"I don't know. I saw them take pills outta Troy's pockets, and they took pills outta Boney's socks."

"They not going back?"

"They didn't say anything to me about going back. Why? What's wrong?"

"Somebody snitched. I'm going back tomorrow. I gotta get ready."

"How'd they know to do a shake down? We just had one a week ago, so somebody must have said something. That wasn't no random shit. Ooohhh! You know what, I saw John in the doctors's office yesterday. He was in there a long time too."

"He don't know. I never gave him shit."

"But you be giving Dietrich shit. You know that's her boy."

"She wouldn't have told on me."

"I didn't say she did, but she prolly told him. Know what I mean?"

David paused to think about it. He knew Dietrich was naive and most likely meant no harm but probably did say something to her friend in passing conversation. After David had packed all his things, he went into the day room where they were playing pool. David saw John approaching the day room. He grabbed a metal pool stick and berated John with it. John ran but was no match for David's long legs. He chased John around the ward, beating him mercilessly with the pool stick. John ran into an adjacent room where he could not escape because the door was locked. David had him cornered. Blood was everywhere on the ceiling, on the doors, the walls, and the floor.

The next day Bryce found a tooth under a chair. When security finally arrived, John had to be taken to the hospital and David was escorted right away to another ward on maximum security. The pool stick was in the shape of an *S*. It had taken David several years to get to the less restrictive side of the hospital. Now he was going back to square one.

CHAPTER 23

On the minimum-security side, the hospital geared the patient's treatment more towards moving back into the community. There were trips to the movies, bowling, ice skating, roller skating, shopping at the mall, and going out to restaurants. Sometimes they would have lawyers and other officials in the mental health industry come in and talk to the patients to give them an outsider's view of what it would be like to live in the world with a mental illness. Through these methods, they tried to offer hope; but those who had been in this system for most of their lives knew otherwise. The doctors and social workers often said that most mental illnesses exhibited symptoms around the ages of eighteen to twenty-five. Bryce met many who had been diagnosed as children and who had been in and out of the mental health system since then. Clayborn was a revolving door, and there were always rumors about who had left and who was coming back and why. This was the norm. And although they were not supposed to, staff would let you know about who was never going home.

After a while, Bryce gathered that those who would most likely die there were pedophiles. The goal was to rehabilitate a person; teach them how to cope with their symptoms, triggers, and other issues; and eventually let them back out to be a productive citizen. Pedophiles could not be rehabilitated, so they remained there. Bryce met a lot of people that she became friends with, played cards with, and talked to that she knew if she met them on the outside she wouldn't give them the time of day.

However, the first thing she learned being at this place was that she could not move as herself. She was constantly being watched. If someone showed any signs of strange behavior, it was reported to his or her doctor and treatment team. Anything could be misconstrued as a symptom of a mental illness. If you didn't want to talk to certain people, you could be paranoid. If you ordered too much canteen or ate too much, you could be anxious. If you didn't eat enough or losst too much weight too fast, you could be depressed. If you got into a fight and whipped someone's ass, you could be labeled as aggressive and deemed not fit for the community, and on and on. Living in Clayborn, you were at the mercy of the doctors and people who would claim to know you through the lenses of many years of schooling. Many of them probably could not crack an egg properly. Bryce saw that it was a game. There were certain things they needed her to say and do. There were many things that were taboo and would keep you there longer.

The staff was a complete team from the nurses to the social workers to the doctors to the therapists to the psychologists. They all worked together and discussed everything about each patient. All it would take was one disgruntled customer to plant the seed of mistrust in a patient's treatment team. Depending on what the issue was, one person's opinion could hold you up for years. Bryce learned that she had to please them all to keep her movement flowing. This went against who she was, but she knew she had to play this game to one day get out. She learned how to be a chameleon and how to be a good liar.

She had a lot of firsts at Clayborn, one being her talks with a therapist. She also got engaged for the first time. She had never been to therapy before and never desired to go. Like everyone else, she had issues that needed to be worked out but would just figure something out on her own, or she would talk to a friend who would give her insight. This was her favorite thing to do whenever confronting a problem because the people she talked to knew her and cared about her. There was no textbook involved. She had to learn to navigate therapy as well. Her first therapist's name was Emily. Emily was a smart young white woman from Kansas. She knew her stuff but had had little life experience, and Bryce picked up on this right away. When talking to her, Bryce felt like she had to put a filter on everything she told her about. If she didn't, Emily's "spidey senses" would go up; and she would get alarmed and tell the doctor.

Bryce figured out a way to divert attention away from herself. She inquired about all the things Emily had learned in school about being a therapist. After a while, she had Emily bringing her all kinds of print outs and information on everything from *O* magazine to the *DSM-V* (the periodical listing of mental illnesses as outlined by leading psychiatrists). For homework, Bryce would read a print out. In her sessions, they would discuss what she had read and apply it to something she was going through. Emily would always tell Bryce how intelligent she was. Bryce didn't take it as a compliment.

Clayborn was a state institution that paid little, so most therapists were still in school or interns. They would only be there to gain experience in their field then they would move on. Most therapists would only be there for about six months at a time. Just when Bryce would get comfortable or used to someone, they would leave and she would be assigned to someone new. All this moving around made Bryce put her guard up. She would tell her therapists some things, but most times she would just make something up or tell them what they wanted to hear. She always remembered the goal of getting out and moving on.

Although Bryce was determined not to get involved with anyone, she got lonely and fell for this guy named JJ. JJ was brown skinned, short, and handsome. He was very intelligent, loved football, and had a thing for this white girl named Dietrich. Bryce and Dietrich didn't get along. Bryce tolerated her but couldn't stand her. Every day Dietrich would try to take over the TV. She was narcissistic and very controlling, but all the men from the security guards to the patients loved her. Bryce couldn't figure it out. Dietrich had a personality disorder and wasn't exactly a looker, but she had these big breasts and long legs. She would always say flirty things to all the black guys like "Don't you want some company?" or "Can I sit next to you?" They would eat it up like it was cake while Bryce just sat there and watched. Then she heard about Dietrich sucking JJ off in the laundry room. Instantly he was smitten. Bryce was jealous. She watched the two, plotting on how she could get JJ away from Dietrich. She talked to him more and more and realized that they had a lot in common. Bryce told herself she was going to take him from her.

"JJ, what do you see in her?"

"See in who?"

"Your girlfriend."

"Who's my girlfriend?"

"Dietrich."

"That's not my girlfriend."

"She sucked you off in the laundry room."

"Who told you that?"

"Everyone knows. It's community information. Is it true?"

"Why you wanna know?"

"I'm curious. Plus, I like you."

"*You like me?*"

"Yeah."

JJ just stared at Bryce for a moment.

"I like you too."

Bryce raised an eyebrow.

"Okay, so what you gonna do about it?"

"Whatchu want me to do about it?"

"I want you to leave Dietrich alone."

JJ laughed.

"You calling shots like that?"

"I'm just telling you how I feel."

"You like me that much?"

"Yeah."

"Okay. I'll leave her alone, but you can't tell anyone we had this conversation."

"What do you see in her anyway?"

"Don't worry about that."

210

A few months went by, and JJ and Bryce were a couple. Dietrich had moved on to another man on the ward, but she could tell that JJ was still interested. Bryce was determined not to lose. The two spent more and more time together. They played pool on the ward, and Bryce always asked for pointers.

"Show me how to bank it off the railing."

"Okay, first, you gotta get low. Get your eyes level with the ball. Make sure the cue is straight, then pull back, and hit the ball like this. It's easy."

"Okay, let me try. Guide my hand."

Bryce only wanted JJ to get close to her. She would miss on purpose, so he'd lean down and do it again. Since they were locked up, this was almost as exciting as sex. They stole hugs and kisses in the laundry room. Whenever JJ would wash his clothes, Bryce would sneak in and fold them before he got there. When he would go to check on his clothes, they would be neatly folded and piled up on top of the dryer. He would be so surprised and would chuckle.

"Damn, you folded my drawers too!"

Bryce was falling fast. Whatever he asked for, she would do; but her limit was sex. If they got caught, they would go back to maximum security; and the set back could last years. Sometimes JJ would hint or joke about sneaking off somewhere, but he wasn't willing to take the risk either, or so he was telling Bryce. Then JJ got some good news. He would be leaving soon. Bryce was happy for him but sad to see him go. She would cherish every moment until the time came. They talked about it often, and Bryce would pay attention to all the details about *his* discharge; so when her day came, she would be well informed. He wanted to move to Prince Georges County. Bryce had never heard of it but continued to ask questions. JJ said he had family out there and wanted to escape the chaos that got him into trouble. Instead of going back to the Eastern Shore where he was from, he opted to go to PG County.

Bryce tried to relish every moment with JJ she could. They agreed that him leaving would not be the end of their courtship. Bryce knew her day was coming too. She just didn't know when. She made sure that she and JJ would stay in touch even if he would be out and she would be in. JJ's discharge processed rather quickly. A director came to talk to him, and he went to see the group home and program. He liked it and chose to go there. He had his in-house trial, and his treatment team sent all the appropriate paper work to his judge. The judge sent his paper work back within two days, and JJ was approved to leave. The whole time he never discussed the process with Bryce. He just went on being her friend. Then his social worker came to him and told him to pack his bags because he'd be leaving tomorrow afternoon. JJ followed instructions; and when everything was packed and ready to go, he went back into the day room to be with his Clayborn girlfriend.

They spent the whole evening together, and soon all the other patients had gone to sleep. It was just JJ, Bryce, and two staff left. JJ told Bryce to follow him into the back room where the doors were made of plexiglass. There was a computer, an exercise bike, a table, and four chairs. The exercise bike was behind a wall, so it was like a blind spot in the room. They sat across from each other and continued their conversation. The staff didn't bother them because they could see them through the glass doors, and they were carrying on a conversation of their own. Then JJ turned their conversation to sex.

"You never told me what your favorite position was."

"Missionary. I'm boring."

"You like to fuck, or you like to make love?"

"I like to start out making love. Then when I get used to my partner after a while, I wanna fuck. What about you?"

"I like to fuck. I wish I could fuck you right now. In fact, my dick is already hard."

Why did he tell Bryce that?

"I never told you this before, but whenever I'm around you, my pussy gets wet. I enjoy talking to you. It turns me on."

"Oh yeah?"

"Yeah."

"Show me."

Bryce looked around.

"Go over there behind the bike and jerk off for me."

"Hold on."

JJ went behind the bike, pulled out his penis, and stroked it for Bryce. She tried to contain herself so as not to arouse the staff.

"Damn. I'm getting wetter."

"Come over here and bend over and let me put this dick inside you."

Bryce looked around again.

"Hold on. All right, here I come."

Bryce slipped behind the bike and pulled her pants down. She turned around and bent over. JJ put it in and pumped four times and then yanked out. Bryce turned around to see what was wrong and saw that there was a puddle of seamen in JJ's hand. Their eyes met, and JJ darted out of the room. Bryce pulled up her pants and followed him, asking what was wrong, only to meet one of the staff at the door. She wished that it lasted longer but was glad it didn't. One more pump and they would have gotten caught.

The next day JJ was distant. Bryce tried to talk to him, but he wasn't interested. He told Bryce he was leaving but made it sound like he'd just found out. He promised to write and call. Bryce told him to step into the kitchen so they could sneak one last kiss and hug, but he wasn't interested in that either. Bryce was confused. After he left, they stayed in touch. They talked every morning and every afternoon. Soon JJ got a job and bought Bryce a ring. He sent it to her taped to a letter folded in fours. In the letter, JJ asked Bryce to marry him one day. She stood there beaming, and everyone wondered what her problem was. Bryce examined the ring. It was bent from going through the mail. It was petite and silver with a small clear stone in it.

Bryce was so surprised that she didn't care about its flaws. She would have to size it, though. It would only fit on her pinky. She wore it around the ward but didn't tell anyone that she was engaged. It was long distance, but Bryce didn't care. She thought she was in love.

The years went on; and Bryce went from ward to ward, advancing each time. Five years went by before a meeting with her doctor and treatment team informed her that she would be leaving soon. She was so relieved. She remembered thinking that she might never get out, and now her day was on its way. Her social worker told her what she would have to do once she got out. A five-year conditional release would be in place. In the penal system it was called probation. Bryce would have to see a psychiatrist once a month and a therapist once every two weeks. She could have no weapons, drugs, or alcohol. If it was ever suspected that she was indulging in any of these things, she would be tested via urinalysis. If her test came back positive, she would be sent back to the hospital and have to start all over again. If her therapist or doctor ever reported that Bryce had become a danger to herself or others, she would be sent back to the hospital.

Another five years? Bryce didn't know if she could do it. She couldn't believe how fast the time went by on the inside. She decided to just get outside the front door and try her hand. Hopefully, the time would go by as smoothly as it did inside.

Her social worker also said she would have to live in a group home. She would start in what they called an in intensive house where staff would be there around the clock. Eventually, she would be stepped down to a less restrictive environment in another group home. After staying there for a while and getting approval from her outside treatment team, she could move into her own place. Bryce asked lots of questions because she didn't know what to expect. The team had answers for them all. She thought about money and wanted to know if she could get a job. Her social worker explained that being in Perkins was not a punishment. She was there strictly for treatment.

Being on the outside, she would be treated the same way. Her team there would guide her through the maze of job interviews, résumés, management of her money, and just the mechanics of every day living. Their services were what they called wrap around; and everything would be funded by the state, Medicare, or Medicaide. She would have to draw Social Security (SSI) or Social Security disability insurance (SSDI). The state would determine how much she would get every month. Her social worker said the amount may be anywhere from $500 to $2,500 a month. Getting SSI or SSDI every month would pay for her room and board at the group home. Each program was different, though. Some programs would give the consumer a stipend from his or her SSI check every month. Some would not. Some programs would allow you to work and then take a percentage of your paycheck besides getting your SSI or SSDI every month. Some programs would let you keep %100 percent of your earnings. Bryce would have to talk to and visit a place to discover how they operated and what would be the best fit for her. She wrote down a whole list of questions to ask when she would go to visit a program.

The team told her she could also choose where she wanted to go if it was in the state of Maryland. Each county and Baltimore City had programs all over. Bryce could discuss her goals with a program director who would come into the hospital to talk to her. If she liked what she heard, then she could set up a time to visit the program and group home. The programs and group homes were connected. They worked together to ensure that the consumer had a place to go every day and a place to rest his or her head each night.

When she got out, Bryce went to a place called Armistice in PG County. She chose PG County because JJ was there and she was hoping to be closer to him. She had a ring, so she just knew that they would be together. They kept in touch via the phone for a little while. However, when JJ moved to a less restrictive house, he stopped calling and didn't give her the new number. She called him one day, and his roommate informed her that JJ moved and he didn't have his new number. Bryce was so hurt, but she got over it.

Bryce didn't like living with Armistice. Almost everyone in the program was older, and they seemed to lump everyone together. It wasn't like in the hospital where you were treated as an individual. There was no wiggle room. If something applied to someone who was severely ill, it also applied to the people who were highly functional. Bryce didn't think that was fair. For example, the first house she went to live in had a counselor who cooked all the meals. Her own mother never cooked for her, so Bryce felt like an invalid. She complained right away, and they let her cook.

At first, they had Bryce helping the counselor. Then they gave each roommate a day to cook. Then, since this was her first time drawing SSDI, the government gave Bryce a lump sum of $10,000 in back payment. From the time you apply for SSI or SSDI until the time you actually get it can be almost a year; so when you do get it, you get back pay. She had never had that much money before and wanted to get a car and a job. They told her no and that she would have to wait on both accounts. They also said that she could only have $2,000 in the bank; or else, she would no longer be eligible for the program. Now you do the math. Bryce got a safe.

In the hospital, she met all kinds of people who had been in and out of the system for years. They all had horror stories about group homes and programs out in the community. One lady said she was living in a group home; and when she got her back pay, she spent her money to fix up her room. She bought a stereo system, a TV, and a computer. All the doors to the bedrooms had locks, and the only person with a key was her. They did keep a spare key in the safe in case something happened to the consumer's key. She came home from the program one day and unlocked her door to find that her room was completely wiped out. The only thing in there was the bed. She reported it to the group home's director and she said that they were not responsible for people's belongings. There was nothing she could do.

There was a guy who got his lump sum and put the cash under his mattress. He came home one day to find nothing. There was nothing they could do for him either. Another consumer would carry his lump sum around with him in his pockets. A counselor who worked for the program called him into the office to see why his pockets were bulging all the time. When the consumer told him he had money in his pockets, the counselor told him he was afraid for him and to leave the money with him so he wouldn't get robbed. The consumer trusted him and emptied his pockets. When he returned at the end of the day, the counselor was gone. When the consumer reported it, it was his word against the counselor's word. When the guy got irate about his money, they said he was a danger to himself and others and sent him back to the hospital.

Bryce now had to do five years on the outside. She thought she would go crazy without a job. Not that she had any bills to pay, but all that sitting around was driving her crazy. She needed something to do. She needed to be productive. After two years, they finally let her get a job. She was referred to the program's vocational department. She talked to the lady running the program. They had two offerings: a job as a room attendant at a hotel or a job as a waitress at a restaurant. Bryce had been a waitress before, and her grandmother had been a maid. She wanted to go forward instead of backwards, so she went with what she knew. The owner of the restaurant sat on the board of directors for the county's Alliance for the Mentally Ill and was invested in helping the mentally ill who needed jobs and wanted to integrate back into the community. Bryce interviewed with him and nailed it. She got the job and made $100 a day as a waitress. She worked part-time and then switched over to full-time.

At the restaurant, she did well enough to train people. They had her training a guy named Dwayne. Bryce didn't want to do it because it was too busy. She did it anyway. She didn't like Dwayne at first because he was petty. This restaurant had a rule that trainees didn't get tips because they were getting paid a training rate. All tips went to the trainers. Dwayne knew this, and Bryce would keep an eye on what her customers were leaving her. Her tips would disappear, and Dwayne would give them to her, but she would have to ask him for the tips each time. It was feeling like an up hill battle trying to train him. Plus, he had no experience as a server, so she was teaching him the restaurant's way and the basics of serving.

And he was slow. He would take an order for a table of two writing everything down then repeating the entire order back twice while his whole section filled up. Then he would get mad when you wouldn't help him, but he always acted like he knew what he was doing.

Dwayne and Bryce talked a lot during training and remained friends. She was attracted to him and went over to his mother's house. He lived with his mother. During the days, Dwayne would wash her car for her. She thought that was sweet. Besides the guys at the carwash, no man had ever washed her car for her before. He always said, "Only real men wash their own cars." Then one night it happened. They were in his room, and they kissed. He seduced her; and when she pulled out a condom, he looked as if he wanted to cry. Bryce's weakness was always men. She didn't want to see his tears, so she put away the condom. She guessed that this meant that they were officially together now.

Sex with Dwayne was always boring. Like most men, he would only seek to serve himself. She never came, never had an orgasm, but he came every time. One time he asked her if she came, and she said, "Uuuhh-huh." She was just happy to have someone to talk to, happy to have someone pay attention to her, happy to have someone pay her car note every month. Although he lacked a lot, he got really close to what her ideal of what a man and a relationship should be. She would later find out that he was just acting. Bryce missed two periods. She went to the doctor and found out she was pregnant. Dwayne was elated. He went to all of the doctor's appointments and made it home every morning.

The restaurant they worked at was open twenty-four hours. Dwayne worked the graveyard shift, and Bryce worked in the mornings. He didn't have a car, so Bryce would let him drive her car to work at night. Then he would come home, and Bryce would drive herself to work. The only thing she hated about this arrangement was that she had to sleep alone at night especially while she was pregnant. However, he was only one phone call away at work. During this time he never let her down.

CHAPTER 24

As the months crept on and Bryce's belly got bigger, Dwayne got more and more hostile. Whenever they would lie down together, he would lie on top of her and try to squash the baby. Bryce would get so upset. All she could imagine was her baby suffocating inside her. She would tell him to stop, and he would; but one night, after she had cooked dinner, out of no where, he was just so angry. Everything she said inflamed him. Then he got up in her face like a drill sergeant and challenged everything she said. Bryce stood her ground and challenged him right back. This went on for ten minutes.

Finally, he backed down, took the keys off of the kitchen counter, and went to work. She couldn't believe it. They had argued before but never like that. The only thing he didn't do was hit her. She could understand it. Here, she was letting him use her car every night, cooking for him every night, and having sex with him whenever he wanted it and this is how he would act? Why the sudden change?

Bryce thought bringing a man's baby into the world would bring them both joy. She could feel the shift in their relationship. She thought maybe there was another woman, but when would he have time? When he wasn't at work, he was at home. And if he wasn't in front of her, he was only a phone call away. He always picked up his phone when she called. Besides arguing with her, he did nothing suspicious or shady, so she assumed she could trust him.

He came home after work and acted like nothing happened. There was no apology or even acknowledgment of him getting in her face, so Bryce didn't bring it up either. They both just went on.

"What do you want for dinner?"

"Fried chicken."

"You had that last night."

"Well, it was good. Did you make enough for leftovers?"

"No. But there's some more in the freezer. I'll just have to thaw it out."

Bryce put the frozen chicken in a sink full of warm water and sat down to watch TV.

"You not gon cook?"

"It's thawing out. I'll start dinner a few."

Dwayne went into the bedroom to do some push-ups. Bryce followed him but went to the bathroom inside the apartment's bedroom. She was a little tired from being pregnant, so she just sat there with her panties around her ankles and watched Dwayne do his push-ups.

"Ninety-one, ninety-two, ninety-three . . ."

"Damn. How many you gon do? You usually do sets of sixty-five."

"Mind your business."

Bryce got upset.

"You never told me to mind my business before. We live here together, so your business *is* my business."

"You need to watch your fucking mouth."

"Don't cuss at me!"

"I say what I want."

"You never said what you want before. Why the sudden change?"

"Stop asking so many questions."

Bryce paused.

"I don't get it. Lately, you been all up in my face. I'm pregnant, and you don't even seem to care anymore. Do you still want the baby?"

"It better be mine. I'll see when it comes out. If it don't look like me or my mother, I'm out."

Bryce couldn't believe how irate he had gotten. She knew he was on the brink of hitting her. That was her deal breaker, so she forced his hand.

"So what you gon do if the baby looks like me? You still gon be out?"

"I told you what I'm gonna do!"

"What if the baby looks like my mother? Whatchu gonna do!?"

"Don't question me!"

"Whatchu gonna do, huh?! Whatchu gonna do?"

Dwayne crawled over to Bryce. He was eye level with her; and when he got close enough, he smacked her as hard as he could. Bryce was silent. She held her face to feel wetness around her eye. She wasn't crying, so she wasn't sure if it was blood or tears. All her notions about what he would do had come true.

"Did you feel that? I need $300!"

"Where am I going to get $300 from?"

"Well, find it then!"

"You're not even making sense. Every month you pay my car note. Now you're asking for $300? How that sound?"

Bryce sat there for a moment and just allowed him to rant. She wiped herself and got up. She flushed the toilet. She washed her hands and put in her contact lenses so she could see. She walked over to the bed and sat down. Dwayne had become quiet too. He was confused because she wasn't saying anything. She took off her clothes and put on her pajamas. When she looked in the mirror while putting her contact lenses on, one side of her face was swollen. Dwayne was watching her like a hawk. She wanted to take a picture of her face and call the police; but she knew if she did that, she would agitate him further.

All she could think about was her baby and him hitting her again. She knew she had to play it cool, so she put her legs under the covers and sat up in bed to watch TV. She was waiting for him to go to sleep. He got under the covers and lay in bed next to her. They said nothing the whole time. She watched TV for twenty minutes and then looked at him to see if he was asleep. He felt her staring and jerked his head around to let her know that he was wide awake. She felt trapped. She waited some more, and he did the same thing. Bryce got up and went to sit on the couch in the living room. She turned on the TV there. Dwayne followed her but went into the kitchen. He popped the top off of a Heineken and finished it in big gulps. He left the empty bottle on the counter. He could see everything she was doing by peering over the breakfast bar. He stood by her Martha Stewart knife set and eyeballed it.

Bryce gulped her saliva and put both hands over her stomach. He finished another Heineken. Then he went into the freezer and pulled out a tray of ice cubes. He filled up a Zip loc bag with ice cubes and wrapped a wash clothe around it and then approached his baby's mama.

"Here, put this on your face."

"I don't need it. I'm okay."

Bryce ignored him. Then he sat down next to her on the couch. Almost two hours went by. This would go on all night if she let it.

"I'm craving some ice cream."

"It's two o'clock in the morning. Where you gon get ice cream from?"

"The restaurant. The restaurant's open. I want some vanilla ice cream with chocolate sprinkles. I'm going to get some. You coming with me?"

Bryce got up and put on some clothes. She didn't bother to take her rollers out. She just left her silk bonnet on. Dwayne got up. He left his pajamas on and threw on a hoodie.

"I'll sit in the car."

"Okay."

She drove him to the restaurant where they worked.

"I'll be right back."

"All right."

Bryce hurried to the bathroom and called 911.

"911, what's your emergency?"

"My boyfriend has assaulted me, and I'm afraid he's going to hit me again."

"Where are you, ma'am?"

"I'm at the restaurant on Route 5."

"Are you okay?"

"Yes."

"Where is your boyfriend?"

"He's outside in the car. I'm Iin the bathroom. He doesn't know I'm in here."

"What kind of car is he in?"

"A dark- gray Nissan Altima. It's sitting right in front of the restaurant."

"I'm sending an officer out. Stay on the phone until he gets there."

"Okay."

Bryce waited for a few minutes.

"The officer is outside. You can hang up the phone now."

"Okay. Thank you."

Bryce took several pictures of her face in the bathroom's mirror. The swelling had gone down, but her eye was still puffy. Bryce cautiously went outside to see Dwayne in hand cuffs.

"Bryce, they gon take me to jail! What are you doing?"

Bryce turned her head to look away. She could feel her eyes watering up. She didn't want him to see her cry. She felt bad but knew she had to separate herself.

"Is this the man you called about, ma'am?"

"Yes."

She went to the back of the restaurant where no one was and sat down to put her hand over her mouth. A few minutes later, the officer came back there to talk to her.

"Would you like to filel out a police report?"

"Yes."

He handed her a piece of paper with writing on it and a pen.

"Here, fill this out. If you have any questions, just ask and I will assist you."

"Can you take a picture of my face? This is where he hit me."

"No. I don't see anything wrong."

Bryce was surprised but said nothing. She didn't make an issue of it because she knew she had already taken pictures of her face. She felt invisible. It was not that busy; and although she recognized some of her co-workers, no one said anything to her. No questions like *What you'll doing up here in the middle of the night?" "Why is he in handcuffs?" "What happened?"* No one seemed to care. After she filled out the police report, Bryce gave it to the officer and went home like nothing happened. She was exhausted.

The next morning she called her rental office to have the locks changed. She told them what happened and said she had a police report. She said it was an emergency and she needed her locks changed right away. They said someone would come over within the hour. She would have to pay $75, though. Bryce said it was no problem. All she wanted was a receipt. She went around to the rental office to pay the money and get her receipt. Once the locks were changed and she had a new set of keys, she packed Dwayne's stuff. She remembered that the officer told her she would have to be in court the next day to obtain a restraining order, so she moved quickly so as not to be late for court. He still had the totes he used to move in, in the closet.

She took all his shirts and pants off the hangers and threw them into the totes. She followed suit with his shoes and other belongings on the shelf up top in the closet. The totes were large and heavy, so she pulled and pushed them across the rug to the door. She didn't realize how much stuff he had. There were only two totes, so she put the rest of his things in trash bags. When everything was piled up by the door, she began the task of loading up her car. She could barely see out of her rearview mirror.

She showered, got dressed, and drove to Dwayne's mother's house. When she got there, she didn't see any cars in the driveway and didn't bother to knock on the door or ring the doorbell. One by one, she unloaded each bag and tote, piling them up in front of his mother's garage. When the task was complete, she lifted her arms, stretched, sighed, rubbed her belly, got into her car, and drove off to court.

When she got there, she was surprised to see how crowded it was. The courtroom looked like the same one she had seen on TV called *The People's Court*. She found a seat in the back and looked around. When she heard her name called, she approached the front of the courtroom. She stood in front of the podium to the right and saw Dwayne approach the podium to the left. The judge spoke,

"You wanna tell me what happened?"

"Well . . ."

"No, not you, him."

Dwayne spoke. He explained his side of the story, making Bryce look like the bad guy. He said she provoked him into hitting her; and although she knew she did, she still knew he was wrong. After he gave this long-drawn-out testimony, she started her side of the story. She tried to remember all the important details. The judge reviewed the evidence and granted Bryce the restraining order. He told them both to stay away from each other and that they would have to reconvene in court at a later date. Bryce was afraid but found some solace in her now having a restraining order.

When her next day in court came, she was almost late. She had printed out the pictures of her face from that night. This courtroom was located at another courthouse farther away. Bryce didn't mind driving, though. When she got there, it was crowded just like the other courtroom had been. She found a seat in the back and checked her e-mail account while waiting for her name to be called. She listened to the judge's voice with her head down.

"Please refrain from using your cell phones. That includes checking your e-mail and texting."

Bryce never lifted her head. The judge raised her voice.

"That includes checking your e-mail and texting!"

Bryce looked up and the judge was looking directly at her. She turned her phone off and put it away. Her mind was frazzled, but she tried to pay attention to the cases before hers. It was quite interesting. People were complaining about many things robbery, vandalism, being owed money but she didn't hear about any domestic violence cases. She felt like she may have been the only one.

When she heard her name, she stood up and shuffled across the bench, feeling like she was in church. She saw Dwayne coming into the courtroom from a side door. He was in chains and handcuffs. Finally, something made sense. He took his place at a desk on the left side, and Bryce went to the right. She was so ready to explain to this judge what had happened and show her the pictures she took that night. The judge asked Dwayne how he was pleading. Dwayne said, "Guilty."

Some other words were exchanged, and he was led out of the courtroom. Bryce thought, *That's it? I don't even get to say what happened?* She was confused and looked around. Since she was standing there by herself, she looked at the judge. The judged told her he would be sentenced at a later date and that she could leave now. Bryce couldn't believe it. How long would he be in jail? Would justice really be served? Although he had pled guilty, she went home feeling defeated.

Bryce went on going to work. Normally, when Dwayne was late or didn't show up to work, her co-workers would ask her about him. Once she would tell them where he was or what happened, they would seem to be more at ease. But this time, Bryce noticed that no one was asking about Dwayne. It was as if they already knew what happened. She hadn't discussed the case with anyone, and his absence didn't seem to affect anything anymore, so she just left it alone.

She continued to work hard and save money. After all, she had to prepare for her first child. Her SSDI check was paying the rent, and her weekly wages went mostly to her car payment and car insurance. Together, they amounted to about $800. When Dwayne was living with her, she had bought a brand-new car. Initially, he paid the car note, so somehow they made ends meet. But after she had to put him out, she didn't even realize that she was missing his $400 monthly contribution until things began not to add up. Eventually, her rent was three months late. She was working as much as she wanted to and still getting her check, so she didn't worry about it. She thought she could catch up at some point, but she never did.

She wanted to have a baby shower. She searched for places to hold the event. The owner of the restaurant where she worked overheard her talking and said that she could have her baby shower there. The back of the restaurant was not occupied during the middle of the day, so he said that would be the best time. All he wanted was a day and time. Bryce was relieved. She searched her cell phone for people to invite. She bought enough invitations for seventy people. She invited everyone from old high school buddies to co-workers, family, and friends she had met along the way. Everyone seemed happy for her. This would be an occasion she would always remember. She was so excited.

She went to the library and put together plenty of games to entertain her guests. The menu was simple but sufficient. It was provided compliments of the restaurant's owner. It included chicken strips, garden salad, several types of dressings, potato salad, cole slaw, chilled sodas, juices and water, and cookies and cake for dessert. Everyone had a great time and brought Bryce gifts for her new baby, but she noticed that the only people who showed up were her co-workers and her family. There were enough of them, so she didn't let that concern her.

The guys from her job loaded her car up with the gifts, and she told them to make themselves to-go boxes full of leftovers from the party. Bryce made sure they got all the soda and juice they wanted too. It was a wonderful day and came together perfectly, but she went home to an empty house. Before unloading her car, she wondered how she would bring this baby into the world all by herself. She wasn't sure if she could do it. She remembered that her cousin told her when she was pregnant the first time that when you have a baby people will help you. Even if you don't know how, you will make things come together sometimes if you keep the faith it will all work out. She tried to find comfort in that advice.

She was eight months now and getting close, so she took a leave of absence. She typed up a letter letting her boss know that she would be back six weeks after the baby was born. Her manager accepted it and said goodbye. Bryce went home with nothing to do. She lived off her tips and made cash money every day. With no money coming in, her finances dwindled even more. She was so caught up in the hype of having a baby, though, she didn't worry about it the way she should have. At the time, she was getting $300 in food stamps. She took the time off as an opportunity to step up her cooking game. She wondered what she would spend $300 on at the grocery store. The first time she got that amount, she filled up two carts with everything she could think of, especially meats, chicken, steaks, ground beef, and turkey. Her freezer was stocked. She was careful not to get fat, though. She would look up recipes on her phone, and most fed four to six people. Since Bryce lived alone now, she had to calculate how to reduce the recipes down to one or two people. She bought quarter pans to bake bread instead of the usual loafing pans and tried to make just enough for herself.

She was cooking almost every day. Her second trip to the grocery store, she bought things she normally was too frugal to spend money on. She would buy all kinds of expensive spices, sauces, and cooking wines. She cooked nothing that she had cooked for Dwayne. She wanted to experiment. Never mind buying $40 canisters of formula for the baby. She didn't even think about that.

She went to use the bathroom one day and wiped herself. A huge pile of a light yellowish substance came out on the tissue. She wiped again. More came out; but this time, the pile was longer. This had never happened before, and she never stopped to think that maybe her body was preparing itself to give birth. She wiped until it was gone and moved on like nothing ever happened.

About a week later, she started having pains. She thought the pains should be equal in intervals and get closer together as she approached birth. These pains were random. She would get a few close together then not feel anything until hours later. That made no sense to her. She imagined someone having her voodoo doll and sticking it in the stomach at a random pace. When she couldn't take the pain anymore, she went to the hospital to find out if she was in labor. She drove herself there.

She checked in, and they asked her to have a seat. She wasn't having any pains. An attendant came over to escort her to labor and delivery. She asked how far she had to go. The attendant said that labor and delivery was on the fourth floor all the way at the opposite corner of the hospital. Afraid that she might have pains on the way walking there, she asked for a wheelchair. The attendant looked at her as if she had two heads. Bryce was insulted. He knew she was having a baby, and he was going to make her walk? She thought that was inhumane. She insisted, and he clammed up and walked off to find a wheelchair. When he came back, he wheeled her up to the fourth floor. She looked at the man and thought about her father because they favored one another. He was just slightly shorter.

IRMA'S GUN

When she got there, she sat on a cold table with a thin white sheet of paper on it. The attendant said the doctor would be in soon. A middle-aged man with light-brown complexion, average height, and curly brown hair strolled in and looked at Bryce with childish eyes. He introduced himself and then let her speak first. She told him she was having random pains and wanted to know if she was in labor. He just looked at her. She went on,

"The pains are not consistent. They come randomly. In fact, I haven't had any pain for about six hours. Is that normal?"

The doctor didn't say a word. Bryce could feel herself getting upset. She became flustered.

"Am I in labor?"

He said he would prepare a room for her and that a nurse would come in and talk to her. Then he left. She sat there all alone and angry. Bryce hated being lied to even if it was by omission. A nurse came in and walked her to a room next door. She noticed that the sign above the door said Blood Transfusions, but she didn't ask any questions, afraid that she would be lied to again. The nurse told her to take off all her clothes, even her bra, and place them on the chair. She said she could put on a white paper gown and to put the opening in the front. She gave her some socks to wear and pulled out the stirrups on the bottom of the table.

Bryce was still not having any pains. She always imagined having a baby as being this laborious event. She felt so uneasy and wanted to leave because she felt that no one was addressing her needs. This was not how she wanted to bring a baby into the world. When the nurse left, instead of taking her clothes off, she tried to leave. As she walked pasted the desk, the secretary asked her where she was going. Bryce said she was leaving. The secretary told her she could not and to go back into her room. Bryce told her she felt uncomfortable and wanted to go to another hospital. The secretary called security. Bryce stood there to listen.

The next thing she knew, about fifteen security officers came in and grabbed her arms. They walked her back into the room and told her she could not leave. A female security officer told her to take her clothes off. There were men in the room, so Bryce wondered if she was about to get raped. She refused to undress in front of the men, so the female officer made them leave.

It was just Bryce and several female officers in the room. She undressed and put the gown on. She sat there silently until a different nurse came in. This nurse said she would administer oxygen to Bryce before she had the baby. Bryce still was not having any pains. The nurse told Bryce to lie back on the table. Afraid that the scowling officers would clobber her if she didn't, she lay back. The nurse put what looked like a clear suction cup over her mouth. Bryce fell asleep instantly.

CHAPTER 25

When she woke up, she was furious and didn't know why. She saw a nurse standing at a computer near her bed. Her heart was beating fast, and she gasped for air. Bryce looked down and saw that her belly was flat. She had a line of staples in her stomach below her navel. She still felt no pain. The nurse asked her if she was okay. Bryce wanted to cry but could not. Here, she was almost all alone and her baby was gone. She didn't get to see her or touch her or anything. There was a void inside her that echoed loudly, but no one could hear it. Her mind went blank, and she just lay there looking at the ceiling. A different nurse came in and helped her remove her gown. She was as careful as could be. She handled Bryce like a delicate new born bathing for the first time. She wiped her down, but Bryce noticed that she was already clean, so she wondered what she was doing. She started with her neck. Tenderly moving in large circles, she went from one side to the other, making her way down her chest, under each breast, and across her stomach.

Bryce felt like this was more an act of contrition than a bath. She didn't know this woman, but somehow this woman knew Bryce. She walked over to the chair where her clothes were and brought them to Bryce. She even helped her put them on. The nurse announced that she was leaving and. Bryce wanted to thank her but was silent. With head bowed, she just sat there waiting for instructions.

A third woman came in and escorted her to a different place. When Bryce asked where she was going, the woman stalled with small talk until they were locked inside the psych ward. When the doors slammed shut and automatically locked behind them, she informed Bryce that she would be seeing a psychiatrist in the morning. Meanwhile, she would be staying here.

Bryce tried her best not to panic. Having experience with these matters, she knew acting the way she felt inside would only make matters worse. Then she tried to recall. Did she say something to anyone at this hospital about once being a patient at Perkins? She did not. She knew she didn't because she was too distracted by everything else that was going on. How did they know? She had been set up, and now her baby was gone.

The woman took her to her bedroom. She told her to put her belongings on the bed. The woman rifled through her little bit of things and told her she was okay.

"Do you have anything in your pockets?"

Bryce patted her pockets to see.

"No."

"Okay. We're done here."

The woman left Bryce by herself. Bryce gasped for air again. She had to get away. She walked out to the desk and excused herself.

"How long am I going to be here?"

"Talk to your doctor in the morning. He'll give you an assessment."

Bryce walked away. She knew they couldn't keep her forever, but how would this affect her conditional release? If Perkins found out, would they try to send her back? She got nervous. What the hell was going on? For a moment, she had forgotten that she had just given birth. Two days went by before she asked about her baby.

"Can I see my baby?"

"She's in the NICU. I'll take you at two o'clock."

"Okay."

IRMA'S GUN

Bryce watched the clock on the wall. When two o'clock came, she went back up to the desk.

"Can I see my baby now?"

"Okay, here I come."

The pair went down a flight of stairs and around two corners. Going through the back entrance, they were there. The woman introduced Bryce to the NICU nurse, and she led Bryce to a tiny bed surrounded by clear plastic.

"Here's your baby."

Bryce stood there and stared. She was beautiful. She had her father's nose and ugly feet. Everything else belonged to Bryce. She was wrapped in what Bryce had traditionally seen as a dish rag. It was white with a big blue stripe and a red stripe. She was wrapped up tight as a mummy sleeping peacefully. Bryce pinched at the cloth and pulled it back. The lump of blotchy reddish, light-brown skin moved. One little leg after another, she stretched and then extended her arm as if she wanted to shake her mother's hand. Then she stretched and separated each finger and put her thumb up to her mouth but didn't suck. Bryce thought about a comedian who did the same thing, saying he would blow up his hand and smack somebody. Bryce believed she was really going crazy. The baby was smiling the whole time with her eyes closed. Bryce just looked at her. She never picked her up. She only gazed.

The woman who had brought her there was still waiting for her, so she returned to the ward with her. Bryce was numb, and her mind was blank. Later on that day, the hospital's social worker came to Bryce to let her know that social services would be taking her child. When Bryce asked her why, she said someone had given an anonymous tip that a child's life had been put in danger. She started asking questions.

"Who would have done that? How was her life in danger? Why didn't anyone come to me to ask me what happened?"

"That's not the way it works. When someone gives a tip like that, the child is taken on a temporary basis."

"So I can get her back?"

"Possibly. First, an investigation has to be done. If it is found that you are safe and you have a home and way of providing for her, she will be given back to you. However, if the contrary is found, she will be sent to a foster home or adopted. A counselor from DSS will be here shortly to advise you of your options in seeing and bonding with your child in the meantime."

"I get to see her again?"

"Yes. You can set up appointments to spend time with her under the supervision of DSS. They just want to make sure you will be a fit mother."

They continued to talk. Then the social worker left. This time, though, she wasn't alone. Being on the psych ward of a hospital was a little different than being at Clayborn. It was way smaller, and there were just two rooms and the bedrooms. Around 8:00 p.m., they made everyone line up for meds.

Bryce pondered how they knew she had been diagnosed. When they ask her what she takes, should she lie and say nothing or ace the talk with the doctor and get out of there? Or should she tell them what she takes because they already know and she wants to appear to be compliant? Bryce played the middle.

"I can't remember. I don't know what you're talking about."

"*You can't remember*? Well, just wait for the doctor. He'll give you something."

Bryce had slipped away for the moment. She went back to the common area. Several other people were there, and she waited for someone to start up a conversation with her as she sipped her apple juice. No one came over, so she eavesdropped. All the conversations were basic but familiar. Everyone seemed to know everyone.

"Have you seen Joan?"

"No, I haven't seen her in a while, but I heard she was here and just left."

"Oh, okay. What about Pearl?"

"She's not doing too well. I heard she got into a dispute with her group home and was homeless. She'll probably be here soon, though."

And the familiar went on and on. Bryce thought only Clayborn was a revolving door, but apparently it was that way here too. Recidivism ran rampant in this whole system. And now Bryce was caught smack in the middle of it. She finally talked to the doctor. He asked her a bunch of questions and decided on a diagnosis,

"You have bipolar disorder.'

How do they come up with this stuff? This would make the third diagnoses she received since being thrown around in this system. She was careful not to tell this man she had been in Clayborn because he might throw the book at her, so she went along with it, trying to coast her way through.

"How long will I be here?"

"We just want to observe you. Then we will make an assessment and let you go. It shouldn't be more than a week."

"*A week?*"

"It'll be here before you know it."

Bryce sauntered off in a tacit fit of rage. She just wanted to get away from him. At least, he didn't say a month or a year. The bottom line was that she just didn't want to be here. Then one nurse asked her if she wanted to see the father of her child. She hadn't seen Dwayne since court and didn't want to see him now. The nurse went on.

"He says you have a gun."

"What would I be doing with a gun? You checked my belongings when I came in here. You know I'm not strapped."

"What should I tell him?"

"Tell him to leave me alone."

"Will do."

She bounced away with a smirk on her face. And how did *he* know she was in the hospital? She hadn't called anyone. She didn't write anyone. And why did he think she wanted to shoot him? Finally, discharge day came, and Bryce almost ran out of there. This hospital life was not for her. When she got home, her apartment was a mess. Clothes, dirty dishes, and paper were everywhere. The first thing she did was clean up. She needed her space to reflect her mood.

The next day she got ready for court. The social worker from DSS told her to be in court to contest having her child being taken from her. Bryce had been in the hospital all week and wasn't prepared, so he requested an extension. It was granted, and she came back in two weeks.

When she returned, the judge kept calling Adriana "the grandmother's child." Bryce felt like she didn't exist anymore.

When she got home, she contacted DSS. She told them she had a child in their system and wanted to visit her. She was told she could visit twice a week. Bryce made the appropriate appointments. She went there eager to see Adriana. She gave her Dwayne's last name simply because he was the father. She knew one day Adriana would inquire about her lineage. She wanted her to know where she came from even if her father was a piece of shit.

She went into the room, and Adriana was sitting in a car seat on a table. The foster parent left a carry-all bag with diapers, bottles, wipes, a blanket, and some toys. Bryce paused to look at her daughter and then reached down to lift her from the car seat. This was the first time she'd ever held her. While she cradled her in her right arm like a football, Adriana was still asleep. Bryce didn't care. She was just happy to be holding her. Adriana opened her eyes.

"Aaaaayyyy. . . You awake?"

Bryce called her daughter A because this was her first child.

"You hungry?"

Adriana rolled her eyes back and stared at her mother, yawning and stretching at the same time. Bryce retrieved a bottle from the bag to feed her. A imbibed the formula like she hadn't eaten in forever. As she did, she looked away from her mother and into the double mirror that Bryce was standing in front of. Bryce turned around to see if she would turn her head. She moved to another part of the room same thing. Bryce's feelings were hurt. Why was her child looking away from her? She checked her breath, but she was okay, so it wasn't that. When the milk was gone, Bryce put the bottle back in the bag and tried to hold A in an upward position. A fussed like a scorn lover, so Bryce put her back in football position, and she quieted down. She remained there for an hour, spending time with her daughter, hoping she would have her home one day. Little did she know, she would not.

Bryce repeated this routine twice a week for a month. Since she didn't have a baby at home and she was getting desperate for money, she went back to the restaurant. She told her manager she was ready to come back to work, but the manager said there was no room on the schedule for her. Bryce thought, *What does that mean?* She figured she would just come back at a later time. When she did, she asked a different manager for a schedule. This manager told her she no longer worked there. Bryce was in shock. How could you fire someone who had just had a baby? She went over her history there. Did she have any problems with anyone? She always thought she had a good rapport with everyone from the owner to the managers, servers, and dishwashers. What could have happened in such a short time?

Bryce went home and thought about it. She was so tired of running from this ghost. It never occurred to her she could look for another job. Besides, the same thing would just happen all over again anyways. She was a gerbil in a wheel. She sank into a deep depression. She stopped cooking, stopped going to therapy, stopped going to see her doctor, and stopped caring. She would just sleep all day. Then one day she got up to take a shower; but before she reached the bathroom, there was a knock at the door. It sounded like the police. Bryce looked through the peephole, and two officers were standing there. She cracked the door, and they stormed in. One was male, and the other was female. The man rushed past Bryce and headed straight for the safe. Nothing was in it. Bryce had spent all of her funds trying to keep afloat while she wasn't working. The female officer was rude.

"Ma'am, you're getting evicted today. Gather what you can and vacate the premises."

Bryce heard a commotion outside. There was a huge white truck, and several black men poured out of the back of it filing into the small apartment, removing things, and putting them on the front lawn. They started with the living room furniture. Bryce went into the bedroom and slipped her bra on underneath her shirt. She grabbed her purse and threw her cell phone and car keys into it. She put on her sneakers and walked briskly outside to her car. She was officially homeless. She drove into the heart of the city just to rest. Nothing crossed her mind but failure. She drove for ten minutes before stopping in a parking lot. She put her hand over her mouth, and her eyes darted back and forth.

She had been close to homeless before, but this was it. She wished she could cry, but nothing would come out.

She reclined her seat back and stared at the roof of her car. They would be coming for that soon too because she hadn't made a payment in two months. With no real address now, maybe she could buy some time. A tow truck rambled by, and she imagined he was looking for her. She thought, *He probably knows I'm homeless now and doesn't want to put me out of my car. Besides, it's getting cold.*

Bryce thought about killing herself. She had never been suicidal before, but this was her breaking point. She worked too hard and was too loyal to have something like this happen to her. She never contemplated asking anyone for help. She didn't want help. She wanted this to stop. And since she couldn't make it stop, she would take control of the only thing she could her life but how would she do it? She couldn't buy a gun because she had been diagnosed with a mental illness. She might buy one off the streets. She went to the first place where her grandfather used to live and waited.

She saw two older men talking to each other. She approached them and asked if they knew Ms. Molly from "years ago." They paused and said yes. Bryce was in. She talked about how she used to live here with her grandfather Sam and he used to make her give out gum and chips to all the neighborhood kids. Right away, both guys chimed in, "Yeah, we know Sam. He used to live right there." They both pointed to the spot where his apartment used to be. "We were working at the ship yard when he lived around here."

"Hey, do you know where I could get a gun?"

"Yeah. I can get you one right now. How much you looking to spend?"

"I just need a little something to tide me over. How much they cost?"

"I can get you one for a couple hundred."

"Okay. I can afford that."

Then the second man pulled the first man away. They briefly discussed something and then came back. The one that Bryce was talking to almost had tears in his eyes.

IRMA'S GUN

"Oh naw, I can't get you no gun."

"What? What do you mean? You just said you could get me one for $200."

"That was a mistake. I can't get you nothing. I'm sorry."

Both men walked off and left Bryce alone. Again, she wanted to cry but could not. She had to find another way. She remembered how a rapper named Pimp C died. He had drank a concoction of codeine-laced cough syrup and pills and then went to sleep. He never woke up. Bryce rushed to Rite Aid. She went to the drug aisle and found some cough syrup. She checked their labels, and none of them had any codeine. She guessed that after so many deaths they must have altered the formula. She read the backs of boxes and bottles randomly. She came across Tylenol.

Warning: Can cause death via liver failure

Bryce bought a two pack on sale. It contained two big bottles for $5. She also bought a big bottle of water. She went back to her car and downed one whole bottle. She wondered if that would be enough, so she started on the next bottle. She was halfway through when she got sleepy. She figured it was working; so she stopped, finished the water, and lay back in the driver's seat to go to sleep. She woke up four hours later feeling high. Her vision was blurry, and she was completely out of it but not too far gone to know that she didn't want to wake up. What was she going to do now, and how long would this take? Not wanting to bring attention to herself, she moved. She drove to a nearby McDonald's and got into the back seat. By this time, her stomach was cramping up. She didn't think she could take the pain. She called 911.

"911, what's your emergency?"

"I'm having a terrible stomach ache. I need help."

"Did you eat something bad?"

"No."

"Are you injured? What do you think is the source of the pain?"

"Uuuhh . . . I don't know."

"I'm sending an ambulance out. Where are you located?"

"At the McDonald's on Biddle Street. I'm in a dark-gray Nissan Altima."

"Stay on the phone until the paramedics arrive."

"Okay. I'll try."

Bryce curled up into the fetal position and waited in the back seat. She rocked back and forth at the pain. Finally, a medic tapped on the window and opened the back door.

"What did you eat?"

"Nothing. I just took some Tylenol. I had a headache."

"What's all this stuff in the car?"

"Uuuhh . . . my stomach."

"Let's go."

Two medics put Bryce on a stretcher and wheeled her into the ambulance. She squirmed the whole time. On the ride to the hospital, she felt every bump. The ambulance would rock and jump a little, hitting potholes. To Bryce, it felt like a midget was in her stomach pulling strings. She held on tight. When she got to the emergency room, they admitted her right away and took her to a bed in the back. She lay there by herself for what seemed like an eternity. She pushed the button on the controller near her bed for assistance.

"Yes. May I help you?"

"I'm in pain."

"Okay. I'll be right there."

A nurse came in to check on Bryce. She told her that her toxicology test came back. She asked her how much Tylenol she took. Bryce said a handful and that she had a really bad headache. The nurse looked at her and paused.

"The report said you had eight hundred times the recommended amount in your system. Was the headache that bad?"

"I may have taken a little extra. I was really in pain."

The nurse said she would return with some Tramadol and that Bryce was being admitted to the hospital. Relieved that she would have a place to sleep for a night or two, she said okay; and the nurse left. Bryce turned over back into her original fetal position and groaned while she waited for the Tramadol. Soon after, another nurse came in with two cups. One was filled with water, and the other had two little pills in it. She said nothing. She just handed the cups to Bryce. It was as if they already knew each other. Bryce was quiet as well and accepted each cup one at a time with shaky hands. When she was finished, she regained her normal bearings and faced the wall. Two men in white came in and transferred Bryce from one bed to another and then wheeled her to a room upstairs. She didn't even pay attention to her surroundings. She just kept her head buried in the pillow as she felt the motion of the gurney gliding through the hallways and turning each corner.

When she arrived, they transferred her again this time to a lower more stable bed in a room with an empty bed. Bryce sat up on the edge of the bed and held on to the sheets around her. As she looked at the floor, she wanted to cry but could not.

Then a doctor came in. He introduced himself and talked for several minutes about who knows what. Bryce couldn't concentrate. She was in so much pain. He was smiling at her like he knew her, and she wondered why. The last thing he said before he left was that she would have to drink a cup of unpleasant-smelling and tasting liquid to reverse the reaction of all the Tylenol she had taken. He said the whole process would take about three days and she should be fine. Her liver had been affected; but over time, it would heal if she took care of herself. Her wished her well and promised to return at the end of the process to give her an update. Then he left.

As the pain lessened, a short dark-haired nurse came in. To Bryce, she looked like she was still in high school. Bryce wondered what she was going to do to her. She handed her a Styrofoam cup with a bent white straw hanging out of it. She explained that she would have to drink this every eight hours to reverse the effects of the Tylenol. She warned her that it was nasty but she would just have to get used to it. Bryce reluctantly accepted the cup and pinched the straw with her thumb and index finger. It smelled like liquid fart in a cup. She sampled it. The texture was slimy and tasted like liquefied bugs. She imagined being on *Fear Factor* and this was her punishment. She inhaled deep and then took huge gulps of the red juice until it was gone. The nurse stood there watching her.

"Are you finished?"

Bryce opened her mouth, stuck out her tongue, and handed the nurse the cup all in one motion. The nurse accepted it and left the room. Bryce fumbled with the buttons on the remote to the television. Nothing good was on, so she turned it off and sat there. She looked at her clothes folded in a neat pile on the chair. She grabbed her hoodie and zipped it up. Putting her hands inside the pockets, she could feel her keys in her right pocket. She took them out and eyeballed them. There were two sets: her house keys and her car keys. She put the house keys in the palm of her hand and caressed them. Then she threw them into a waste basket by the bed. Then she lay down, pulled the sheets across her body, and tried to take a nap.

She repeated these steps three times with the different nurses before got nauseous. She would throw up randomly in a pink pan by her bed. There wouldn't be much that would come up because she had no appetite. It would be mostly water and juice. On the second day, the short dark-haired nurse who looked like she was in high school came in to give Bryce a cup of the infamous liquid and change the pink pan next to her bed. Bryce felt something coming up, so she reached for the pink pan. The short nurse pulled it away as if to tease Bryce, so she threw up on the floor. Bryce was irate; and as she fussed, the nurse walked out and left her there along with the vomit on the floor.

Why were the doctors so nice and the nurses so cruel? There was always this confusing dichotomy going on in her life. Everything would appear to be a go. Then just like that, something would happen out of no where, and she'd be halted. She couldn't even throw up without being interrupted. The janitor on that floor came in and cleaned up the mess. Bryce went back to sleep. On her last day there, a team of doctors came in. They were all tall white men. The doctor was an older man, bald with glasses. Then there was a handsome strapping man with black hair down to his shoulders. The third man looked like a mafia don with a protruding belly and a dark-brown buzz cut. Together, they symbolized a unified fort that could not be infiltrated. They looked happy to be there; and although she had gotten better, Bryce was still out of it. She sat there with a slumped back, looking at the floor and listening.

"We tested your blood, and the Tylenol is out of your system. Your liver still needs to heal, but as long as you drink plenty of water and stay away from alcohol, you'll do great. You should expect a full recovery."

Bryce thanked him in her mind, but outside she was silent. To her, the three men were unusually happy. Did they take some kind of pleasure at seeing her unhappy? She didn't know and didn't care. She didn't want to leave because she knew she had nowhere to go, but she knew she couldn't stay there forever. She got up to take a shower before she hit the road. She put her clothes on and took one last look at the room. Then she left. She went to the desk to get her discharge papers and walked down to the entrance level to wait for a cab.

"Where are you going, ma'am?"

"To McDonald's on Biddle Street."

CHAPTER 26

When she got there, her car was gone. Frantically, she went inside and asked for the manager.

"There was a dark-gray Nissan Altima parked outside a couple days ago. What happened to it?"

"Read the sign outside. It will give you more information."

Bryce walked briskly outside and searched for a sign. When she found it, she breathed in before reading. It read:

> 20-minute parking for customers only
> Violators will be towed at the owner's expense
> All vehicles will be towed to the Auto Barn on
> W. Lafayette Street in Baltimore, MD.
> The telephone number is listed below.

Bryce called immediately. When she asked about her car, the guy on the other end said it would cost her $15 each day and that they would only keep the car for thirty days. After that, her car would go to salvage. Bryce had only been gone three days, but she knew there might be other fees and taxes. Thank goodness, she was still getting her SSDI check.

She was in the city, so she just walked to the corner to wait for a cab. She got in and gave them the address to the Auto Barn. When she

IRMA'S GUN

got there, she got out of the cab thinking she could just walk into the place behind this tall locked fence, but there were four dogs barking like crazy, guarding the property.

Bryce got scared. She didn't have the shelter of a car to run to. She was just out there all alone. She wasn't exactly a track star either, so running would prove futile. After looking around, she realized that they were inside a fence which was inside the outside fence. Once someone unlocked the gate, she could go in unharmed. She rang the bell. A woman peered out. Then a few minutes later a man came walking out to open the fence.

"Are you here to pick up a vehicle?"

"Yes."

"Okay, go inside the office and tell them your name. Do you have your driver's license?"

"Yes."

The dogs continued to bark, and Bryce went in cautiously. The same lady she saw looking out of the window asked her the make and model of her car. Bryce gave her the information she wanted, and she looked something up in her computer. She told her she owed $167, which included a three- day lot charge, towing expenses, and other fees plus taxes.

Bryce needed her car. She asked no questions. She just handed over her bank card so the lady could swipe it. She gave Bryce the keys and location of her car and told her which lot it was on. Bryce thanked the woman and went looking for her car. When she found it, there was dust all over it like it had just come from the set of *The Dukes of Hazzard*. She didn't care. She was just happy to be out of harm's way. She got in, started it up, and drove off. She didn't even go to the car wash. She just drove it around dusty.

Another three days had gone by, and Bryce wondered where she could go to wash up. She usually went to the public bathroom in Mondawmin Mall. She had a small bucket she got from the dollar store. She would take that in along with a bar of soap and a wash cloth. She would fill the bucket halfway because it wouldn't fit all the way into the sink. She would go into the handicapped bathroom because she had

ty of space in there to do her thing. Most times, if she wasn't able to
wash her clothes, she would buy a new outfit from Rainbow for under
$20 so she could change her clothes after she washed up. But today she
didn't want to go to Mondawmin Mall. She knew she was wearing out
her welcome, and soon the security guards would be on to her. She tried
to think of where else she could go. Then she remembered that the cab
company she used to work for had a bathroom in it.

She went to go see the mechanic she had become friends with; but
when she got there, they said that Kenny was at his grandfather's bar. She
asked if it was still in the same place, and they said it was, so she went
by there. The mechanic was behind the bar serving drinks, and his
grandfather was engaged in a game of pool. Bryce strolled in casually.

"Hey, remember me?"

"Yeah, how could I forget? 197 the dispatcher used to call you
baby."

Bryce conversed for a while because she didn't want it to look like
she was only there to use their bathroom. She almost offered to play
a game of pool but remembered that she wasn't smelling the greatest.
When it appeared that everyone had let their guard down, she asked to
use the restroom.

"Sure. It's right there."

She locked the door and took all her clothes off. She lathered up
from neck to ankle and then began the process of wiping down. Rinsing
the washcloth off was most time-consuming. Then she heard someone
banging at the bathroom door. It was the mechanic's grandfather.

"Come on outta there! What you doing? I don't allow no foolishness
in my bar! If you don't come out, I'm coming in!"

"Bout in a minute. I had to do a number two."

Bryce still had soap all over her bottom half. What would she do if
he walked in and saw her naked? They both would have a heart attack.
She hurried as fast as she could, wiping her legs down, leaving a thin
film of soap that later caused her to be ashy. She slipped into a red-and-
white dress, which was shorter than she anticipated. She wished that
she had bought some white leggings to wear underneath.

"Coming out!"

She threw on some white sandals and fumbled with the clasps. When she finally came out, Kenny's grandfather was visibly upset.

"What was you doing in there, getting high?"

"I don't get high, sir."

"Well, what was you doing? Ain't that much shitting in the world!"

"I'm gonna leave now."

"Good. I think that's the best thing."

Bryce hurried up and got out of there before he called the police. She told Kenny she would call him later, and he said bye. When later came, he called her first,

"Hey, you all right?"

"Yeah. Just a little shaken up. Tell your grandfather I'm sorry I had to leave like that."

"Oh, don't worry about him. He's an old grouch."

"I was taking so long in the bathroom because I was in there washing up."

"Washing up? For what?"

"Kenny, I'm homeless right now."

"What! How'd that happen?"

"I just had a baby, and then I got fired from my job. I couldn't pay the rent, so I got evicted. I don't have anywhere to go. I sleep in my car."

"Whatchu do for money?"

"I get a SSDI check every month."

"Oh yeah. How much?"

"Almost $1,000."

"I got a room. You can stay with me. Just give me $400 a month and buy your own food. I can handle the rest."

"Really? Are you sure?"

"Yeah. I know you from when we used to work together. We'll get along just fine. I got some house rules, though."

"Okay."

"Be in by midnight. I gotta get some rest for the next day's work. No company. I don't want no niggas and bitches over my house or knowing where I live. Uuummm . . . I already said buy your own food. Don't keep the lights on unless you really need to, and if you cook, make sure you wash the dishes. And just clean up after yourself. I mean you's a grown woman. You know what to do. You kept your place clean, didn't you?"

"Of course."

"I know you did. Imma get you a key tomorrow so you can come and go. Can you pay me the $400 up front in cash and on the first every month?"

"Not a problem. I'll have it for you tomorrow when you give me the key. What's your address? I want to put it in my phone."

"Let me see your phone."

The mechanic typed his phone number and address into her phone and then gave it back.

"See you tomorrow."

Bryce said bye and gave him a hug to thank him for rescuing her. She was relieved that she now had a place to stay that she could afford. She went straight to the ATM to get $400 to prepare for the next day. She was tired, so she wanted to go somewhere that had a camera so she could take a nap in her car and be safe with the $400 on her. Her dress had no pockets, so she lifted up her dress and folded the money in half. She placed it inside of her underwear where no one would ever find it. It was a little warm that day, so she rolled the window all the way down, reclined her seat, lay back, and took a nap in front of 7-Eleven. She had pulled up right in front of the store. There was a camera pointed directly at her car so she would sleep well. When she awoke, the first thing she did was check her dip. The wad of cash looked thin, so she unfolded the money to count it. There was only $200 there. She thought that maybe she had misplaced it even though she knew she did not.

She stared at the camera. It was still pointing towards her car. She looked around and saw a police car. The officer inside was the same one who came to investigate the night she'd gotten robbed in the cab. Apparently, she had been robbed again. She backed out of the parking lot so fast she almost hit another car. She was headed for the ATM again to get $200 for Kenny.

When she moved in, all she had were the clothes on her back. The mechanic's place was small but homey and neatly kept. He showed her,

IRMA'S GUN

her room. There was a wooden night stand with a lamp on it, a single-sized bed with tan sheets, a dresser with a small TV on top, and a small white plastic trash can in the corner. This would be home for a while and, but Bryce didn't mind because it certainly beat sleeping in her car. The mechanic was hospitable.

"I'll get you a blanket."

"Thanks, Kenny."

"I know you get a check and everything, but you should look for a job in the morning. I know you can still work part-time while getting that check. That way, you can save up your money and eventually get a place of your own. I don't mind you staying here, but this arrangement can't be permanent. I have family who comes in and outta town from time to time. Usually, they stay in here, so after a while, Imma need my spare room back, okay?"

"Gotcha."

"As long as we understand each other."

The mechanic went to get her a blanket as she sat on the bed wondering what she was going to do. She called her bank to check her balance, and the automated system told her that she was $50 in debt. Bryce was shocked. How did that happen? Well, she took out $400 initially for the mechanic, then she had to take out another $200 because she got robbed, and then her car insurance was taking out $395. Her SSDI check was only $945. It was the beginning of the month, and she didn't have gas money or money for food. What was she going to do for the next thirty days? She had to make something happen.

Kenny left out for a while. Bryce opened the blanket and made up her bed. Then she walked around the rest of the apartment. It was a little dusty, so she found a feather duster and dusted. She went into the kitchen, looked in the freezer, and found some ground beef. She took it out and put it in some warm water. Then she found a jar of spaghetti sauce, but she couldn't find any pasta. She had about $10 left, so she went to the corner store and bought a box of spaghetti, an onion, and a green pepper. Then she had about $7 left, so she splurged on two packs of Kool-Aide, a five-pound bag of sugar, and a large pitcher. When she went to pay for it, she was short. The cashier let her go for $0.43. Bryce thanked her and promised to pay her back next time she saw her. The cashier said it was okay and waved a friendly goodbye.

Bryce returned to her new home and got busy. She put on some boiling water for the spaghetti and found a large pan for the ground beef. She rushed to chop up the onion and green pepper and found some oregano and garlic powder. When she looked in the refrigerator, the mechanic had a loaf of bread and some butter. Bryce smeared some butter on four slices of bread and sprinkled some garlic powder on top and spread them out on a piece of aluminum foil to put in the oven once the spaghetti was almost ready. She put a tiny amount of oil in the heated pan and sautéed the chopped-up vegetables until they were tender. She put the halfway frozen ground beef on top of the onion and green pepper and chopped it up so the ground beef could thaw completely. She sprinkled some oregano and garlic powder on top of the ground beef. Then the mechanic walked in.

"Mmmm . . . what's that smell?"

"I'm making some spaghetti, and there's some garlic bread in the oven."

"What? You cooking dinner?"

"Yeah. You let me stay here. It's the least I can do."

"Aawwww, baby, you ain't have to do that."

"Yes, I did."

"Well, when is dinner gonna be ready? I'm hungry."

"Give me about fifteen minutes."

"Let me go wash up. I'll be back."

"Take your time. I still gotta make the Kool-Aide."

"What flavor you get?"

"Cherry."

"OKAY."

When the mechanic returned, he was in his pajamas. He had taken a shower and shaved.

"You want me to make the Kool-Aid?"

"Naw. It's in the refrigerator. Have a seat."

Bryce made Kenny a plate and sat it in front of him. Then she poured him a glass of chilled Kool-Aid. He didn't pray or anything.

He just devoured the food as if it were his last meal. Bryce made a plate for herself but instead watched the mechanic eat. He never looked up.

"Is it okay?"

"Mmmm, huh?"

She made herself a plate and sat across from him and picked at her food.

"What's wrong? Why you not eating?"

"Just got a lot on my mind that's all."

"You sure everything's okay?"

"Yeah. I'm sure."

They finished eating, and Bryce washed the dishes and cleaned up the kitchen. When everything was put away, the mechanic went to his room and went to sleep. Bryce went to her room and turned on the television. She couldn't concentrate. All she could think about was Kenny, so she took off all her clothes and crept into his room. She stood there at the threshold for a minute. He was laying on top of his covers, snoring. She walked in and lay down next to him, putting her arm gently across his body. She softly pressed her body against his. He stopped snoring and opened his eyes.

Before turning over, he paused. Then, underneath Bryce's arm, he rotated his body until they were staring into each other's eyes. No words were exchanged. They kissed. Bryce slowly unbuttoned his pajama top and felt on his chest. They continued to kiss. Then he came out of his shirt. He pulled down his pajama pants and kicked them off as he got on top of her. He pushed himself inside and wrapped his arms around her body. They made love until the next morning.

"Damn, girl, Imma be late for work."

"Want me to make you some breakfast?"

"No. Just make me some coffee and put some of that left over spaghetti in a plastic container so I can take it for lunch. I'm about to get in the shower real quick."

"Okay."

Bryce followed his instructions and threw on his pajama top and her underwear. He kissed her before he left and said he would return around five. He also informed her that there were chicken thighs in the freezer.

Then he asked her if she knew how to make chicken and dumplings. Bryce promised to have it ready for him when he got home. Then she asked if he had a can of biscuits. He said no, and Bryce paused. She would be forced to tell him about her financial situation.

"Kenny, I'm in a bit of a pinch."

"Whatchu mean?"

"Well, I get $945 every month. You already know that, but this month I gave you 400 for rent. When I took the money out the day before I paid you, somebody robbed me for half of it, so I had to take out another $200. Then I had to pay my car insurance, which was almost $400. That left me in a hole $50 deep with my bank. I don't have a job yet, so I don't know what I'm going to do for the rest of the month. I need gas money, and I don't know how I'm going to eat for the rest of the month."

"Well, how much gas you got in your car?"

"'Bout a half tank."

"Well, you're not a big person, so I know you don't eat a whole lot. Just cook for me like you been doing and eat on that. I'll keep the fridge stocked."

"And what about gas? I need to get around so I can look for a job."

"How much you need?"

"Forty dollars should hold me for about a week or so."

The mechanic reached into his pocket.

"Here. Get some biscuits outta this and keep the rest for gas. I'll give you some more when you need it."

Bryce kissed him on the lips.

"Baby, thanks. Imma hook those chicken and dumplings up for you, okay?"

"I'll be back at five."

They kissed like old lovers, and Bryce was happy that she had found not only a place to stay but also a good friend and lover. She forgot all about her past and just wanted to start anew. The one thing she learned this time was to never sleep on a good friend.